Best Man
by
Matt Dunn

Matt Dunn was born in Margate in 1966, but escaped to London and then Málaga, where he worked as a newspaper columnist and played a lot of tennis. He now lives in Brighton.

Previously he has been a professional lifeguard, fitness-equipment salesman and, most recently, an IT headhunter, where his skill in re-writing CVs made him think he might have a talent for fiction. *Best Man* is his first novel; he hopes it won't be his last.

Best Man

Matt Dunn

**POCKET
BOOKS**

LONDON • SYDNEY • NEW YORK • TORONTO

First published in Great Britain by Pocket Books, 2005
An imprint of Simon & Schuster UK
A Viacom company

1   3   5   7   9   10   8   6   4   2

Simon & Schuster UK Ltd
Africa House
64–78 Kingsway
London WC2B 6AH

www.simonsays.co.uk

Simon & Schuster Australia
Sydney

A CIP catalogue record for this book is available
from the British Library

ISBN 0 7434 9551 9
EAN 9780743495516

Typeset in Bembo by Palimpsest Book Production Limited,
Polmont, Stirlingshire
Printed and bound in Great Britain by
Bookmarque Ltd, Croydon, Surrey

For my parents, Sheila and Frank Dunn.
Thank you for having me.

Chapter 1

'So, as I was saying, we're back at her place, and it's getting to the Clash point . . .'

'Clash point?'

'Yeah, you know, "should I stay or should I go", and we've been making the usual first date small talk – job, family, past relationships.'

'Past relationships? I hope you gave her the abridged version?'

'So somehow we get on to the subject of marriage and infidelity, and she tells me this story about a guy she knows from university. You know the type: the college Casanova, good looking, funny, a real ladies' man, went out with most of the girls in his year.'

'Bit like you then, mate.'

'Piss off! Anyway, to everyone's surprise, straight after graduation this guy marries the dullest girl on their course, moves out to the suburbs, does the whole two-point-four children thing. However, he works as an estate agent in London, and this gives him the perfect excuse to spend long hours in town while the wife stays at home to look after the kids.'

'With you so far.'

'He's always kept in contact with his other female friends

from college — most of them ex-girlfriends, of course. One by one he meets up with them in town for lunch or an early evening drink, when he pours his heart out over a bottle of Hard-done-by, telling them how he feels trapped in the marriage, has no life outside of work, and that the physical side has all but disappeared. They're generally looking at him all misty eyed before they've even finished their first glass.'

'Crafty bugger!'

'Exactly. So, when the time comes to leave, he says that he's just got to pop into a house round the corner and value it — five minutes, that's all — he's got the keys on him, and do they want to come and have a look? What woman can turn down the chance to have a nose around a complete stranger's home, and so before you know it the two of them are strolling around the empty property, with him pretending to make notes while bemoaning the state of his marriage.'

'What, "South facing reception room, I'd leave her if it wasn't for the children"?'

'That sort of stuff. And hinting how he wished that he and that particular girl had been closer at college, whilst she's making all these "you poor thing" type noises. Anyway, the last room they get to is of course the bedroom . . .'

'And?'

'And what do you think? She makes him an offer on the spot, which he gladly accepts!'

'So what did you say when she told you this?'

'I said what she wanted to hear of course: "What a bastard!"'

It's Friday afternoon, the sun is shining, and the three of us are sitting in our favourite drinking establishment in Chelsea, Bar Rosa, snacking on tapas and sipping that bottled Spanish beer that costs twice the price of normal lager yet has only half the taste. Nick hasn't been focused on work all day, and I never need an excuse for an early finish, so we've shut the office and, on the pretext that we are his most valued clients, extricated Mark from his firm of stuffy accountants. As is traditional, we're talking about my previous weekend's date.

'Too right,' agrees Mark, absent-mindedly fingering his wedding ring. 'What a bastard!'

'What a lucky bastard, you mean,' says Nick, enviously. In his mind, anyone getting more than their fair share deserves his jealous admiration.

'Best of both worlds, if you ask me,' he continues. 'Don't you agree, Adam?'

Nick, sporting a 'designer' shirt with a pattern that could probably trigger epilepsy, nods expectantly, his lanky frame perched awkwardly on a bar stool. Underneath his short dark hair, everything about Nick's face is exaggerated, as if his features are competing for attention: big bushy eyebrows, a mouth that wraps a little too far round to the sides, and a nose that doesn't quite point in the same direction as everything else.

More high street than high fashion, Mark is wedged into the chair opposite, fatherhood and corporate life having broadened both his responsibilities and his waistline. At times, he looks like a man fighting a losing battle, his mousy brown crew-cut receding as the years advance, and his once good-looking face now rounder, and occupied by an extra chin.

I scratch my head thoughtfully. 'Well, no, actually. I can't condone the infidelity aspect.'

'What do you mean?' says Nick, incredulously. 'You go out with loads of women.'

'Yes, but not at the same time. And I'm not married.' I take a sip of my beer. 'But I suppose it's a pretty good trick.'

'Not that you've ever needed tricks, eh?' says Mark, reaching across the table to slap my face Morecambe and Wise style. I'm too fast for him, and knock his hands away with a mock-threatening and poor mock-cockney 'Leave it!', nearly spilling my drink in the process.

Bar Rosa is run by a gay American couple, Pritchard and Rudy – better known to the three of us as Richard and Judy but, of course, not to their faces – and we're here so often that they've become our good friends now. At that moment, Rudy appears at the other end of the bar, looking at his watch and miming surprise when he sees the three of us in so early.

'Anyway,' continues Mark, 'that guy she was talking about doesn't know when he's well off.'

Nick frowns. 'How is he well off? Having the dutiful wife at home to look after the kids, or the extra-marital shagging?' he asks, not unreasonably.

Mark looks at Nick, shakes his head, and sighs exaggeratedly. 'So,' he says to me, 'going back to . . . what was her name again?'

'Evelyn. Eve.'

'Doomed from the start,' observes Nick.

'Sorry?' says Mark.

'Duh!' says Nick, making that face where you stick your tongue under your lower lip, and reminding me instantly of when he was eight years old, when we first became friends. '*Adam* and *Eve*?'

I do have a thing about girls' names. You've got to sound right as a couple. No rhyming, joke names, celebrity, literary or, as in this case, biblical allusions.

'Ah,' says Mark. 'Point taken. Was she attractive?'

I feign shock.

'Good kisser?'

'Tongue like an electric eel,' I say, repeating my favourite *Blackadder* line.

'Good in bed?' asks Nick.

When I huff indignantly, Nick looks at me, incredulously.

'So you didn't?'

I remove an imaginary bit of fluff from my sleeve. 'Er, might have done . . .'

'And?'

I look at them both and shrug. 'And what?'

'And what was she like?' Mark leans forward in his chair, causing me to shift a little uncomfortably in mine. I settle for what I hope will be an end-of-conversation reply.

'Well, if you'll excuse the pun, a bit of an anti-climax, actually.'

'An anti-climax?' exclaims Nick. 'What were you expecting, the sword-swallowing abilities of a top porn star? How exactly did she disappoint?'

'Jesus! What do you want? A blow-by-blow account?'

'Please!' says Mark, a little too keenly.

I shake my head resignedly. 'Well, she was just a little too . . . reserved.'

'Reserved?' exclaims Nick. 'You mean she didn't let you . . .'

I hold up my hand to silence him. 'Nick! Please!'

'What?' he says, gulping down a large mouthful of beer. 'You can't say something like that and then not give us all the facts.'

I look for support from Mark, but he's already nodding in agreement with Nick.

'Well, let's just say I kept looking down expecting to see a mortuary tag on her toe.'

'Ha!' smirks Nick. 'That might have been your fault, you know.'

'True . . .' I concede, grinning back at him. '. . . But doubtful!'

'You know,' says Mark, lowering his voice conspiratorially, 'speaking of climaxes, there's one sure fire way to find out what a woman's like in bed.'

'Sleep with her?' suggests Nick.

'No. Well, *yes*, obviously,' says Mark. 'But, apparently, *before* sleeping with her, you can tell a lot about what she's going to be like by . . .' He pauses for effect. 'By the way she sneezes.'

Nick and I look at each other, and then back at Mark, before Nick does the honours.

'Such as?'

'The way she, I mean, what she's like when she . . .' He reduces his voice to a whisper, despite there being nobody at the adjacent tables, '. . . orgasms.'

'What?' exclaims Nick.

'Orgasms. *Comes.*' Mark beckons us closer, as if he's about to divulge state secrets. 'For example, if she sneezes really loudly, with lots of facial expression and body movement, then she's going to be the same way when she, you know . . .'

Nick and I stare transfixed at Mark, who, sensing he's got our full attention, ploughs on. 'If she tries to hide it, or it's one of those pathetic little "achoos" that hardly registers, or worse still, it's no more than the "ach" part, then she'll be afraid to let herself go.' He leans back in his chair, obviously pleased with this little pearl of wisdom.

'Thank you, Yoda,' says Nick. 'And in your vast sexual experience, is this a fact?'

Mark opens his mouth to answer, but Nick cuts him off. 'Oh, hang on, you'd have to have slept with more than just the one woman for a valid scientific study.'

'Sod off!' counters Mark, always the master debater.

'Sneezes, eh?' I say, mentally running through a quick review of my evening with Evelyn.

Mark nods. 'Apparently.'

Nick stares at him, disbelievingly. 'You're making it up!'

'No, if you must know, I read it in *Cosmopolitan* the other day,' admits Mark, who then pales.

Nick starts to laugh. '*Cosmopolitan*? Oh, so it must be true,' he scoffs. 'And what were you doing reading *Cosmo* anyway? Isn't it a,' he continues, emphasizing the word, '*girl's* magazine?'

'It — it was Julia's copy,' stammers Mark. 'She'd

left it lying around and I just picked it up. To be honest, it made a pleasant change from *Accountancy Weekly*.'

'So,' I say, raising one eyebrow, 'your wife's started reading *Cosmo*, has she?'

'Better nip that in the bud, mate. And quickly!' advises Nick.

'And she's just leaving it,' I make speech marks in the air, 'lying around?' I shake my head slowly.

Mark frowns. 'Why? What are you talking about?'

Nick and I are on a roll now. 'Watch out, mate,' he says. 'Dangerous thing, a woman who reads *Cosmo*. Once Julia finds out there's such a thing as a female orgasm . . .'

I nod. 'Let alone more than one type . . .'

Nick looks at me quizzically for a moment before continuing. 'Exactly. You're in big trouble. It wasn't left out by accident, you know.'

I put a hand on Mark's arm. 'Was it open at any particular article?'

'Any passages underlined?' asks Nick.

'Fuck off!' says Mark, the panic rising in his voice. 'Julia and I are very happy. There's the small matter of another baby on the way, you know.'

'Okay, okay,' I say. 'Calm down. Just teasing.' I turn to Nick, to give Mark a bit of respite. 'But seriously, what about Sandra?' Sandra is Nick's girlfriend. 'Does she prove Mark's, sorry, *Cosmo*'s theory?'

'Now I think about it,' says Mark, before Nick can get a word in, 'I can't remember ever having heard her sneeze.'

'At least not with Nick there,' I add.

Nick snorts. 'Ha ha. Very funny.'

'So,' says Mark, clapping me on the shoulder, 'another potential Mrs Bailey bites the dust,' and I wince inwardly at the memories that phrase still brings. I was engaged once, a few years ago, although only for a few days. 'I take it you're not going to see her again?'

I think about this for a second. 'I shouldn't think so.'

Nick exhales loudly. 'Why not?'

I think about this for two seconds. 'She just didn't do it for me.'

'Again – what exactly did you ask her to do?' asks Mark. I yawn exaggeratedly and ignore him.

Nick shakes his head. 'What does a woman have to do to actually qualify for the position of *girlfriend* with you nowadays?' he asks. 'You can't still be comparing them all to . . .'

I give him a look that stops him mentioning Emma's name. 'No. Not any more. It's just . . .' I mull this over for a moment, as although it's a question I've asked myself a number of times, I'm still nowhere near a definitive answer. 'I guess they've just got to have that . . .' I can't quite think of the word, '*thing*, or whatever you call it.'

'You want to go out with a girl with a "thing"?' laughs Mark. 'You've been spending too much time on those Internet sites again.'

I pick a peanut up from the bowl on the table and flick it at him.

Mark notices that his beer bottle is empty, and checks

the clock on the wall. 'Sorry, chaps,' he says, adopting a haughty tone, 'but time and tide wait for no man,' adding, 'and nor does the number 211 bus,' when he sees Nick and I exchange confused glances. Despite living almost next door to a tube station, Mark insists on commuting in to the West End from Ealing by double decker, a journey which even Sir Ranulph Fiennes would think twice about.

'Why on earth do you have to travel everywhere by bloody *bus*?' asks Nick, the idea of any form of public transport so obviously abhorrent to him.

'I like travelling by bus, Mr Small Penis,' replies Mark, nodding through the window at Nick's Ferrari, which is double parked on the street directly in front of Bar Rosa. 'Much better than spending every morning stuck in a traffic jam, or playing sardines on the tube. Besides, statistically speaking, buses are the safest form of transport.'

'No they're not,' says Nick.

'Yes they are,' says Mark.

'Bollocks!'

'Bollocks yourself!'

'This is great, chaps,' I interject. 'You can't beat a good, intellectual discussion.'

'Okay,' continues Nick, 'if they're so safe, why does everyone always use that phrase "*You could get run over by a bus tomorrow*"?' He sits back smugly on his stool.

Mark retrieves his battered briefcase from underneath his seat and stands up. 'Not if you're on it!' he replies triumphantly. There's really no arguing with logic like that.

Mark waves goodbye to Rudy and walks out of the door. On his way past the window he stops next to the sculpture in red that is Nick's car and, checking to see that he's got our attention, points at Nick's new personalized number plates and mimes the international *wanker* sign. Nick just raises his left hand and slowly extends his middle finger.

'Why on earth did you get those embarrassing things fitted?' I ask, as Mark disappears off towards the bus stop.

'No point in having a Ferrari if nobody knows it's yours,' he says, a look of almost fatherly pride on his face.

'But *you* know it's yours,' I reply. Nick just shrugs.

As usual, we're sitting at one of Bar Rosa's window tables, firstly so Nick can keep an eye on his car, as much to spot the traffic wardens as the approving glances, and secondly (although firstly in my case) so we can check out any women who might walk past. Today the scenery is especially good, as it's a warm afternoon, which increases the amount of tanned midriffs and plunging cleavages on display.

Nick's vocabulary includes a variety of alerts to any particularly interesting sights, his favourites being 'hands up!' whenever a girl with overly prominent nipples is approaching, and, of course, a 'bit of a Monet' for those women who look great from a distance but not so good close up. He always adopts the tone of a World War Two squadron leader when he does this, i.e. '*hands up at two o'clock*', or '*bit of a Monet coming out of the Sun*', the Sun being the pub on the opposite side of the road. However, today he's unusually oblivious to the passing attractions.

As I work my way hungrily through a plate of nachos, I notice that Nick has hardly touched his food. As usual, he's drinking his beer straight from the bottle, but for some reason hasn't done his usual trick of stuffing a slice of lime down the neck, thus making it impossible to comment upon his liking for girly drinks. I'm about to ask him if he's okay when he looks up at me and shifts nervously in his seat.

'Listen, mate,' he says. 'Now that Mark's gone, there's something I need to talk to you about.'

'Corporation business? Should I be taking minutes?' Nick and I run a small Internet company, PleazeYourself, headquartered in a small office suite in a small business centre just off the King's Road, from which we make a small fortune.

'Nope. It's,' he clears his throat and lowers his voice, so I have to strain to hear him over the noise from the bar, 'ahem, personal stuff, actually. Sandra and I, we're . . .' His voice tails off, and he downs the rest of his beer before continuing. 'You know how when you've been going out with someone for a while.'

'Define "a while".'

'Oh yes. Sorry. I forgot that might be hard for you to imagine. But Sandra and I, we've kind of fallen into a routine, you know, it . . . it's all got very comfort-able. She's there when I go out in the morning, and always around when I get back home.'

'That's because she doesn't have a job.' I say, thinking

except for spending your money. I'm not Sandra's biggest fan.

Nick ignores me and carries on. 'Well, we were lying in bed last night, and she made us do this thing she'd read about.'

I shudder. 'Steady on. I'm not sure I want to hear this.'

He looks at me disdainfully. 'No. Nothing like that. We each had to write this list about what we wanted out of life, and then compare the two. Some sort of compatibility test.'

Bloody *Cosmo* again, probably. 'And?'

'And she got really upset.'

'Because?'

Nick swallows hard. 'Because she'd written stuff like "get married, have children", whereas . . .'

This should be good. 'Go on,' I say, taking a large swig of beer.

'Whereas I'd put "villa in the south of France, pet pot-bellied pig".'

I just about manage to prevent lager from coming out of my nose. 'Ah. Probably not what she wanted to hear, I imagine.'

He shakes his head. 'Quite. So I thought I'd better do something about it. You know, think about my priorities, make a decision.'

I'm sure he's going to tell me they're splitting up and he wants a hand moving her stuff out of the flat, or changing the locks. Nodding sympathetically, I prepare the now traditional 'plenty more fish in the sea' speech.

'So,' he announces, before I can deliver it. 'We're
. . . I'm . . . getting married!'

The bar suddenly seems deathly silent. Out in the
street, the birds have stopped singing. A piece of
tumbleweed blows past the open doorway, and somewhere in the distance a dog barks.

'What?' I splutter. 'To *Sandra*?' For a moment I
think, no, *hope*, that I can't have heard him properly,
but he's smiling like an idiot, so I must have.

'Of course to Sandra,' replies Nick, thankfully
mistaking my disbelief for surprise.

I realize that the look on my face isn't exactly
conveying my delight, and I fight to hide my astonishment. Not knowing what to say, I get a sudden
flashback to five years ago, Mark and Julia's wedding,
a drunken Nick lurching up to me, putting his arm
around my shoulders and gesturing towards the happy
couple.

'Just me and you now, mate,' he'd slurred. 'The last
of the musketeers!'

'It's mohicans,' I'd replied, only slightly less the worse
for wear.

'What?'

'It's *Last of the Mohicans*. You're getting confused
with *The Three Musketeers*.'

He'd struggled to process this piece of information.
'Yeah, but at some point there must have been just
two musketeers left?'

'Yes, but the thing to describe the last of anybody
is mohi— Oh, never mind,' I'd said, realizing I was
also arguing against the combined forces of Jack

Daniel's and Johnnie Walker. But as we'd stood there, gazing at our friend, I'd known exactly what he meant.

'That's right,' he exclaims, snapping me out of my reverie. 'So, will you do me the favour . . .' *Oh my god, I know what's coming. Quick, try and look pleased*, I tell myself, and force my mouth into some approximation of a smile. '. . . of being my best man?'

My mind starts to race. *Now's my chance*, I think. *Decline gracefully. Tell him what you think of Sandra.* But instead of condemning the idea as sillier than, well, most of the other decisions Nick makes in his life, to my surprise I find myself congratulating him, telling him that I'd be honoured, and we clink our bottles together loudly. Nick grins broadly, suddenly finding his appetite again, although I seem to have lost mine.

I'm still reeling from Nick's news when Rudy appears at the table, all white teeth and perma tan.

'Are you guys celebrating something?' he drawls.

I raise my eyebrows at Nick, who nods his consent. 'Nick's getting married,' I say, still not quite believing it myself, and pretty sure that 'celebrating' isn't the word I'd choose.

Rudy doesn't miss a beat. His face drops and he gazes imploringly at Nick, resting a hand on his shoulder. 'But, Nick,' he asks, 'are you sure you're doing the right thing? I mean, denying your true feelings?'

Nick falls for it. 'What do you mean, my true feelings? Sandra and I—'

'No, I mean your true *leanings*. Sandra will find out. They always do.'

Nick looks confused. 'What are you talking about?'

'It's okay,' continues Rudy. 'A number of my ex-boyfriends were married before they could admit to themselves and the world where their loyalties lay. It was like a final denial to themselves.'

Nick turns bright red as realization dawns. He looks lost for words for a few seconds, before selecting a couple of choice ones.

'Fuck off!' he says, with a grin.

Rudy starts to laugh, and despite my recently darkened mood I can't help but join him.

Suddenly, Nick's mobile rings, and when he sees the number displayed on the screen his face drops.

'Shit!' he says loudly, looking at his watch and then at the two of us. 'Fuck!'

'Tourette's playing up again?' says Rudy, causing us both to snigger.

Nick ignores him and hurriedly answers the call.

'Hello, honey,' we hear him say. 'Yes. No, I hadn't forgotten. Be right there, hon.'

Rudy and I exchange knowing glances as Nick hangs up sheepishly. 'I'm just going to the toilet,' he says to no one in particular, and heads off towards the gent's.

'And how do you feel?' Rudy asks me, once Nick's gone.

For a moment I think he's off on another of his mickey-taking routines but he actually looks quite sincere.

'Pardon?'

'You're not exactly jumping up and down with happiness. Everything okay?'

I do a good impression of a goldfish, my mouth moving but no sound coming out. 'I just . . . I mean, it's all a bit *sudden*, don't you think?' is the best I can eventually manage.

Rudy looks at me, enquiringly. 'Is that all?'

'Come on, Rudy, you've met Sandra. She's . . . Well, she's hardly his type. Mind you,' I add, 'I'm not sure what Nick's type actually is.'

Rudy sits down next to me. 'So what are you going to do about it?'

'What can I do about it?' I say, weakly. 'This is Nick we're talking about. Once he's made his mind up . . .'

Rudy sighs exasperatedly. 'Here's an idea. Just tell him what you think. Is that too easy for you?'

'Rudy, you just don't understand. We're English and we're male. Talking about stuff, especially stuff like this, just isn't in our nature.'

'But surely he'd listen to you.'

I shake my head. 'There's only one person Nick listens to nowadays, and she's hardly got his best interests at heart.'

'Maybe he's in,' Rudy clears his throat and adopts a Barry White voice, 'lurve.'

Horror crosses my face. 'With the Wicked Witch of the West End?'

Rudy corrects himself. 'Smitten, then. She is very attractive.'

I nod. 'Maybe. And that's the problem.'

'How do you figure?' asks Rudy.

I look around, checking that Nick's not on his way

back yet. 'Well, he's not the best-looking of guys, right?'

Rudy laughs. 'I've seen Picasso portraits with more regular features.'

'Exactly. And most of his other girlfriends . . . well, let's just say a few of them were born in Grimsby,' I say, emphasizing the first half of the word.

Rudy looks puzzled. 'You mean butt-ugly?'

'Well, over here we prefer the term *aesthetically challenged*.'

He rolls his eyes. 'Your point is?'

I nod towards Nick's car through the bar window. 'Look at when he bought the Ferrari. Mark and I tried to talk him out of it, and, if anything, that made him more determined. He got obsessed with the idea, particularly when he saw how everyone else responded when he told them. Since he's made all this money, he's realized he can buy into a new Nick. An Armani-suited, Breitling-wearing, Ferrari-driving Nick.'

Realization dawns on Rudy's face. 'And Nick judges himself by how other people react to him. Or rather, what he's got.'

'Precisely. Every now and again, he gets a notion about something he believes may make him *appear* a little better, and then decides to go through with it without really considering the consequences. It's as if he likes the look of it, the immediacy of it, without wanting to open his eyes to the possibility that in the longer term it might not be the most sensible thing to do. I mean, a car is one thing, but . . . getting married? And to Sandra?' I look at the ceiling in despair.

Rudy folds his arms. 'Jeez! You're really worried about this, aren't you?'

'I know him, Rudy. What he's like, how he thinks. And anyway, you heard him. He calls her "hun"!'

'As in "Atilla the"?' says Rudy. 'Come on, Adam. He's your oldest friend. You've got to tell him what you think, if only because you'll never forgive yourself if you don't.'

'But he's asked me to be best man.'

Rudy smiles. 'So *be* the best man. Surely the best thing you can do is try and stop him from ruining his life.'

I stare at him for a while before replying. 'You're maybe a bit too perceptive for your own good.'

He winks conspiratorially as Nick arrives back at the table. 'It's in the genes.'

Nick eyes us suspiciously. 'What are you two talking about?' he asks.

'Er . . .' I stammer. Fortunately Rudy rescues me.

'I was just wondering where Adam bought his jeans,' he replies.

Nick looks at us strangely and checks his watch again. 'Right,' he says, picking his car keys up from the table. 'Must dash.'

Rudy nudges me, and I take a deep breath. 'Stay for another beer?'

Nick shakes his head. 'No can do. Off to look at rings.'

'Sounds like my kind of afternoon!' smirks Rudy,

as he heads back behind the bar. Nick and I grimace
simultaneously.

'So, have you set a date yet?' I manage to ask, trying
in vain to prolong the conversation.

'Yeah,' replies Nick. 'Sandra thought it would be
nice to do it on my birthday.'

I'm confused for a moment. 'But that's . . .'

'I know,' he grins, walking away from the table. 'Six
weeks' time!'

Nick's already halfway out of the door before I can
think of anything else to say. I watch through the
window as he squeezes himself into the Ferrari and,
evidently having selected 'dragster' on the automatic
gearbox, screeches off towards his intended, or rather,
intended's, destination. And, standing there, I suddenly
realize that Rudy's right. In hindsight – which is
always 20/20 – I wish that someone could have told
me.

You see, Emma and I weren't right for each other
– a fact she made quite clear in the letter she left for
me on my kitchen table. I won't bore you with the
details, although I can still recall every single word
that she wrote, or rather typed, in Times New Roman
twelve point. On my computer.

One sentence bears repeating, though: 'You always
told me that people should never compromise in relationships.' Even in my distraught state I was impressed
by this: throwing my own logic back at me, although
I still can't work out how *she* was having to compromise. After all, I was the one who'd been prepared to
take on . . .

Anyway. That's just sour grapes now. At least she gave the ring back, although what good was it to me any more? I could hardly do the walk of shame into the jewellers and return it, or keep it for the next 'one', could I? Instead, I ran to the end of Brighton pier and threw it out as far as I could into the stormy grey water.

When I told them, Nick and Mark came straight round. I even showed them her letter, which they read, one after the other. And then, before I could stop him, Nick theatrically ripped it up right in front of me.

'You know, I think she did you a favour,' he said, earnestly. 'We never thought she was right for you, but we couldn't tell you that, could we?'

Open mouthed, I asked them why not, but Mark just shrugged. 'Because she seemed to make you happy.'

'Oh well,' Nick grinned. 'Plenty more fish in the sea.' And I actually laughed at his insensitive observation, because, despite the pain I was feeling inside, I knew he was right.

But later, worried that Nick had destroyed the last piece of contact we might ever have, I switched on my laptop and found where she'd saved her letter. And it was then, as I read it through one last time, that I realized the fundamental problem with real life: There's no backup copy.

Nick's my best friend, Sandra's not right for him, and someone really needs to let him know before it's too late – because you can bet that Sandra

won't. And even though there's not much time to
get them 'disengaged', how hard can it possibly be?
After all, he's only known her for a few weeks.

Chapter 2

I finish my beer in a bit of a daze and walk home, pausing only to nod goodbye to Rudy, who indicates the tyre marks where Nick's Ferrari had been parked and mouths what I guess is 'talk to him'. Back in my flat, I head straight for the bookshelf in the hallway, where I find my copy of *The Best Man's Bible*, which I'd bought to check on my duties for Mark's nuptials. I leaf through the book a couple of times, but nowhere can I find the chapter titled 'Stopping the Wedding'.

The night when Nick first met Sandra was little more than a month ago, a dark and stormy night – no, honestly – when Nick and I went to a black tie benefit that Mark's firm were sponsoring in aid of London Zoo's Adopt an Animal charity, at the Natural History Museum of all places. Strange choice of venue, perhaps: an event trying to raise money to keep animals in captivity alive held in a place that's famous for displaying the remains of their long-dead relatives.

The evening hadn't got off to the best of starts. I was running late, as it had taken me ages to get a taxi because of the weather, and I was still trying to get my bow tie done up in the back of the cab as I headed round to collect Nick. By the time I got to his flat he was already waiting impatiently on his doorstep but, as befitted Nick's usual sartorially challenged style, he was sporting a *white* dinner jacket.

'Shurely shome mishtake,' I said, looking him up and down while trying my best Sean Connery accent, but unfortunately sounding more like one of those deaf people who have learnt to talk without ever hearing real speech.

Nick stared back, indignant. 'What?'

'Nothing, mate. It's just that I didn't know we were going to be playing blackjack with Blofeld this evening.'

'Fuck off!' He said, sticking out his lower lip to indicate his hurt feelings. 'Back in a minute.'

Nick disappeared back up the stairs to his flat, and reappeared, literally sixty seconds later, more properly attired in black.

'Better?'

I stared at him, incredulously. 'You've got *two* dinner jackets?'

He shrugged. 'Well, you never know . . .'

'Nick, most people don't even own one, let alone two. And what exactly is the correct protocol for wearing one or the other, anyway?'

He grinned at me. 'Whether your mates take the piss. Besides, if you want to impress the *lay-dees* it helps to have the right gear.'

I shook my head despairingly. 'Mate, you need the help of Richard Gere.'

We headed off through South Kensington and up towards the museum, where the driver, who'd watched the goings-on with more than a little amusement, deposited us outside the huge building. Strolling nonchalantly up the stone steps we walked inside, the doorman checking us off on his list as we swaggered past him.

'I didn't know so many of your ex-girlfriends were going to be here tonight,' Nick whispered, and I felt a momentary sense of alarm before noticing his smirk and seeing where he was pointing. Towards the dinosaur hall.

'Let me buy you a free drink,' I said, helping myself to a couple of glasses of champagne from a tray proffered by a passing waiter. I handed one to Nick, which he downed in one, and we headed off in search of Mark. We soon spotted him in his ill-fitting suit, his bright red cummerbund concealing the fact that he couldn't do the top button up on his trousers any more, a detail he'd made the mistake of telling me on the phone earlier. I caught his eye and he excused himself from the group he was talking to and ambled over. We clinked our glasses loudly and downed what was obviously expensive champagne with little respect for its vintage.

'Been here a while?' I asked him, having noted his slightly rolling gait.

'An hour or two,' he replied, stifling a burp.

Nick surveyed the room, which was full of London's richest and, it had to be said, oldest. 'So, how much would these tickets have been, anyway?'

Mark lowered his voice. 'Two hundred quid, mate.'

My jaw dropped. 'Two hundred quid? I thought it

was "adopt" an animal, not pay for it to live at the Savoy.'

Nick made a sweeping gesture. 'Look at this place,' he said. 'It's full of people with more money than sense!'

'You should fit in perfectly, then,' I said, digging him in the ribs.

'Just enjoy yourselves, and don't tell anyone you got in for free, will you?' Mark slurred. 'I've got to go and be sociable.' Dextrously grabbing another glass of champagne from the now returning waiter, he staggered back towards the people he'd left.

Nick and I helped ourselves to more drinks and discussed our strategy, quickly deciding that the best course of action was to get as drunk as we could in as short a time as possible. As Nick headed off to find the toilets, I liberated more champagne from the bar and began scanning the crowd for any potential female company.

After downing the best part of a bottle, I'd decided that the only unattached women there were probably single because their husbands had recently died of old age, and they weren't long for this world themselves. I'd also started to worry about Nick, who'd been gone for half an hour. I collared Mark, and we were discussing whether we should go off and look for him when he appeared, looking like he'd got his fast-forward button pressed down, clutching a brown envelope in one hand and a scrap of paper in the other. I greeted him as I would any long-lost friend.

'Where the fuck have you been?'

'Sorry, boys. Got sidetracked,' he said, triumphantly

waving the scrap of paper in the air, on which we could see what looked like a name and a telephone number.

Nick's never been a great chatter-upper of women. He's not the most charming of guys, and his usual idea of an opening gambit is to 'casually' throw his Ferrari key ring on the table in front of any woman he fancies. In my book, any woman impressed by this approach . . . well, horses for courses.

Much to his annoyance, neither of us took the bait. 'Aren't you going to ask me what this is?' he said, eventually.

I grabbed it from his hand and held it up to the light. 'Hmm. I'd say it's a scrap of paper. Mark?'

'Yup, definitely paper,' Mark agreed, taking it from me and examining it closely. 'And I write on the stuff every day. I should know.'

Nick snatched it back impatiently. 'I've just met someone and got their phone number.'

'What's he like?' said Mark.

'Fuck off, fat boy. It's a *she,* obviously. And she's gorgeous.'

I sighed resignedly. 'Come on then. Tell all.'

'Well, I was off looking for the toilets,' he gabbled excitedly, 'so I went through this door by the bar, and in the room there's this desk, and behind this desk was this gorgeous woman.'

'Name?'

'Sandra. And we got chatting, and it turns out that she's working for the charity people here tonight, and so—'

I held my hand up. 'Hold on,' I said, a dreadful realization dawning. 'Which one?'

'What?'

'Which one?' I repeated, louder this time.

'Which charity? I don't know what it's called. Anyway, that's not important. So, she—'

'No.' I stopped him, and reverted to sentences one word long. 'Which. Animal. Did. You. Adopt?'

Nick looked at me sheepishly. 'Er . . .'

'Please tell me you didn't?'

'Um, a monkey,' he replied, his eyes wandering guiltily to the envelope in his other hand.

'A monkey?' I shook my head in disbelief.

'Yeah.' He peered at the front of the envelope. 'Capuchin, to be precise.'

Mark frowned. 'Isn't that a kind of coffee?'

'And dare I enquire how much?' I asked, guessing the phrase 'pay peanuts, get monkeys' wasn't applicable in this case.

'Well, I . . . I thought we could put it through the business,' stammered Nick.

'Put it through the business?' I said, incredulously. 'Bollocks!'

'Why not? Good . . . PR and all that,' he replied, in a straw-clutching kind of way.

'Well, you put it through your half of the business then.'

'Good PR? I can't quite see how,' said Mark, his champagne intake putting him a few seconds behind the conversation.

'So anyway, me and Sandra got chatting—'

'How much?'

Nick rocked nervously from one foot to the other. 'Only a thousand. Anyway, as I was saying—'

Mark suddenly caught up. 'I thought a "monkey" was five hundred pounds? Or is that a "pony"?'

I was almost speechless. 'You spent a thousand pounds sponsoring a . . . a *monkey,* just so you could get a girl's phone number?' I would have liked to say that I didn't believe it, but knowing Nick it certainly wasn't out of the question. Despite earning well, the school of life has taught me the value of money. Nick, however, had obviously been off sick for that particular lesson.

'Not just for her phone number,' he said, slipping it guiltily into his pocket.

'So what else? Do you get to take the monkey home at weekends?'

'Not exactly.'

'Do you get to visit it, feed it, anything like that?'

'Er, nope.' His eyes flicked back to the envelope. 'You get a certificate.'

'A certificate?'

'Yeah,' he said, suddenly perking up. 'And, you get to mention it in any advertising you do.'

'Nick. We run an Internet porn site. How is that going to work? "Dear Customer, please select us as your preferred masturbatory medium because we sponsor an animal at London Zoo"?'

We stood in an uneasy silence for a while, until Mark suddenly piped up. 'I've got it,' he announced. '*Fed up spanking your own monkey? Spank ours!*' And I laughed, despite myself.

Nick, on the other hand, was looking like he'd been told off by his mother. 'Well, I'm sure it's tax-deductible,' he offered.

I sighed wearily and found myself actually looking at Mark, hoping that yes, maybe this did make some financial sense. Unfortunately, he was still too pleased with his joke and too full of champagne to offer any serious advice.

'Admit it,' I said, turning back to Nick. 'You just did it because you fancied her.'

'Um . . .'

I peered over his shoulder, back in the direction he'd come from, and drained my glass.

'Well, let's have a look at her then,' I said. Shaking my head, I started to head off out of the hall, but Nick grabbed me by the arm. Quite firmly.

'No way,' he said. 'I don't want you stealing her off me before I've even had a chance to go out with her.' And I remember looking at his face, thinking he was joking, but seeing instead just how serious he'd been.

Then, two weeks later, when Nick marched proudly into Bar Rosa clinging to this girl like they'd had an accident with the superglue, I had to stop myself from doing a double take. He'd been right – unusually for him, she *was* gorgeous. Tall, expensively dressed, her long blonde hair scraped back off her angular face – open any copy of *Hello!*, turn to the society pages, and you'll see her type, usually draped around Lord *Nobody-of-Note* at some charity polo bash.

'This is Sandra,' he announced, albeit quite

unnecessarily, and with a silly grin on his face. 'Sandra
– Adam. Adam – Sandra.'

She looked me up and down for a few moments,
keeping hold of my hand for longer than felt comfortable.

'Hi, Sandra. Nice to finally meet you,' I said.

'Hello, Adam,' she replied, in a voice that could cut
glass. 'Nick's told me all about you.'

I raised my eyebrows and looked across at Nick,
slipping effortlessly into that 'best buddies' routine.
'Most of it probably true.'

'I hope so,' she said, with a glint in her eye that
instantly made me feel awkward, and that, strangely, I
hoped Nick hadn't seen.

We found a table in the corner. 'What would you
like to drink, hon?' Nick asked her. Hon? I tried to
catch Nick's eye, but with no success.

'My usual,' she replied.

'Two glasses of champagne please,' Nick asked
Pritchard, who'd suddenly materialized next to us.
'Adam?' he asked me, as I watched Sandra sizing
Pritchard up.

'No, I'm fine with my *beer*, thanks,' I replied,
wondering when Nick had started drinking champagne in the middle of the week.

I'm a great believer in my instincts. I can normally
tell what someone's like within a few moments of
meeting them, and I certainly know almost immediately if we're going to get on. Just as Pritchard and
Rudy say they have a 'gaydar', where they can immediately tell anyone who's their way inclined, I have a

similar sixth sense, a 'bitch sense' if you will, when it comes to women; and with Sandra my hackles, wherever they are, had definitely started to rise. And when I think back now, I realize that it was her smile that unsettled me the most: a smile that, although frequent, and revealing perfect white teeth, forgot to tell the rest of her face to join in.

'So, what do you do, Sandra?' I asked her, as she sipped her champagne.

'Oh, I'm in between careers at the moment,' she replied dismissively.

'Oh really? Which two are you in between?' Perfectly normal question, I thought, but her answer was just another of those surface-only smiles.

We chatted for a while, mostly about Sandra, her hanging on to Nick's arm and Nick on to her every word. Strangely, I'd initially found myself trying to think of a way to excuse myself without being rude, but the novelty factor of seeing Nick with an attractive woman soon overcame my urge to leave. Then Rudy came over, smiling broadly, and refilled their glasses.

'On the house, Nick,' he said, hovering at the table.

I stood up. 'I'll do the honours, shall I? Sandra, this is our friend Rudy. He and Pritchard own this place.'

'Oh really?' Sandra suddenly seemed more interested now Rudy had been elevated from the status of barman. She smiled and held out her hand, and Rudy kissed the back of it.

'Nice watch,' he said, noting the gleaming Cartier on her wrist.

The smile clicked off, and she quickly removed her hand from Rudy's and settled it back on to Nick's arm.

'Thanks. It was a present.'

Rudy and I both stared at Nick, who was blushing slightly. 'Well, Sandra said she didn't have a watch, and we were out shopping, and I could tell she really liked this one—'

Sandra stopped him by putting a finger on his lips. 'Now now, Nicky. I'm sure your . . . friends don't want to hear about our private lives,' she said, emphasizing the word 'private'.

Nicky? Eeugh! I thought, as Rudy and I looked at each other knowingly.

'Join us for a drink?' I asked him, leaning over and patting the seat next to Nick, who edged along awkwardly.

Rudy smiled. 'No can do – I've got to go downstairs to the cellar with Pritchard and flush the pumps. Care to give us a hand, Nick?' he added, mischievously.

'Please,' said Nick, 'there are ladies present.'

I looked round at him, waiting for the joke, but none came.

We sat in an awkward silence for a few moments, until Sandra patted Nick on the arm. 'Excuse me,' she said. 'I'm just going to use the ladies'.'

'That's normally Adam's speciality,' said Rudy, putting an arm round my shoulders and giving me a squeeze before heading back to the bar.

'Thanks a lot,' I replied, moving my chair so Sandra

could get by. Nick reluctantly let go of her, and we watched her walk away from the table.

'So,' he turned to me, once she was out of earshot. 'What do you think?'

Now, there are two rules between best friends concerning girlfriends, and as it was looking like Nick was seriously considering Sandra as someone who could fulfil this position, I decided that I had to apply them. Rule number one is, of course, never sleep with your best friend's girlfriend, past or, obviously, present. It will create an unspoken issue between the two of you, particularly in terms of performance issues, size comparisons, and so on.

Rule number two, appropriate in this case, is never give your honest opinion, even if asked, of your best friend's current girlfriend, fiancée or wife. At least not until they've parted company, and even then, the only acceptable comments are along the lines of 'We never liked her anyway' or 'You could do better'.

So when Nick asked me what I thought of Sandra, what was I to say? That I didn't like her? That I didn't trust her? That my initial impression after a few minutes was that the watch, the champagne, and the lack of career marked her out as a gold digger? Or that, dare I say it, she was out of his league, especially given his puppy dog eyes whenever he looked at her?

I settled for a 'She seems nice', and watched him sip his drink nervously, his eyes flicking repeatedly towards the toilet door, as if he feared she might never come out again. Eventually, she returned to the table,

and, without sitting down, made it clear that she wanted
to leave.

'So, Nicky, did you decide where we were going
for dinner?'

'Well, I thought we could maybe eat here?' he
suggested, tentatively.

'Oh, I'm not really keen on these Spanish . . .' she
looked around dismissively '. . . finger-buffet places.
What about somewhere like . . .' She named a horren-
dously expensive restaurant in Knightsbridge.

'Sounds good,' Nick replied, looking at his watch.
'Let's go and see if we can get a table.'

And with that they'd left, Sandra giving me a couple
of those little air kisses either side of my face that
didn't actually make skin contact – something I was
actually quite glad about.

'Bye, Sandra. Nice to have met you,' I lied, adding,
'Bye, *Nicky* . . .' Nick shot me a murderous glance.

I watched them go, and then walked to the bar to
settle up.

'Who was that bitch?' Rudy asked me.

'That, unfortunately, was Nick's new girlfriend,' I
said. 'And don't call me bitch.'

'You'd better look out for that one,' he said, as we
saw Nick hold open the Ferrari's passenger door for
her. 'I think she's set her sights on our friend.'

And as I watched her fixing her make-up in Nick's
rear-view mirror as they drove away, one question
leapt to the front of my mind: a question I was worried
I already knew the answer to.

What did she see in Nick?

Chapter 3

With *The Best Man's Bible* failing to provide any inspiration, divine or otherwise, I put it back on the shelf, and, with Nick's announcement still playing on my mind, get out my mobile phone and select 'calendar' from the menu. Today is April 4, it says – not three days earlier, sadly – and Nick's birthday is on May 17. With a rising sense of panic, I scroll all too quickly through the six intervening weeks. Time to think.

By early evening I'm no closer to a strategy, so I decide to stroll round to my gym, the 'amusingly' named Slim Chance, to work out my frustrations on weightier matters. It's one of those huge health clubs on several levels, although not metaphysically, you understand. Heading in past the smiling receptionists, I take the lift up to the top floor.

Walking past the dance studio, I'm disappointed to see that there are no aerobics classes taking place, even though, unfortunately, and despite my numerous anonymous suggestion forms, it doesn't have a spectator area. I change quickly and head into my regular venue, the cardio-theatre, where a huge bank of television sets on the wall at one end broadcasts a selection of news, music and assorted programmes to the exercising faithful on the machines below. Each bike, treadmill, or cross-trainer has its own control box, into which you plug your headphones (£9.99 from reception), before selecting your channel and setting off on your workout.

My personal favourite time here is the soap slot, between 7.30 p.m. and 8.30 p.m. on a weekday evening, when West London's fitness-conscious (or, I suppose, non-television owning) women love to sweat away in front of *Coronation Street* or *EastEnders*. Personally, I can't stand the soaps, and it means that I'm reduced to listening to my personal CD player whilst all the televisions are tuned to one or the other of these programmes, but fortunately the gym scenery usually makes up for what's on the screens in front.

I survey the alternative entertainment on offer before deciding which exercise machine I'll use, workout specificity sacrificed for the best vantage point, of course. Today, however, despite arriving in time for *Emmerdale,* the selection's not so great, so I settle for a bike at the back of the room, where at least I can get a good view of the whole gym.

I plug in my CD player, which I've loaded with some fast-beat Ibiza-style mix where all the 'songs' seem to blend into one another (it's a feature of the CD, honestly, and not just me sounding like my dad), select a course on the digital display and start my workout. At the same time, I try and work out what I'm going to do about Nick.

He and I have been best friends for as long as we both can remember – the kind of friendship where the other person always acts as the reference point for the major events in your life. Stories always start, 'Nick and I were . . .' or 'Nick, do you recall . . .' or similar. Our parents lived, still live and will probably die next door to each other in Margate, a town so neglected that it shouldn't be twinned with anywhere. It's more in need of fostering.

Like me, Nick was an only child, but we were so close that we didn't feel it, and perhaps because of that we've always looked out for each other. We'd gone to the same schools, been in the same classes even, and when the time came to choose a college Brighton had seemed a good option for both of us – relatively close to our respective homes, and offering a good enough degree course, business studies, which should have led to something positive in terms of potential careers.

Not that either of us had any idea what we wanted to do with our lives at that time, except work our way through our grant cheques whilst not-working our way through college. It was there that we'd met Mark, having all answered the same ad for a house-share in Albion Terrace, a run-down Victorian street just off the seafront. The three of us had hit it off immediately, mainly because we shared a childish sense of humour.

Of the three of us, Mark was the only one who seemed to take studying seriously. He was on the accountancy course, and seemed to us to have been born into the profession. I remember one drunken night, one of many drunken nights (but one of the few I actually remember), we'd had that 'dream careers' discussion, where we'd all had to decide on our ideal job if qualifications (and talent) were no object. Mine was easy: photographer for *Playboy* magazine, and Nick soon settled on Ferrari test driver. That same night, Mark admitted, sadly, that he had always wanted to be an accountant. We've never let him forget that.

We stayed in that house for the whole four years, loving the Brighton life. On sunny afternoons we'd skip lectures, pile into Mark's car and head up on to the cliffs at Beachy Head, where we'd sit for hours, watching the sun set over the horizon and emptying the endless cans of beer that we'd emptied our bank accounts to buy. Nick and I would perch right on the cliff edge, our legs dangling over the crumbling chalk, seeing who dared sit the furthest out. Mark always stayed a few feet back, blaming his vertigo but really just preferring to keep both feet on solid ground.

Once we'd finished our degrees, lured by the big noise and bigger salaries of the capital, we'd moved to London, where Mark had already got a position with one of the top accountancy firms. Together the three of us had rented a flat in Chelsea, where Nick had taken a job with an IT company and I'd joined an advertising firm. And then, four years ago, while Mark was progressing steadily towards both parenthood and his partnership, Nick and I had set up Please Yourself. We've never really looked back.

You know that *Monty Python* sketch where the old

guys are sitting around remembering how tough they used to have it? I can see the three of us like that in years to come, sipping piña coladas on the beach, talking nostalgically about life gone by. Oh, except for the fact that we didn't ever have it tough.

A harsh bleeping sound signifies the end of both my reminiscence and my exercise programme, but instead of heading for the weights machines I find myself hitting the 'start' button again, because just getting on to the bike in front of me is this – at least from behind – gorgeous woman wearing the smallest pair of Lycra shorts. I'm a huge fan of Lycra; I think it must have been a guy who invented it, and whoever he was should be given a medal for services to mankind. I can just imagine him showing his invention off at the annual scientists' convention:

'Gentlemen, I present my latest discovery – it's a super-elastane material with high-tensile properties.'

'And how do you think your invention will benefit mankind? In the field of engineering? Or medical science, perhaps?'

'Why, neither. Rather, I forecast that in the future it will be dyed the most garish colours and used to harness all manner of sweaty breasts and buttocks.'

She's obviously doing some type of hill workout, because every few minutes she stands up on the pedals for – I count – thirty seconds, affording me a fantastic view of her pert behind.

A quarter of an hour later, and I'm flicking through the various workout choices on the LED screen in front of me – interval training, fat-burning – frantically searching for one labelled 'coasting downhill', when suddenly the gym empties. *EastEnders* is over, and the only soap being attended to now is in the showers. I'm knackered, but Lycra-lady is showing no signs of stopping, so I consider my options for a moment. I'm too tired to start another session, so instead I walk over to the stretching area, where I do some half-hearted exercises, hoping that she might come over and join me when she finishes her ride.

By the time I'm in danger of becoming so loose I won't be able to stand up, she finally gets off her bike. I've sat so I can monitor her progress in the mirror without being caught staring, and I congratulate myself on my positioning as she towels herself down in full view and then comes over to where I'm sitting.

I'd been worried she might be, to use one of Nick's incredibly sexist terms, a 'butter face' – one of those women who looks fantastic from behind but when she turns round she's really ugly, i.e. great body, 'but-her-face . . .' Not so with this one. Short dark hair, a cute nose, a bit like that new BBC news presenter who everyone claimed got the job due to her looks and not her journalistic experience of sitting and reading an autocue.

There are three mats, and I've purposely taken the middle one so she has to come and use one next to me, and I feign indifference as she sits and starts her cool-down. I'm just about managing to touch my toes and can't help but stare as she effortlessly leans forward and rests her forehead on her knees.

She looks up and meets my gaze. 'Hard?'

'I'm sorry?' My eyes widen inadvertently.

'Exercising after a busy week at work. It's hard.'

Not having had a busy week at work for a while, I smile back.

'You're looking good on it, though,' I say.

She straightens back up and dabs with her towel at the sweat glinting sexily off her top lip. 'Thanks,' she says, blushing slightly.

'Good workout?' I ask her.

'Not bad,' she replies, mid stretch. 'I'm just trying to get back into shape after . . .' Her voice tails off.

'After?'

'Oh, you know.' She looks at me for a moment as if considering how much to reveal, and then drops the towel, metaphorically speaking. 'I've just broken up with someone and I'm going through one of those re-focusing times. I've only recently moved to London so I thought I'd join a gym, as I don't really know anybody here.'

Hmm. Newly single? New in town? Has possibil-ities. 'Well, now you know one person, at least,' I say, holding out my hand. 'Adam, by the way.'

'Samantha,' she replies, and we shake hands, rather formally seeing as we're both sat on the stretch mats, sweaty, and not wearing very much.

We chat for a while, Samantha twisting her body into more and more convoluted positions, me trying to keep not only my interest from growing. Eventually she stops her routine and regards me nervously for a moment, as if she's running me through some sort of approval process.

'Listen,' she says, 'I don't normally do this, but . . .' she takes a deep breath, 'would you like to go out for a drink some time?'

'Er, yes, why not. That would be nice,' I reply, after the briefest of pauses.

'Well, when might you be free?' she asks. 'Tonight?'

I hesitate for a few seconds, wondering whether I should really be trying to sort things out with Nick instead, and for a moment Samantha looks as if she's worried she might have overstepped the mark, or put me under a little too much pressure.

'That's if you're not busy, I mean,' she adds, unconsciously stretching her leg up behind her ear.

Nick can wait for this evening, at least. 'No,' I say, smiling at her. 'I mean, no, I'm not busy. Tonight's good,' and we arrange to meet in an hour at a bar on the Fulham Road.

I walk back towards the changing room, wondering whether I've got time for a quick Jacuzzi, but when I see that there are already a few people in there I decide against it. That's the problem with those communal ones – you can never be quite sure where all the bubbles are coming from. Instead, I spend some time in the shower, careful to wash thoroughly in preparation for this evening, and as I get dressed I play back our brief conversation in my head, just to make sure I've got the facts straight. Samantha. *Sam.* One of my rules broken already – women whose names can be shortened into a masculine form. It makes it more difficult down the line to say 'I love you' if those three words are followed by something male-sounding. Oh, and while I'm on the subject, never ever go out with a girl with the same name as your mum. Crying it out in bed just doesn't . . . Well, you get the picture.

I head out of the gym and walk slowly back to my flat, exhausted from my extended exercise session, and when I get in I notice the answerphone light flashing insistently. It's Evelyn, my date from the previous Saturday, wondering if I'm interested in a 'repeat performance' tonight. Feeling slightly guilty, I delete the message and get ready for my date with Samantha.

Ever since I was a baby women have been picking me up. I'd been one of those few newborns lucky enough not to exit the womb a dead ringer for Winston Churchill, and my mother was always being stopped in the street so complete strangers could hoist me out of my pram to fuss over me. In my formative years to walk down the street was to run the gauntlet of constant hair-ruffling, cheek-pinching and prickly kisses from old ladies, normally accompanied by an *ooh, isn't he cute*, or *he'll break a few hearts when he's older*. All this female attention must have made a big impact, because this is something I've worked hard to maintain all my adult life.

Now, aged thirty-one, that babyish charm is long gone, but through a combination of hard work – admittedly in the gym rather than the office – dressing well and, of course, close attention to personal hygiene, I've managed to maintain a respectable level of attractiveness, which means I do pretty well in the competitive dating world. I don't mean to brag, but just as some people are good at games or have an ear for music, this is my speciality. I'm one of those people for whom the sum of the parts is greater than the whole, and believe me, I work hard on all my parts.

You know how you occasionally see pictures in the newspaper of brothers or sisters of celebrities, and they share certain facial characteristics with their more famous relative but just don't quite have that star appeal, or whatever you call it? Well, next time you see one of those pictures, think of a pre-Bond Pierce Brosnan (somewhere between the Remington Steele and Mrs Doubtfire years should just about do it), and then, using the same formula, imagine how his younger brother might look, and that's me.

I'm just under six feet tall – five eleven and a quarter, in fact. That's 181 cm in new money. It bugs me slightly that I haven't made the six foot mark, although I can't quite see the sense in having this standard. Roll on metrication, then I won't have to feel miffed at not being a 'six-footer'. After all, no one's going to say 'He's a shade under one hundred and eighty-three centimetres', are they? I'm currently tipping the scales at around twelve stone, which apparently is my 'ideal weight'. Ideal for what? Not being a fat bloke, I guess.

And here's my confession: my name's Adam Bailey, and I'm a date-a-holic. That's right – I go out with women. Quite a few, Nick and Mark will tell you. Okay, short-term and serially, if you want to define it even further. It's not that I'm trying to avoid any of this serious 'relationship' stuff – quite the opposite, in fact – I don't have any issue with commitment. It's just that too often I start seeing a girl and we get on fine, but there's the rub. We only get on fine. No spark. No violins playing, no fireworks going off overhead, no aching hearts when we're apart, hoping when the phone rings it's her, that sort of stuff. There might be nothing at all wrong with the poor girl, but for some reason I just know it's not going anywhere. I then get hung up on the slightest of issues, which means it's never going to progress past more than a couple of dates. They might range from the unreasonable – discovering that she has fat ankles – to the very unreasonable – maybe pronouncing 'espresso' with an 'x', as in *ex-presso* – but as soon as I notice something like this I'm off. Call me fickle, and I'd agree with you.

It's not that I don't want to settle down. It's more that I'm not prepared to settle. Compromise. Call it what you like, but only Miss Right is going to become Mrs Bailey. And I don't mind how many frogs I have to kiss.

I study my reflection in the hall mirror before I leave. I'm dressed straight from the pages of *GQ* – untucked, fitted black shirt, a pair of what I guess are called smart-casual trousers, new underwear, black, recently-shined shoes, hair just on the trendy side of unkempt, and I've lightly doused myself with Issey Miyake, which (thanks, for once, *Cosmo*) I believe to be a smell that meets with almost universal female approval. A quick check of the wallet for those two first-date prerequisites – cash and condoms – and I'm off.

I always arrange to meet first dates at the venue itself, instead of picking them up in the car beforehand, mainly to avoid all those awkward dropping off at home issues afterwards. If I'm not interested in extending the evening, it's much easier to get into separate cabs outside a bar or restaurant than be sitting outside her house in my car trying to think of excuses not to come in. Plus, if the evening becomes mind-numbingly boring, and trust me, many of them do, I can seek escape in a bottle or two of good wine without worrying about driving home. It's also because I'm quite strict on this drinking and driving stuff – my policy is that if you drive and then drink, you should drink so much you can't find your car again at the end of the evening.

I arrive at the bar early, find a table with a good view of the door, and order my 'usual', a Jack Daniel's on the rocks. I drink this for two reasons: firstly because it looks pretty cool, and secondly because I actually like it, and I'm on my second drink by the time Samantha walks in. She's ten minutes late (not a good sign – I was starting to get a little worried), and I watch her as she stands nervously by the door for a few seconds before I wave her over to where I'm sitting. She looks good – a simple blue but very low-cut dress that means I'll have to try hard not to stare down her front all night, and I notice with satisfaction that quite a few heads turn, both male and female, as she makes her way over towards me. I ready my best charismatic smile and stand up to greet her with a kiss on the cheek. She smells good, and reddens slightly as I tell her so.

We order a bottle of wine and chat for a while

about the usual innocuous things: her parents, friends, her work. She tells me that she's an assistant research technician for a drug company, and then I make the mistake of saying 'So what exactly does an assistant research technician do?'

I pride myself on being a good listener, which turns out to be just as well given the amount Samantha's got to say for herself, as she embarks on an explanation, in minute detail, of the process of bringing a drug to market, the testing procedure, everything down to deciding on the appropriate size and shape for the tablet itself. Maybe it's because she's nervous, or more likely I've plied her with too much wine, but by the time we're on our second bottle she just doesn't stop talking.

'Wow,' I say, twenty minutes later, stifling a yawn and having gathered enough information to go into competition with Pfizer, 'I'll never look at an aspirin in the same way again.'

And then things take a turn for the worse. 'So,' she asks, fixing me with a slightly out-of-focus stare, 'what star sign are you?'

Oh NO! Horoscopes. And so soon. This is definitely a conversation I don't want to get into, and the more interest anyone shows in the subject, the less I'm interested in them. *Libra*, I always reply, *well balanced*, in a 'hilarious' reference to the scales, although it's not as if I'd say *fishy* if I was Pisces of course. *So you're the creative, analytical type*, they say, or some such rubbish. *No*, I reply, *it just means I was born at the end of September. But it's all to do with the tides*, they never tire of telling me, *and as your body is seventy per cent water* . . . , but by that point I've already zoned out.

And even worse is when they try and guess, which is what Samantha attempts to do before I've had a chance to answer her.

'Don't tell me . . .'

'No, honestly, it—'

'Leo, yes?'

I sigh, and lie. 'Yes, how did you know?' I say, feigning curiosity. After all, she does look good in that dress.

'Oh, it's just a knack I have,' replies Samantha, looking immensely pleased with herself.

I try to change the subject rapidly, but it's something she wants to hold forth on, and after a further half an hour my neck is aching with the effort of nodding every few moments as she comes out with yet another 'fascinating' astrological observation. It's time to take stock of the evening, and I can tell that given the eye contact, body language and more importantly the amount of alcohol she's consumed, my chances of sex later are pretty high. But even though her earlier feats of flexibility are still fresh in my mind, I decide it's just not worth the effort of trawling through the rest of the date.

By the time she gets on to Feng Shui, even a brief fantasy involving her in various positions on my furniture fails to rescue the evening for me. With a clarity of foresight that Russell Grant would be proud of, I can suddenly see my future, and Samantha's not in it. I decide to invoke my escape clause, and excuse myself to go to the toilet where, from the sanctuary of the cubicle, I call Mark on my mobile asking him to phone me back in five minutes.

Back at the table, and after a further ten minutes on how Samantha had her fortune told recently, during which I'm cursing Mark, who's probably looking at his watch and sniggering, my phone finally rings. I apologize along the lines of *Oh sorry, I should have turned it off*, but I tell her it's work, it might be important et cetera (fortunately, we haven't had time or the opportunity to talk about what I do). Answering the call, I feign growing shock as I repeat *Oh really, oh no, I'll be right there*, and all the while Mark is on the other end of the phone going *You cheeky git, I keep saving you like this, what's she like anyway – nice tits? Ow!* I'm guessing Julia has just thumped him, and I hear her call him a sexist bastard as I end the call.

I switch the phone off and turn to Samantha, a look of annoyance on my face as I explain. 'The office alarm is going off. They can't get hold of my business partner so I have to go and meet the police there. I'm really sorry,' I say, calling the barman over so I can settle the bill.

Her face drops. 'Oh, that's okay,' she says. 'Do you want me to come with you?'

Oops. I feel a little guilty now. 'No, thanks. It might take a while. I'll get you a cab.' And at least I do one decent thing, in a sea of indecent things, as I walk her outside, flag down a taxi and pay the driver to take her home. As we kiss goodbye, she presses a scrap of paper with her number scrawled on it into my hand.

'Call me?' she says, more of an enquiry than a request.

I smile and nod, but as the taxi pulls away I make a mental note not to go to the gym on a Friday evening for a while. Callous? Maybe. But what was the alternative? Lead her on just to sleep with her, then never call her again? Or waste another couple of hours just to be honest over coffee and tell her? And tell her what? That I don't want to see her again because she tried to guess my star sign? Would she have believed that? Would anybody? Come to think of it, do I?

I think about getting a taxi myself, but walk instead, as tonight's one of those warm, late-spring evenings when the Chelsea streets have a nice buzz, the cafés and bars just beginning to spill their exuberant clientele out on to the pavements. As I stroll back along the King's Road, feeling slightly but pleasantly drunk, I find myself noticing how like me these people all are: thirty-something, probably with good jobs, nice houses, and, by the look of them, the same objective in life: having a good time. But as I look closer, I'm suddenly struck by a sobering realization. They're all couples.

Chapter 4

Saturday night finds me driving towards Ealing, where Mark and Julia are having a party at their house. It's been planned for weeks, but has turned into an impromptu engagement bash given yesterday's developments. I've arranged to get there early, ostensibly to give Mark a hand but actually because, with only six weeks to go until the wedding, I've realized that it's me who'll be needing help if I'm going to do anything about Nick and Sandra.

I drive one of those cars that give you more *bang for your buck*, as our American cousins say. You know the type: those normal saloons with huge turbocharged engines, oversized spoilers, and insurance premiums to match. It's Japanese, a Subaru Impreza, or 'Suburban Impresser', as Nick sneeringly calls it, and I love it. It's not as ostentatious as the Ferrari, but give me a twisting country road and most other cars, including Nick's, become little more than a distant dot in the rear-view mirror.

Although it's not the best looking of vehicles, I do find it attracts a lot of attention, especially from those tall grey cameras mounted by the side of the road.

And even though London's current congestion levels mean that I can rarely get it out of second gear around town, at least it doesn't constantly break down, unlike a certain piece of Italian engineering.

Blipping the accelerator, I edge my way along the Fulham Road, cursing the heavy Saturday evening traffic. The crawl up past Earl's Court takes an age, and I'm starting to worry that I haven't left enough time for my pre-party pow-wow, but once I get past Tesco the road begins to clear, so I turn the stereo up and put my foot down.

Accelerating off the Hammersmith flyover, I can feel my anticipation building for the coming evening. The conversation with Mark aside, I'm looking forward to seeing the other guests, a mixture of old friends and colleagues from years gone by, many of whom I haven't seen since Mark and Julia's wedding. Plus, Mark has taken the fantastic step of banning children from the event, which means young India, my goddaughter, has been packed off to her grandparents for the night, and the other guests, by now mostly married couples with kids of their own, have been ordered to get babysitters in. I'm therefore hoping for a throwback to the famous parties of old, where the last ones standing would usually be Nick, Mark and me, watching the sun rise through the beginnings of our hangovers.

Mark's house is one of those large Victorian red-brick places just off Ealing Common that would be described, in a good way, as a 'pile', bought just before Ealing became fashionable. Pulling into the driveway,

I'm slightly dismayed to see that there are no other
cars there, and am just about to dial Mark's mobile
when I see him arrive, piloting his ageing Renault
people carrier expertly through the narrow gate and
parking an inch away from the Impresser's back
bumper. His stereo is blaring heavy rock music through
speakers normally used to the sedate tones of Radio
Four, and he sits there grinning at me as the car shakes
impressively with the sound. I shout at him to turn
it down but he can't hear me so I walk round and
open his door, wincing slightly at the volume.

'Hello, mate,' he says, switching off the engine,
which miraculously kills the music too. 'Did you say
something?'

'Just "turn it down". I'm surprised you're not deaf.'

'Pardon?'

'I said, I'm . . . oh, ha ha! Very funny. What are you
doing with such a flashy stereo in such a middle-aged
man's car anyway?'

'Drowns out the wife and child shouting at me.'
He grins. 'In Espace, no one can hear you scream.'
This is obviously a joke he's used before and thinks
is extremely funny, judging by his amused expression.

I notice that Mark is sporting a black eye. 'Crikey,
mate. Julia's got some left hook,' I say, but he informs
me it's actually the result of a game of fetch with Max,
his Labrador, the previous day.

'They've got solid skulls, you know,' he says, gingerly
fingering his eye socket.

Unloading the crates of beer and boxes of wine
from the back of his car we stagger with them through

the house, which I'm pleased to see for once doesn't
have the entire stock of Toys Я Us strewn over the
carpet. I follow Mark into the conservatory, where
he's set up one of those large plastic bins full of ice,
into which I unload one of the crates, pausing only
to open a couple of bottles, one of which I pass to
him.

I'm just about to launch into my concerns regarding
Nick when a freshly scrubbed Julia appears, her short,
spiky hair still wet from the shower. She's looking
radiant, I tell her, as she kisses me hello, simultaneously pinching both my backside and my beer.

'Should you be drinking in your condition?' I ask
her, half seriously.

'My *condition*?' she says, patting her stomach, which
isn't yet showing any sign of their impending arrival.
'It's not an illness, you know,' she adds, taking a huge
swig from my bottle.

As Julia busies herself in the kitchen, Mark and I
pretend to be organizing the music, but in reality just
use this as an excuse to drink a couple more beers
out in the conservatory. Conscious that the clock is
ticking, I prepare my opening gambit.

'So,' I begin. 'Nick's getting married, then . . .' I
leave the sentence hanging, to see what he has to say.

'Yeah,' nods Mark, unfortunately following it with
'and speak of the devil', as we hear the unmistakable
sound of the Ferrari arriving with a roar and a spray
of gravel. As Nick and Sandra breeze in through
the front door, Mark breaks into a grin and heads
off to join in the communal backslapping. Hiding my

disappointment at a missed opportunity, I concentrate on cramming the last few beer bottles into the cooler, but what happens next makes me shudder, and it's nothing to do with the tub full of ice in front of me.

'Aren't you going to congratulate me, Adam?'

I look over my shoulder to see Sandra standing in the doorway, proudly sporting an engagement ring with a diamond big enough to be seen from space. I take a deep breath, fix a smile and turn round.

'Yes, of course,' I say, walking over towards her. 'Congratulations.'

As I lean in to give her a peck on the cheek, Sandra turns her face quickly towards mine, and kisses me full on the lips. I pull away awkwardly, staring at her in disbelief, just as Nick comes bounding into the room like an eager puppy, Mark and Julia following in his wake.

'Hello, mate,' he says, putting his arm round Sandra and giving her a squeeze. 'Mine's a cold one.'

After what's just happened, it crosses my mind to contradict him, but then I notice that he's nodding towards the cooler. Still a little stunned, I wordlessly pass him a beer, then have to hide a smile as he tries unsuccessfully to twist the cap off. It's not that kind of bottle.

As Mark heads off to answer the front door, Julia produces her new digital camera and ushers the three of us together for a photograph, the flash glinting brightly off the ring on Sandra's left hand.

'Look at that,' says Julia, examining the screen on the back of the camera. 'All this modern technology and I still manage to cut Nick's head off.'

'Probably best,' shouts Mark from the hallway, as he lets some other guests in. 'Don't want to ruin a perfectly good photo.'

'Oh well,' says Sandra, taking the camera from Julia and squinting at the display. 'At least it's a nice one of you and me, Adam.'

I grunt something intelligible in reply.

As we make our way through to the front room, Sandra hangs back to wait for me. 'Shame I didn't spot you first, eh?' she adds, in a whisper, before heading off to join Nick.

By the time the party is in full swing, there must be fifty people milling about in the house; only Pritchard and Rudy haven't been able to make it this evening, due to some last-minute staffing issues at Bar Rosa. As usual, Nick is holding court and bragging about his Ferrari, which he's made sure he's parked right outside the front door so no one can miss it, making the assembled estate-car- and people-carrier-driving dads insanely jealous. Sandra stands next to him, clutching his arm and showing her ring off to the throng of admiring wives and girlfriends.

I take up a position close to the beer cooler, in order to minimize bottle-empty time, and watch the goings-on around me with interest, particularly because also at the party is my friend Mike and his new fiancée, Mel. Mike and Mel are always very nervous of me at occasions like this, because they know that I know that they met through an Internet dating service and for some reason they're embarrassed about this.

I've promised them that their secret is safe with me,

but of course I've told Nick, which has the same effect as taking out an ad in the papers, so whilst they think the three of us have a secret from everyone else, in actual fact everyone else knows, but keeps this a secret from the two of them.

Apparently this Internet dating is a hugely popular option for us over-thirties, and single women in particular, either those who still haven't found Mr Right, those just looking for Mr Bit-of-all-right, or those newly divorced who find themselves back on the market unexpectedly. The advantage, Mike explained, was that you can get to a very intimate stage very quickly once you've set your sights on a prospective partner, via the innocent medium of 'e-chat', building up a profile of your intended through their keyboard dexterity without even having to go to the trouble of meeting them. Some people even go to the extent of buying a little web cam once they've agreed to go forward, he informed me, so they can clap eyes on the e-hunk or e-babe of their dreams.

Mike admitted that this had helped him avoid several awkward dates, because his particular aversion, women of, shall we say, larger stature, was quite easy to spot once the albeit low-resolution pictures were beamed through.

The amazing thing, it seemed to me, was that, given the fact that the whole process is accelerated, it means that once you've actually met the partner with whom you've been corresponding, you're almost guaranteed to sleep with them on the first date. You may even have had email sex with them already, although apparently having to use one hand to type doesn't give the same immediacy of relief as phone sex. Then, if the actual date proves to be unsuccessful, either due to bad sex or bad breath, you simply break off all future computer contact and your date disappears off into cyberspace again.

So I of course kept badgering Mike as to how he was getting on, and when he told me he'd met Mel (who became known as Melanie.com to the rest of us) and that things were looking serious, no one was surprised when they announced their engagement some weeks later. The most amusing thing at gatherings like this was to watch them squirm when someone asked them how they met – you'd have thought they would have got that story straight first, and made up something more plausible than the standard 'through work' answer that Mel always goes with. Particularly because Mike's a prison officer.

But for me this sort of approach just takes a little of the romance out of it. Surely the tradition of courtship can't be the same if you're doing it through a modem? And the sad fact is, no matter how much time you seem to spend getting to know someone through the false intimacies of email, and how much you get to like their personality and sense of humour, it still all comes down to whether you fancy them when you eventually put a face to the fingers, and weeks of carefully typed flirting can be overshadowed by one fat arse.

I go through the usual routine of circulating, chatting, drinking and having a pleasant time, particularly as I manage to avoid Sandra for the rest of the evening. Come ten o'clock I've lined up a selection of funky CDs and I'm starting to crank the volume up slowly in the hope that some brave soul will start the dancing. What happens, though, is the exact opposite, as the house starts to empty. I'm sure it's not as a result of my musical tastes, and when I challenge the various couples as to why they're leaving early it seems that they really must get home to relieve the babysitter.

By midnight, even the (so far, but watch this space) childless Mike and Mel have left. Nick and Sandra are in deep conversation with Mark, who's ominously holding his wedding photo album, and Julia is starting to clear up the plates and glasses from around the house. I put down my beer in disgust and head off in search of something stronger to drink, and am in the kitchen trying to find where Mark's hidden his scotch when Julia corners me. She's slightly tipsy, not having drunk much since she got pregnant, I guess, and pins me up against the fridge freezer, knocking off a couple of India's crayonings – drawings being too kind a description – in the process.

'Not pulled this evening, Adam? Losing your touch?' I can smell the beer on her breath, mainly because her face is only a few inches away from mine.

I manoeuvre away from her to lean against the cooker. 'One of the advantages of being unattached is that you can choose whether you want company or not, and tonight the only thing I'm looking for is your tight-git-of-a-husband's whisky. Besides, I didn't notice that you'd invited any other single people.'

'That's because everyone we know nowadays is married. Or getting married,' she says, putting her hand on my cheek, 'except for poor old you.'

I shrug her hand off. 'And that's a bad thing, is it?'

'Now now, Adam! Don't be so touchy,' she says, resting her hand on my arm, although she's the one being too touchy.

'Sorry,' I say, pulling away from her again. 'I'm just a little stunned about Nick.'

'Yes,' beams Julia, as she dumps a load of plates into the sink. 'Good news, don't you think?'

I'm trying to think of a more tactful answer than a simple *no* as Julia pulls on a pair of rubber gloves and starts to wash up, but I can't. 'Well, no, actually.'

Julia fixes me with a puzzled expression. 'Why ever not?'

I'm not sure that I want to get into this now, particularly not with Nick and Sandra in the next room. 'I just think he might be rushing into it a bit.'

Julia regards me quizzically for a moment. 'Are you sure that's all it is?'

'What do you mean?'

'Well, you're bound to feel a little jealous . . .'

I don't follow. 'Jealous? Why?'

Julia clears her throat. 'Well, for the last few years it's just been you and Nick, right? And now Sandra's come along and—'

'And?' I interrupt, bristling slightly.

'Well, I remember when my best friend got married. I was really pleased for her and everything, but there was a part of me that almost resented their happiness, because I knew that things would never be the same between us again.'

'What are you trying to say?' I ask, incredulously. 'That I'm,' I almost choke on the words, 'jealous of *Sandra*?'

'Don't feel bad, Adam. It's only natural.' She gives me what I'm sure she thinks is a reassuring smile. 'Anyway, it's bound to be your turn soon.'

I exhale loudly. 'Why do weddings always make people want to talk about *your turn*? You never hear that same thing said at a funeral.'

She ignores me. 'Seriously, though,' she continues, 'haven't you ever felt close to proposing . . .' she pauses, as if debating whether to complete the question '. . . again?'

'Julia, if you recall, last time I got down on one knee it took me a long time to get back up on my feet again.'

She frowns. 'No, I mean apart from . . .' I look up sharply, and she stops mid-sentence, and turns back to the sink. 'It's just that you've gone out with all these women in the last few years,' she continues. 'Have you never thought that you might have a future with one of the others? Or anyone before?'

I'm worried that she's fishing for compliments and referring back to the brief period that we dated, before she started going out with Mark. We'd had a fling at college, after I'd been to see Sting in concert and brought her back a poster as a present signed 'To Julia, love Sting'. This, while quite impressive enough to get her to jump into bed with me in gratitude, would have been all the more remarkable had it actually been signed by Sting himself, and not one of my more inspired forgeries. I think about my answer carefully, wanting to do it justice, and then reply.

'Nope.'

Julia stops washing up for a moment and glances at me over her shoulder. 'And do you know why that might be?' she asks.

I shrug. 'Still looking for "the one", I suppose.'

'The next one, you mean,' says Julia, a little acidly. 'Mark says you've got so many notches on your bedpost it's in danger of collapsing.'

'Oh, he does, does he?'

Julia looks at me sheepishly, as she considers her next sentence. 'I have a theory,' she says. 'Do you want to hear it?'

Everyone's got one, I sigh to myself, resuming my search of the kitchen cupboards. 'Go on then.'

Julia attempts to balance a glass on top of the already precarious pile of crockery on the draining board. 'Well, it's like this. Everybody starts off searching for their own Miss or Mister Perfect – their ten out of ten, if you like. Some people go through life constantly looking for this and always end up being disappointed, because they never find it. Some people wise up early on and realize when they meet a six or, if they're lucky, a seven, they should grab it with both hands because they might not get anything better. Some other people meet and marry a four or a five and supplement this with a series of affairs to bring their average up.'

'I must ask Mark what score he gives you.'

Julia sticks her tongue out at me and carries on. 'And the problem with this search for perfection, this ten score, is this. It doesn't exist. Well, let me clarify that – it might exist but chances are, unless you're very lucky, you'll never find it.'

Like Mark's scotch, I think, opening the oven door and peering inside. As a last resort, I check behind the microwave and then just give up and help myself to another beer from the fridge.

'You see!' exclaims Julia. 'Eventually you just can't be bothered to keep looking any more, and so you end up having to compromise.'

Ah-ha. The dreaded c-word. I really don't want to have one of these serious in-the-kitchen-at-parties type discussions, so try and introduce a light-hearted note.

'But what if you still enjoy looking? The thrill of the chase, and all that.'

Julia folds her arms and looks at me levelly. 'Adam, you seem to forget that you're dealing with people's emotions here. You might be content to go along and "sample the wares" without getting emotionally involved, but what about them? Your innocent . . . victims? One or two dates might be enough for you to discount them because—'

'They've got funny toes?' I suggest.

Julia scowls at me. 'Whatever. But from their point of view, they might be starting to fall in love, however little. You then dash their hopes and you're not giving them any feedback.'

I really don't like where this conversation is leading.

I keep waiting for her to ask 'What was wrong with us, for example?', which I'm sure she'll say just as Mark walks into the room, so I decide to go on the attack.

'Feedback? But what could I say – "I'm sorry, but I'm dumping you because . . ."' I search my memory for another recent example '" . . . your canine teeth are slightly too long"? That's hardly constructive criticism. It's not as if she'll go away, have the offending fangs reduced at the dentist, and then expect me to take her back. And, anyway, that's never the real reason. My picking on things like her teeth is really just a front for that missing thing – the spark. I'm sure if that's there, then these little things won't seem such a big issue for me. I mean, I can't just say "I'm sorry but *you* just don't do it for me", can I? Surely that's more damaging than a remark about her physical appearance? There's nothing she can go away and do about that, is there?'

Julia looks a little stunned. 'Erm . . .'

'What's best? I lie, and say "It's not you, it's me", or I tell the truth, and say "It's not me, it is actually you"?'

I can almost hear Julia's brain ticking. 'So you haven't ever met up with an ex-girlfriend who's lost weight and thought "Wow – she looks great – perhaps I'll ask her out again"?'

I shake my head. 'Never.'

'Never?'

'Nope. Although that's probably because I wouldn't have gone out with a fat girl in the first place!'

Julia punches me on the arm, hard enough to make

me question Mark's earlier black eye excuse, leaving a soggy fist-print on my sleeve. 'See!'

No, I don't. 'See what?' I try not to rub my throbbing bicep.

'Your whole approach is too shallow in the first place. You spend all day looking at these perfect, air-brushed images of surgically enhanced women on this website of yours and then wonder why you can't ever meet anybody in the real world who matches up to this.'

I look at her incredulously. 'That's rubbish. And do you really want to know why?'

Julia smiles and nods. I take a deep breath and try and construct my answer.

'My . . . serial monogamy isn't because I'm looking for perfection. I'm just an old romantic and want to feel something special with that special someone. Somebody who brings out the best in me. Inspires me, if you like.' I suddenly remember that this is a conversation I had with Mark on the eve of his wedding, when he'd told me how he knew he was doing the right thing. I try and put it into my own words, as much for my sake as Julia's. 'That's it in a nutshell,' I continue. 'I just want to be inspired. What's wrong with that?'

Julia stares at me for a moment, mouth slightly agape. 'That's beautiful,' she says.

'Anyway,' I say, 'I'm hardly leaving a trail of broken hearts behind me, am I? It's not as if once I've chucked these women they become emotional cripples and go and live in a convent somewhere. In fact, many of them have gone on and got married soon after they went out with me. Or in some cases,' I nod towards Julia, 'married the next person they went out with.'

'Hmph!' says Julia, in that annoyingly smug way women have when they are convinced that they've just proved a point, whereas you have absolutely no idea they were even trying to make one. 'Exactly! And how many of your exes are you friendly with?'

'I'm friendly with them all.' And that's nearly the truth. I'm more than happy to remain civil to my exes. In actual fact, it's more than inconvenient not to, seeing as I still bump into many of them on a regular basis in the gym, at the bar and so on.

'Okay, let me rephrase that. How many are you *friends* with?'

'Including you? Er . . . one. Maybe two.'

She's right. I don't think that I've ever ended up as 'friends' with any of them – not in the true sense of the word. Every relationship I've ever had has ended badly, I suppose. It would have, wouldn't it? Otherwise it wouldn't have finished. After all, there are very few happy 'endings'.

'There you go,' she says, gesturing towards me with the washing-up brush, and spilling some soap suds on my shoes in the process. 'I rest my case.'

'No – there *you* go. That proves my point. If I've never met anyone that I've wanted to stay friends with then that proves they haven't been the right one for me, because, and I quote a number of sickly relationship counsellors, "Your partner should also be your best friend", or some such bollocks.'

'Well, that means you should marry Nick then,' says Julia, peeling off her rubber gloves.

I shake my head slowly. 'But there's another problem. I don't want my partner to be my best friend. I already have a best friend. I want my partner to be something different. Why did you marry Mark, for example?'

I regret asking the question as soon as I've finished the sentence, suddenly feeling as if I'm being disloyal to Mark, but Julia seems to be happy to tell me. And, scarily, she doesn't have to think about her answer.

'Because I wanted security. More importantly, I wanted kids. And given the choice between someone like Mark and someone like you . . .' She looks me up and down. 'Children need a role model for a father. Not a male model.'

I'm struggling to work out whether this is a criticism or a compliment when Julia speaks again. 'And besides,' she continues, 'Mark is—'

'Mark is what?' slurs a drunken Mark, as he lurches through the kitchen doorway, perfectly on cue.

'Mark is a selfish bastard for hiding his whisky,' I tell him, and his eyes flick briefly towards the cupboard under the sink.

I march across the kitchen, open the cupboard door and triumphantly remove the bottle of scotch.

'Ah-ha!' I cry. 'Saved by the Bells!'

Chapter 5

Our company, PleazeYourself, is one of the most popular Internet sites in Britain — not that you'll hear anyone admit to using it, though. Say you're in the office one afternoon, searching perhaps for 'flowers for mother's day' on the world wide web but instead, and completely by accident, your fingers slip and type in 'naked Swedish nurses'. . . Well, you just might, if Nick's done his job properly, be directed to our home page. We're a link site, a directory of the pornographic pages that litter cyberspace — log on to Pleaze Yourself.com and you'll be presented with more naked nurses than you can shake a big stick at.

The directory is compiled by a team of 'researchers', students mainly, whom we employ to sit in a darkened room all day and surf the net on our behalf. Ours is the only company where employees are rewarded for looking at porn on the Internet during office hours — once they find somewhere that looks interesting we email the site to explain what PleazeYourself does, and, if they're agreeable, add their name to a link page under whatever classification, or flavour, if you like, of pornography they happen to feature. For example, as of today, if you look under 'voyeurism' on our site we can direct you to three hundred and fifty-seven different sites for your viewing pleasure.

And how do we make our money? Well, whenever someone joins a site they've found by clicking through from PleazeYourself, we cream off a small profit. Admittedly, these commissions are pretty tiny, but, fortunately for us, of the millions of people who log on to the information superhighway every day, many of them simply want to get off. Alternatively – *Why make it hard for yourself?* is our innovative catchphrase – you can choose to pay a monthly subscription to become a PleazeYourself 'member'. Tell us your particular preference – nothing illegal or arrestable, of course – and we'll email you whenever we find a new site that features your fetish of choice.

Either way, Nick and I do very well out of doing very little. We don't have to spend any money on advertising, either (surprisingly, our recently adopted monkey hasn't produced an upsurge in revenues – a fact which I take great pleasure in constantly reminding Nick of), as most of our success has been due to word of mouse.

Nick's the technology guru. His job is to make sure that every time somebody searches for a particular word on the Internet our site comes up as one of the top answers. If curiosity then gets the better of them, and they start to explore PleazeYourself, well, ker-ching. So, if someone is searching for the word 'beaver', for example, Nick's skill is in making sure that we also appear in a list of other classifications about those lovable dam-building aquatic mammals – and you'd be surprised how far some nature lovers get before they realize they've made a 'mistake'. He even wrote Thomas – which is what we call the software program that manages the database technology behind the site. Why 'Thomas'? Well, it's a search engine used primarily for masturbation, so Thomas the Wank Engine it became.

And what do I do in this sordid but successful operation? Well, I'm responsible for the copywriting. Fortunately, our researchers provide me with a brief description of what it is they've found, which saves me having to look at every single site – not something I ever thought I'd admit, but sometimes you can see too much porn – and then it's up to me to write some enticing little phrase to encourage the surfer to visit. After all, how otherwise would you be able to make an informed choice between Luscious Lesbians or Sapphic Sweethearts?

We've told our parents that PleazeYourself is an Internet introduction agency, which is sort of true, and the site almost runs itself, which means that Nick and I can pick and choose our work hours, usually only a few days each week, and still get to earn something approaching a six-figure salary. It's all cleverly disguised by Mark as dividends and expenses, and his skill in fiddling the Inland Revenue, or, as he prefers to put it, exploiting the UK tax laws to our advantage, means that both Nick and I are, to use more of Mark's jargon, quids in. Unlike crime, pornography pays.

The business centre where we're based is a ten-minute walk (or twenty minutes by car) from our respective flats, but Nick still pays extra for a parking space, simply so he can drive the Ferrari to and from work. We don't really need an office – the team of researchers can fortunately sit in their own darkened rooms so we don't have to house them, but I suppose it gives us the impression of being a respectable company with a Chelsea address rather than some seedy little backroom operation. On the front desk sits a full-time receptionist, Becky, who serves all the companies in the building. Nick and I share a large suite on the first floor, outside which Nick's three-days-a-week assistant used to sit, handling all those administrative things that he couldn't, or, more accurately, couldn't be bothered, to do.

It's Monday morning, and, as usual, I'm on my own in the office. Nick rarely makes an appearance before midday anyway, still living up to his college nickname of 'The Lie-in King', and, besides, he'd muttered something about 'wedding stuff' on the phone yesterday. I'm staring hard at my computer screen, my right hand aching, although from nothing more depraved than trying to beat my best Solitaire score, when my phone rings. It's Becky.

'Adam, your ten o'clock is here.'

'Thanks, gorgeous,' I reply. Becky has a crush on me, which I exploit mercilessly, thus guaranteeing I get the best biscuits (chocolate chip shortbread cookies, which are normally only for visiting heads of state) whenever I order coffee or tea in one of the meeting rooms. Minor details like these are important.

I get up and check my reflection in the mirror, straightening my tie as I walk down the stairs towards the front desk. I'm wearing a suit today because we're interviewing for a new PA, although why Nick needs an assistant in the first place I don't really know. I think he bears the expense simply for the pleasure of telling people approximately once a month that they should 'call his PA' to set up a meeting.

His previous dogsbody, Suzanne, had decided that since Nick hardly spent any time in the office then neither would she, and had started diverting all the office calls to her mobile whilst out shopping, having long lunches or going to the hairdressers. Nick wouldn't have found out about this if he hadn't been skiving himself, of course, but he'd been strolling through Harrods one morning whilst talking to her on his mobile phone, assuming that she was hard at work back in the office, when he walked round the corner in the foods department and found her there doing her weekly shop.

Nick finds it difficult to be tough. Unlike me, he doesn't have a lot of experience of breaking bad news to women, and he'd found the sacking meeting particularly hard.

'But what are you supposed to say?' he'd asked me beforehand.

'Try this,' I'd said, as he unsheathed his Montblanc pen. 'You tell her: "Suzanne, I don't know how I'd manage without you"' – I'd watched as he'd scribbled furiously – '"but I'm going to try."' I swear he was halfway through writing the word 'going' before he'd looked up at me.

'Bastard,' he'd said.

Anyway, he's decided to hire some temporary help until he can get someone new on board full-time, so I've volunteered to interview some candidates from a local agency for him, and standing with her back to me at reception is the girl who I guess must be my 'ten o'clock' – Charlotte Evans. I wink at Becky and clear my throat.

'Miss Evans for you, Mr Bailey,' announces Becky, rather formally.

Unlike most other aspects of my life, my job isn't a great opportunity for meeting attractive women (except, as Julia takes great pleasure in pointing out, in a two-dimensional, on-screen kind of way). However, since the agency had sent photos along with CVs, I'd been able to narrow the candidates down to three, more on the basis of attractiveness than qualifications, of course.

The first two, whom I'd met last week, appeared to have used someone else's picture when applying, but when Charlotte Evans turns round to greet me she more than makes up for the others. She's short, verging on what I guess is known as 'petite', slim, and dressed well, an open-necked silk shirt under a cream business suit, showing just enough cleavage to stay on the nice side of tarty. A cascade of dark hair frames her face, which is dominated by slightly oversized lips that on anyone else might look out of place. And when she smiles, it lights up the whole . . .

'Charlotte. Please call me Charlie,' she says, interrupting my reverie. She makes good – and strikingly deep blue – eye contact with me, and I have to concentrate to return the favour.

'Oh. Yes. Hi. Adam,' I say. 'Please call me . . .' I stop, realizing that I've talked myself into a corner.

'Adam?' she says, raising one eyebrow. I just nod, and shake her outstretched hand.

Handshakes are important. In my book, you should maintain a firm grip for just as long as it takes to exchange names, or say 'Pleased to meet you', or whatever pleasantries you prefer. What I can't stand is when people don't apply any sort of pressure whatsoever, or, even worse, want to hang on for dear life, and for more than the duration of the introduction. Let go, for God's sake! I'm not going to run off, and I can much more easily concentrate on what you're saying if I'm not worrying about if and when you're going to release my hand. But Charlie's handshake is firm and she holds on for just long enough. Strangely, I find myself reluctant to let go.

I show her into the meeting room, fetching us both a cappuccino from the machine, but decide to leave the biscuits where they are even though Becky has artfully arranged them on the plate. Her design of one shortbread finger to two cookies is a bit phallic for my liking.

I flick through Charlie's CV, which tells me she has a degree in geology.

'So, Charlotte . . .'

She smiles, sweetly. 'Charlie.'

'Charlie. Sorry. Why geology?' I ask her. 'Bit of a strange choice—'

'For a girl?' she interrupts.

'N-no, that's not what I meant.' I redden slightly. 'I just, I mean, the study of rocks?'

'I like rocks. Particularly diamonds,' she says, breaking into a smile.

Charlie talks me through her CV, covering in particular her most recent secretarial work, and then I remember why I'd been interested in seeing her in the first place.

'So, you do a bit of, um, modelling?' I ask, trying not to look at her breasts, but failing miserably.

'Yes, but just part time,' she says, folding her arms self-consciously in front of her chest. 'Commercials, exhibitions, demonstrations, that sort of thing. It pays well, but it's not what I want to do long term.'

I take the bait. 'Which is?'

'Work here, of course!' she announces, grinning broadly. She has, I notice, perfect teeth.

From here on in I try to keep the meeting as professional as possible, as I start to worry that if she feels I'm flirting with her then she'll think that I do that with every girl I interview. I give her the usual spiel about what the company does and the types of organizations we work with. She's not put off by the industry we're in, laughs at my jokes (at last – someone who does), and I'm going through my customary repertoire of career questions while pretending to make notes. Eventually, I get to my last one.

'So, we've talked about your strengths. Can you think of any weaknesses?'

I've interviewed most of our researchers, so I've probably heard them all by now; the standard *I'm a perfectionist*, or *I find it hard to delegate* – answers that people think make them sound indispensable – but Charlie thinks about this for a few seconds, as if she's never considered the question before. Eventually she takes a deep breath.

'Chocolate.'

I'm halfway through writing this down before I glance up and see her smiling at me.

I look back on this later and realize that this is the point that I become hooked. Furthermore, just before she leaves, something happens that gives me no choice.

'Excuse me,' she says politely, a strange expression on her face. 'I'm just going to sneeze.'

I suddenly remember Mark's theory, and watch her with interest, but when it comes I've never seen anything like it, and sit opposite, watching in fascination as Charlie sneezes. And sneezes. And sneezes. In all, a total of seven, in succession (I count silently, but with rising interest and amazement), the first six identical, but building in volume slightly, the seventh a gigantic, whole-body sneeze that almost takes the froth off the top of my untouched cappuccino.

'Bless you!' I say, passing her a tissue.

Charlie blows her nose. 'Sorry about that,' she says, with an embarrassed sniff.

I walk her out of the office, give her my business

card in case she has any further questions, thank her for coming in, and tell her I'll be in touch.

'I hope so,' she says, and with a last smile she makes her way through the rotating doors and out on to the street. I stand and watch through the spinning glass as she disappears into the King's Road crowds, until a cough from Becky sends me scurrying back into my office.

Some hours later, I'm sitting in Bar Rosa with Pritchard and Rudy, telling them about Charlie.

'There's nothing sexier than an intelligent woman, in my opinion,' I say.

'Yes,' smirks Rudy. 'Especially one with big breasts, I bet.'

Pritchard decides to put me on the spot. 'So, have you asked her out yet?'

I shake my head. 'Nope. I didn't feel it was appropriate, given that it was a job interview and all that.'

Rudy laughs. 'That's never stopped you before.'

'True.' In fact, I can't think of a reason why I didn't, except perhaps that I'd actually wanted to make a good impression.

'So, what should I do?' I ask them. 'She's perfect for the job, but I can't take her on and then ask her out. If she says yes and we get on I'd feel funny about her working for Nick and going out with me. If I tell her she hasn't got the job and then ask her out she might say no just because she's miffed at not getting it. On the other hand, if I tell her she's got the job and then ask her out and she says no, then there might be an awkward atmosphere in the office.' Their eyes, I notice, are beginning to glaze.

'Or,' I continue, 'if I ask her out before I tell her whether she's got the job or not she might feel she has to say yes just so she doesn't jeopardize her chances of getting it. But then if she takes the job and I ask her out and we don't get on and I chuck her, then it will be even more awkward in the office. Alternatively, if she takes the job and I ask her out but she turns out to be no good but we get on, then I can't sack her—'

'What was the first one again?' interrupts Pritchard.

I stop talking, pick up my beer and take a sip, hoping that they can impart some wisdom.

Rudy rests a fatherly hand on my shoulder. 'Do you want my advice?'

'Is it any good?'

He gives me a withering glance. 'Call her, tell her the job's been put on hold but you'd like to see her again.'

I frown. 'Surely she'll then think that the interview was just a ruse?'

'Not necessarily. But it does mean that you can apologize for wasting her time and say you want to make it up to her.'

'And in her disappointment you can console her,' adds Pritchard.

'Or,' begins Rudy, launching into a huge discussion of potential scenarios, each worse than the previous one. After half an hour of this, I call a halt to the subject.

But later that night Charlie solves at least part of the dilemma herself. She calls me on my mobile, and I excuse myself from Pritchard and Rudy's raised eyebrows.

'I may be some time,' I tell them, walking outside with a swagger to take her call; but my heart quickly sinks when she tells me she's been offered a promotional job, which she'll be taking instead.

'I thought I'd better let you know as soon as possible,' she says, 'just in case you'd short listed me at the expense of another candidate.'

I try to swallow my disappointment. 'It was good of you to call. Most people wouldn't have bothered.'

'Well, I'm not one of those people who string people along when they're not really interested, you know. What are they called?' She searches for the right words.

'Prick-teaser?' I blurt out.

Charlie laughs. 'No, actually, I was thinking of "hypocrite".' I hope she can't hear me blush.

We exchange a few pleasantries, and then I'm unusually tongue-tied. 'Well . . .' I hear myself saying.

'Well,' she says. 'It was a pleasure to meet you, Adam.'

'You too, Charlotte.'

'Charlie.'

'Charlie. Thanks for the call.'

'Don't mention it.'

'Okay, I won't.' Aargh! *Just ask her out*, I'm thinking.

'Well, goodbye then.'

'Yes, bye.'

I listen to her breathing for a few seconds, as if she's waiting for me to say something, and then she hangs up. I stand there like an idiot for at least a minute with the phone up to my ear before walking disconsolately inside.

Back at the bar Pritchard and Rudy offer to buy me another drink in an attempt to drown my sorrows. In actual fact, it takes nearly a whole bottle of wine before they're in need of a lifebelt, which turns up in the shape of Fiona, who happens to walk into the bar with a group of her friends.

Fiona and I went out two years ago, for about a month. It wouldn't even have lasted that long if the sex hadn't been so good, but every time I thought about breaking it off we ended up getting it on. I can't remember exactly what it was that made me finally go off her – I think it was the way she said 'pound' instead of 'pounds' as in 'it cost twenty pound' – but eventually I realized that we didn't really have anything in common apart from an amazing compatibility between the sheets.

When I finally dumped her she went mental, delivering one of those 'You'll never find anyone else like me' speeches. *I should hope not*, I recall thinking. *If I wanted someone like you I wouldn't be breaking up with you. And if I don't want* you, *why would I want someone like* you? Of course, I was too much of a gentleman to explain this, rather I took the cowards' 'It's not you, it's me' stance, which, to my surprise, she actually bought. And when I told her I wasn't looking for commitment right now, she said, 'Okay. Let's just sleep together then.'

So nowadays Fiona is my regular 'sex ex'. Everybody should have one. I suppose it's a bit like being a social smoker. You can get by on a daily basis without wanting a fix, but given a particular set of circumstances, a certain time of day, a couple of drinks perhaps in the company of other 'smokers', you catch sight of the cigarette machine out of the corner of your eye, get that sudden craving, and the next thing you know you're preparing to stick your money in the slot. You always wake the following morning with a strange taste on your tongue and swear never again to yourself. Until the next time.

That's how it is for me and Fiona, apart from the funny taste of course, and it's a habit we've both been happy to keep up. But every time it happens (and I use the phrase like it's something I have no control over) she insists on having the 'Why did we ever split up? We're so good together' conversation, and, although I've never been one for faking it between the sheets, I find myself pretending to be asleep just to avoid it.

I wake up at around 7.00 a.m. in Fiona's bed, my head suffering from the wrath of grapes, and suddenly find myself wishing I was anywhere but here. Fortunately, she's sleeping like a baby, so I extricate myself from the tangle of limbs and duvet, get out of bed without disturbing her and stagger to the bathroom. Fiona has one of those mirrors that you see in theatre dressing rooms, with the light bulbs around the edge, and the vivid reflection that this throws back at me is not pleasant: hair like a crop circle, puffy eyes and, oh *no*, what looks like a bite mark on my left shoulder, which I'm both pleased and shocked by at the same time. I make a mental note that it's T-shirts rather than vests for me in the gym this week.

I don't like to shower at other people's houses so I damp my hair down into something approaching dishevelled respectability, find last night's clothes at their various locations around her flat and let myself out of the front door. It would have been wholly inappropriate to kiss her goodbye.

I spend a few moments looking up and down the street for the Impresser before I remember that I left it outside my flat, so I start to walk home, but at that moment a black cab drives past with its For Hire light shining, so I stick a hand up and wave it over. When I give the driver my address he gives me that *Good night last night was it?* look, and drives me home wordlessly, which I'm quite pleased about.

Walking up the stairs, I nod to my neighbour, who's coming out of his flat on the floor below mine. He is, I suppose, a bit of a minor celebrity – a 'gangsta rapper' who's had some moderate chart success with a group called Uzi Street. He calls himself 2-Tuf – you might have heard of him. But I know him better as Kevin, thanks to the time when I answered my front door to a lovely old Afro-Caribbean lady who introduced herself as Mrs Wilson.

'I'm looking for my son Kevin,' she'd said. 'I think he lives in one of these flats but I've forgotten which bell to press.'

At the time, I only knew the old couple who lived upstairs and 2-Tuf, and as there are only three flats in the building it therefore wasn't too hard to guess who Kevin was, or should I say who 2-Tuf really was. It was with great pleasure that I'd met him on the stairs the following day – well, I'd been listening out from my flat just to catch him, actually.

'Yo, Adam, my man. How's it going with the beaches?' he'd said. Or something like that.

'Beaches? Oh, *bitches*. Women, you mean? Fine,' I'd replied. 'By the way, I, er, met your mother yesterday.'

He'd stopped in his tracks. 'Yeah? And?'

'Oh nothing. See you, *Kevin*,' I'd said, moving to go back inside my flat.

'Yo yo yo, hold on, man,' he'd called after me, his accent becoming less homeboy and more home counties. 'What did you say?'

'Nothing, Kev,' I'd repeated, smiling.

'Er, Adam, this is just between you and me, yes?'

'Sure, Kev. I mean 2-Tuf. Anything you say.'

'And anything I can do for you just ask,' he'd said. Which is how Nick and I had found ourselves backstage at an Uzi Street concert the following weekend.

I unlock my front door and pick up my post from the hallway, but it's just a letter from a bank I've never heard of telling me I've been pre-approved for their latest nought per cent APR titanium super credit card. Life is full of these kinds of offers, and whilst they may all look attractive up front, it's the 'zero interest' part which always turns out to be my problem.

I head straight for the shower. Standing there under slightly-too-hot water, trying to wash away that morning-after feeling and a sudden sense of world-weariness, it occurs to me – just for a moment – that maybe this is what Nick's trying to avoid. Turning the tap round to cold I look down at my tooth-marked shoulder and decide that I really must call Charlie back.

Chapter 6

But first things first. It's Wednesday afternoon, Nick's slipped out of the office, and I need to get hold of Mark to have the conversation I tried to start with him on Saturday. He's not at work, and his mobile doesn't seem to be responding. Eventually I catch him at home.

'Networking or not working?' I ask him.

'Not working,' he replies, sounding a little depressed. 'You?'

'Oh, I'm really busy, actually,' I reply.

'You're joking?'

'You started it! What are you doing at home?'

Mark sighs. 'It's a long story. What can I do you for, anyway?'

'Just checking you're on for Bar Rosa tonight.' We go there most Wednesday evenings – well, I'm there most weekday evenings, actually, but Wednesdays is one of our more regular slots, and about the only thing in Mark's life that Julia still lets him do on his own. Nick has cried off this evening, so it's a perfect opportunity for Mark and I to have a chat.

He's thinking about my question when his doorbell

rings. 'Hold on, mate,' he says, keeping me on the line. 'I'm just going to answer it.' I hear his footsteps as he walks down the hallway, obviously carrying the handset with him, and opens the front door.

'Who is it?' I shout down the phone at him.

'Hold on. Who are you?' he repeats to whoever is in front of him.

I hear a muffled exchange, and then Mark comes back on the line.

'They say they're from the King's Church.'

I think about this for a second. 'Watch out, Mark. They might be con artists,' I advise him.

I can almost hear him frown. 'What makes you think that?'

'Well, for one thing, we don't have a king.'

I hear Mark splutter with laughter, apologize to his visitors and close the door.

'What time shall I meet you?' he asks, giggling like a child.

'Well, I'm going there now,' I tell him.

'Give me an hour,' he says, and hangs up.

Two hours later I'm nursing a drink at the bar and cursing Mark's usual timekeeping. As I sip my beer I'm watching Pritchard, who's scaring a couple of hoorays with double surnames and chins to match who had tried to complain about their food. They'd been quite rude to their poor waitress, who was struggling to deal with them in her broken English. In truth, she was really a drama student who did a good Spanish accent but didn't want to drop out of character, hence the problem.

I'd spotted their behaviour and had quietly called Pritchard over to let him know, and then had the pleasure of sitting back and watching him tower over their table, his gruff 'Is there a problem, gentlemen?' eliciting the meekest of responses. I smirk as they eventually get up and leave, Pritchard still looming over them, even leaving a tip before scuttling out into the street.

Pritchard and Rudy had come over to London at the end of the eighties, when they'd tired of the New York gay scene. They'd told us that they'd lost too many friends to AIDS, and decided to come and start a new life where they weren't constantly reminded of death and depression.

'Well, Chelsea's probably the best place to come for that,' Nick had observed.

The building that Bar Rosa now occupies used to be a hairdressers, which seems somehow appropriate. They completely gutted it, redecorated, and now it's furnished in a kind of Conran goes to Barcelona style. Large upturned barrels line the walls and serve as the tables, around which you perch on high, chrome and leather stools. The floor is a dark wood that's been authentically aged and looks like it's been there for a hundred years. There's a long glass and mirror bar down one side, behind which sits the widest selection of tequila I've ever seen. The walls are half panelled in the same dark wood, and display a number of old bullfighting posters. Throw in a couple of those bottles-in-a-basket with wax dripping down the sides as if they've been host to a lifetime of candles, plus an assortment of hams and cheeses suspended for authenticity above the bar, and there you have it.

Pritchard and Rudy complement each other perfectly, although at first glance they make an unlikely couple. Pritchard is about six foot four inches tall, and probably almost as wide, although without an ounce of fat, or so Rudy tells us. He's the kind of chap who you'd never think was gay, and certainly would never dare ask if you thought he might be. With his shaved head and goatee beard he's a formidable sight – and one that's been sufficient to deter any problem drinkers from causing trouble.

Rudy, on the other hand, is possibly the best-looking man any of us have ever seen. Always turned out immaculately in Versace or Gucci, hair looking like it has been professionally cut and styled that morning, each sideburn trimmed to a point so sharp it could take your eye out. He's forever getting phone numbers thrust into his hand from tipsy ladies who lunch, convinced they can 'convert' him, much to his and Pritchard's amusement.

Pritchard and Rudy have been careful enough not to turn Bar Rosa into a gay bar. 'I don't want this place full of fags,' Pritchard had said once, in his booming American tones. He normally beavers away in the kitchen, overseeing a number of flustered-looking chefs, while Rudy loiters behind the bar, occasionally serving drinks but more often laughing and joking with customers while choreographing the gorgeous, white-bloused, short-black-skirted waitresses, most of whom are probably about as Spanish as I am. The food is always fantastic, including excellent tapas, and I'm just about to order myself something to eat when Mark finally walks in, looking like life caught him sleeping with its daughter.

'Cheer up, pal,' I say. 'It's supposed to be Happy Hour. What can I get you?'

'Pint of lager and a reason to live, please, mate,' he replies, gingerly removing his jacket to reveal a bandage wrapped around his wrist.

'Bloody hell! What happened to you? I warned you about spending too much time looking at our website.'

'As if!' He looks around furtively, and in a low voice says, 'Though it is bloody Nick's fault. You know that new mobile phone he gave me? The one you can download music on to.' Nick, ever the gadget man, replaces his mobile with the latest model every few months, usually passing the old ones on to friends or family. He'd shown it off to us when he first bought it, and it's dead flash, if a little pointless.

'Yeah?'

'Well, I'm working from home today, and Julia's gone out shopping, so I'm spending the morning catching up on my calls, and, not wanting to fry my brain, I'm using my headset . . .'

'Very responsible of you,' I say, as I order Mark a beer.

'So I fancy a cup of tea, and while I'm in the kitchen waiting for the kettle to boil I decide to listen to some music on my phone.'

'With you so far.'

'And I'm still connected to my headset, so I put

the phone down next to the kettle, and, thinking I'm still alone in the house . . .'

'Ye-es?'

'. . . I start dancing.'

'Dancing?'

'Just, you know, moving around to the music a bit. And Julia comes back in from the shops, but of course I don't hear her.'

I'm struggling to follow this. 'Because you're listening to the music on your headset?'

'Exactly. And I see the kettle about to boil, so I grab hold of the handle while I wait for it to click off . . .'

'And?'

'. . . and the next thing I know, Julia has picked up the mop and whacked me on the arm.'

I'm completely lost now. 'Er, why?' I ask, taking a mouthful of beer.

'Well, she walks in and sees me, in her words, "jerking about" with one hand on the kettle, and thinks I'm being electrocuted. Remembering her first aid training from when she was in the Girl Guides or something, she picks up the nearest thing she can think of and smacks me with it to knock me away from the current.'

It's all I can do to not spray Mark with beer. 'So what did you do?' I ask, trying unsuccessfully to keep a straight face.

'Well, having spilled boiling water all over my new phone, I couldn't even call for an ambulance if I'd wanted to, so I made Julia drive me to casualty. Heavy bruising, they said. First my dog gives me a black eye, and now *this* . . .' He waits until I've regained my composure. 'Promise you won't tell Nick?'

'Yeah, sure.' *Yeah, right!*

We take our drinks – I carry Mark's just to be sure he doesn't drop it – and sit down at one of the barrels. Still smirking, I'm wondering how soon I can tell Nick the story, when Mark's next question takes me a little – no, a *lot* – by surprise.

'What underpants have you got on?'

I look around to check no one has heard. Fortunately, both Pritchard and Rudy are out of earshot.

'What are you talking about?'

'Just answer the question.'

'Er, Calvin Klein, I think,' I answer, not wanting to appear like a man who knows instantly the type of pants he's wearing. But I am a man about town, so of course I'm wearing my Calvins, though obviously not with the waistband showing above my low-slung jeans, as favoured by certain rap stars and label sheep.

'Thought so. Me too.'

I unsuccessfully try to stop an image of Mark's less than athletic physique clad in only his underwear from springing to mind. 'Thanks for sharing that, mate. And your point is?'

He winces as he tries to pick his pint up with his bandaged arm, and changes hands. 'Think about it – how many pairs of pants do you think Calvin Klein sells a year?'

'I don't have a clue,' I say, although I do have an inkling where this conversation is going. Mark likes to think that he's a bit of an entrepreneur at heart, and is forever bouncing investment ideas off Nick and me.

'Well, it must be, to use a technical term, shitloads,' says Mark. 'So, what if we could create a desirable brand name to rival Calvins in, and here's the clever bit . . .'

I can't wait. 'Yes?'

'. . . socks!'

'Socks?'

'Yeah. We do for the sock business what Calvin Klein did for underpants. We could have all these rock stars photographed with our logo clearly visible below their trouser legs.'

I'm picturing a host of celebrities with Michael Jackson-type too-short trousers, and wondering why Mark keeps using the word 'we'.

'Don't you get it?' he continues, quite animated now. 'Every time someone walks into a shop to buy a pair of Calvins, they also ask for a pair of, um . . .' He stops short of a name for his breakthrough idea.

'Listen, mate,' I tell him, making sure Rudy is nearby, 'I think it's a commendable idea, you trying to get into men's underwear,' Rudy coughs loudly from behind the bar, and Mark reddens slightly, 'but do you know anything at all about the clothing industry?'

'Er, no,' admits Mark. 'But I'm an ideas man, you see.'

'Ideas man? Isn't that another way of saying someone who wants to get rich but doesn't want to do any of the work?'

Mark frowns. 'And the problem with that is . . . ?'

He's got me there. 'Nope – can't see one.'

'Exactly. Got any better ideas?'

'Okay,' I say, 'how about this one? We place ads in a couple of the tabloids saying "Cut your household bills in half – send £20". We wait for the money to come rolling in and send them back . . . a pair of scissors.'

For a minute Mark looks like he's seriously considering this one.

'Yes,' I add, 'I believe I read in the paper this morning that someone just got ten years for that very same idea.'

We're currently running one of these scams very successfully through PleazeYourself. We offer a money-back guarantee on subscription fees, and anyone who emails in asking for a refund receives a cheque for their subscription by return. The 'clever' part is that the money comes directly out of an account named after the site itself, so their cheque has the inscription 'PleazeYourself Pornographic Club' clearly visible. Not surprisingly, very few of these cheques actually get cashed.

As Mark's face falls I can't help but notice the bags under his eyes. He looks up at me and lets out a loud sigh.

'Sorry, mate. It's just been one of those weeks. Accountant's apathy – a bit like writer's block, I guess. Know what I mean?'

I do actually, but as my writer's block usually consists of my failing to come up with a new term for 'breasts', I don't think it's quite the same thing.

'Oh well. A few more years you'll make partner, and then retirement on the golf course beckons.'

Mark shakes his head slowly. 'Not now Julia's having another baby. I'm going to have to keep working at least until he or she's finished university. That's another twenty-one years of this, and just for what? Paying school fees?'

'Mate, sometimes that's just the way it is. I have days when I'm fed up with my job . . .'

Mark interrupts me. 'How can you be fed up with your job when you don't actually do anything except look at porn all day?'

Not surprisingly, I don't have an answer to that one.

Mark stares wistfully into his glass. 'You know,' he says, 'we took on a new client this week. He's the same age as me, and he's just sold his company for four million pounds. And do you know what he does? Recycles old refrigerators. Incredible!'

As Mark slumps in his chair, I see Rudy approaching, and I make a face to warn him not to make any smart comments. Swivelling smartly round, he heads back in the other direction.

'Come on, Mark. It's not that bad, surely?'

'Adam, you don't get it, do you? Unlike you and Nick, I have responsibilities, and therefore have to actually work for a living. Quite bloody hard. And then I meet people like this . . . this *fridge magnate*, who've got it all so easy . . .' He puts his head in his hands.

Giving his shoulder a friendly squeeze, I decide to try what I believe is known as a 'pep talk'. Mark stares down at my hand and gives me a strange look, so I remove it quickly and launch in.

'Remember back at college?' I say. 'You were the one with all the ideas, all the ambition. Nick and I, well, we just kind of drifted along. But you – you've always known what you wanted, and gone out and got it. And yes, while Nick and I might take the piss out of you from time to time—'

'Most of the time,' interrupts Mark.

'. . . the truth is, neither of us would be in the position we're in if not for you. And neither of us could do what you do. *And* be such a good dad at the same time. I'm sure it's only a matter of time before one of your . . .' I search for the right word, 'schemes comes off, and you'll be sitting proudly on top of your own business empire.'

He looks up hopefully. 'You think so?'

I nod. 'Before you know it, you'll be flying round the world in a balloon and crash-landing in all sorts of exotic places! Come on, mate.' I punch him playfully on his arm, causing him to yelp. 'Where's your fucking drive?'

Rubbing his arm, Mark manages a half-smile for the first time today. 'It's at the front of my fucking house, where my fucking car is parked!'

'That's more like it,' I tell him.

Mark breaks into a grin, and we clink our glasses together loudly.

'Are you okay, mate?' I ask.

'Yeah. Thanks. It's just that . . .' He struggles to work out what he's trying to say. 'Some days, I just want to be running my own ship.'

'Is that what you do?' I ask him. 'Run a ship? Don't you sail it?'

He looks at me, considering his answer carefully. 'Fuck off,' he says.

We order more beer, and drink it while I try and lighten the mood a little by telling him about Charlie. Mark, not surprisingly, is fascinated by the sneezing.

'You mean she's a multiple sneezer? That must mean . . .'

'I know what that must mean, Mark. I promise to report back if your—'

Mark raises one finger, wincing slightly as he does so. '*Cosmo*'s.'

'Sorry, *Cosmo*'s theory is true,' I reassure him, and yet for some reason the idea of sharing anything too personal about Charlie with anyone seems, strangely, a little distasteful. Mindful of my missed opportunity at the party, I try to think of a way to steer the conversation on to Nick's forthcoming wedding. Eventually, Mark raises it without any prompting, although not in the way I was hoping.

'Great news about Nick and Sandra, don't you think? I haven't been to a good wedding since . . .'

'Your parents'?' I suggest.

Mark looks puzzled. 'My parents'? No, they were . . . Oh. I see. Very good.' He likes to dissect these little exchanges sometimes. 'But seriously,' he continues. 'Good to see old Nick settling down at last.'

Ah. 'But don't you think he's rushing into it a bit?'

Mark shakes his head. 'Nah. He's been looking to meet someone for ages.'

'Exactly,' I reply, feebly. 'So shouldn't he give it more than a few weeks before taking such a major step?'

'Adam, for someone whose average relationship lasts just a few days, I would have thought that you'd see this as rather a long-termer.'

'Yes, but it's just, I mean, they haven't even lived together for that long.'

Mark shrugs. 'Julia and I didn't live together at all before we got married.'

Yes, but only because her mother wouldn't let you, I think. 'Well – you don't buy the first house you see, do you?'

Mark laughs. 'Nick would!'

I realize that I'm getting nowhere fast. 'I just can't believe he went ahead and asked her without even talking it through with one of us.'

Mark gives me a puzzled look. 'Well, that's because he didn't.'

'What?'

'I assumed he'd told you. He didn't ask her. She engineered the whole thing, apparently.'

I stare at him, open-mouthed. 'What do you mean?'

'Well, apparently they were having this conversation about what they both wanted out of life, and Sandra got all upset and said to Nick, don't you ever want to get married, and he said, yes, one day, and she said, no, I mean to me, and he said, what, now, and she said, yes, and he thought about it for a couple of seconds, and the next thing you know they're out choosing a ring.'

I knew it. 'What? So *she* actually proposed to *him*?'

Mark nods. 'Looks that way.'

I bang my beer bottle down on the table in frustration. 'That's not quite the version of events he told me! Typical bloody Nick though. It's just like when she moved in to his flat. That whole sob story she gave him about how she had to live in Chelsea for work – when she doesn't even *have* a job – but couldn't afford the property prices . . . He was out getting her a key cut before you could say the words "scheming bitch".' I stare out of the window for a few moments, and then a thought occurs to me.

'Oh well – maybe he can get out of it then,' I say, optimistically. 'Surely it's not legally binding if he didn't actually get down on one knee or something.'

Mark scratches his head. 'Er, I dunno. I'm not sure that it's legally binding in the first place until they actually say "I do", is it? But what's the problem anyway? If he loves her and she loves him and they both want to get married, why does it matter who asked who, or who didn't ask who?'

'Because . . .' Deep breath. '. . . He's making a mistake.'

Mark looks at me for a moment. 'What do you mean?'

'With Sandra. He's making a mistake. She's not right for him. She's only after one thing.'

'Aren't most people?' He smirks.

'Stop it. I'm serious. I'll prove it to you.' I wave Pritchard over.

'Hey, fellas,' he says. 'How's it hanging?' he adds, adopting a cod-British accent. 'Isn't that what you limeys say?'

'Not out loud, if we don't want to get beaten up,' replies Mark.

Pritchard makes a mock horror face and turns to me. 'What do you want?'

'I just wanted your opinion on something. What do you think of Sandra?'

Pritchard strokes his chin thoughtfully. 'Sandra? Refresh my memory.'

'You know – Nick's girlfr—' I correct myself, and the word almost sticks in my throat. 'Fiancée.'

'Oh. That bitch? Only after his money if you ask me. I see her type in here all the time. Ask them what their favourite book is, they're sure to reply "cheque".'

'Thanks, Pritchard.'

'No problem. I mean, you're welcome!' He winks and goes back to the bar.

I look across at Mark smugly. 'Told you.'

He laughs. 'Told me what? You're asking me to take an opinion about a woman from a man who doesn't go out with women in the first place. Does that make him more or less objective, do you think?'

I sigh, exasperatedly. 'Mark, do *you* actually like Sandra?'

He pauses for a few seconds before answering. 'Well, it's not me that's marrying her, is it?'

'I know, but the way she looks down her nose at us sometimes, the way she flirts with every guy she meets, how she manipulates Nick, spends all his money. And her voice – sometimes she screeches in that high-pitched way that only dogs can hear—'

'Steady on, matey,' he interrupts. 'You're the one

who's got to stand up and say nice things about her on the day, you know.'

'Yes, but what nice things? I'm not sure she possesses a single decent human quality. Even Nick says that she suffers from a condition known as Reverse PMT – grouchy most of the time, but, if you're lucky, once a month she's actually a normal person.'

'She's got a nice arse!' opines Mark.

'Thanks. I can just see that observation going down well in front of all her family. Hold on – I'm assuming she does have family and wasn't just created by some evil scientist in a lab.'

Mark looks at me over his pint glass. 'She seems to make Nick happy, though.'

'Yes, but that's probably because he doesn't know any better. Since he's met her, it's all "Sandra thinks, Sandra says . . . " It's like he's fallen under the influence of some evil cult.'

Mark laughs. 'Are you sure you've got that last word right?'

'It's the same as his bloody car. He could have got something more reliable, but oh no, as usual Nick has to go for something that's more style than substance.'

'Says the man who goes out with ugly philosophy students!'

'Piss off! This isn't about me. And anyway, at least I don't decide I'm going to marry them after a month.'

Mark shifts uncomfortably in his seat. 'Have you, er, talked to him about this?'

'And said what? "Nick, I hate your fiancée, she's nothing but a nasty, money-grabbing, two-faced bitch"?'

'With a nice arse,' repeats Mark, cutting me off. 'Listen, whatever you think of her, and no matter who asked who, they're getting married, and you have to go along with that. And look on the bright side – at least as the best man you'll get to sleep with the bridesmaids.'

I look at Mark and shake my head. 'That's just a cruel myth designed to tempt people into accepting the role. In my experience, most bridesmaids tend to be either married already, which usually makes them off-limits, too ugly to be married already, which *always* makes them off-limits, or five years old . . . You get my drift.'

He frowns. 'You slept with Julia's sister after our wedding.'

'Ah. But she's the exception to the rule. And besides, she's divorced.'

'She wasn't then. She is now.'

'Anyway,' I say, 'getting back to *Nick*. What would you do if you thought, no, *knew* he was making a huge mistake? I mean, you'd say something if he was about to step out in front of a bus, wouldn't you?'

'Well, that would depend on whether he owed me money or not,' jokes Mark.

'I'm serious, Mark.'

Mark leans back in his chair and folds his arms. 'Yeah, but what you have to understand is this. Most male friendships are based around an ancient and complex structure of mickey-taking. From the first time that Neanderthal man walked around the cave and boasted about the size of his' – he lowers his voice – 'club—'

'Oh. I thought you were going to say "penis",' I interrupt loudly, causing Mark to redden.

'. . . men have engaged in this ritual humiliation of their fellow man. Since then, an unwritten set of rules has developed, passed down from father to son through the mists of time, indicating which lines cannot be crossed, which subjects are taboo.'

I look at him strangely. 'Have you been reading *Cosmo* again?'

Mark ignores me, firmly on his soapbox now. 'This is good,' he continues, 'because it ensures that most male interaction is superficial, thus avoiding the need for violent conflict. When these lines are crossed, for example in a Saturday-night lagered-up "are you looking at my bird" kind of way, the result is all too predictable. However, the downside of this is that, between friends, it's then much harder to ever talk about anything serious, because you're fighting against generations of social conditioning.'

'But say you were worried that he was becoming an alcoholic, or addicted to hard drugs. You'd do everything you could to stop him then, wouldn't you?'

'Yeah, but—'

'She's bad for him, Mark. Why should this be any different?'

'Come on, mate. It's just one of those things, isn't it? Your friends can criticize most things about you: your haircut, the shirt you're wearing, but your choice of *wife*? At the very least that's a hanging offence. And not necessarily by the neck.'

Mark's right. And I know he's right, although I can't

resist having one more try. 'If it was you, you'd want me to tell you, wouldn't you?'

He thinks about this for a moment. 'I'm not so sure. Isn't this one of these situations where you just have to let someone make their own mistakes?' A look of concern suddenly crosses Mark's face. 'You don't think I did, do you? With Julia, I mean?'

'Er . . .' I hesitate just long enough to enjoy the growing panic in his eyes. 'Of course not! Julia's . . . fine,' I say, grinning at him.

'Bastard!' says Mark. 'But seriously, we couldn't tell you what we thought about Emma, could we?'

I look up sharply. 'Even though you thought I was making a mistake?'

He nods. 'Yup.'

'And do you not think it might have been better if you had?'

Mark shifts a little uncomfortably in his chair. 'Well, in retrospect, I suppose so.'

'And do you remember why you couldn't tell me?'

'Because she seemed to make you hap— Ah.'

'Exactly!' I say. But at the same time, I wonder whether I'd have listened.

We sit in an awkward silence for a few moments, drinking our beer. Eventually, I just sigh and shake my head, as I realize that I'm on my own on this.

'Listen,' says Mark, finally. 'People want different things out of life. There are those who buy a Ferrari, perhaps because they're seduced by the lines, the colour, the noise, even though it might not be the most sensible or reliable option. Others decide all they want is something to get them from A to B, and go out and buy a Ford.'

'What's your point?'

'Well, look at you, for example. God knows what you really want, and I don't think that you're even sure yourself, or know if anyone even makes the car for you. Me? Much as I hate to admit it, at this point in my life, I'm just trying to get from A to B. But as for Nick? Well, if you'll excuse the phrase, for better or for worse, Nick's a Ferrari kind of guy.'

Mark walks over to the bar, orders another couple of drinks and brings them back to the table. 'Anyway,' he says, putting a bottle of beer down in front of me, 'at least you've got plenty of ammunition for the speech.'

And while that may be true, I've never actually been worried about what I'm going to say about Nick on the day itself. It's working out what to say to him beforehand that's proving to be the problem.

Chapter 7

Nick spends most of the following day out looking at wedding venues and choosing menus, and then I'm at the gym by the time he makes his fleeting appearance in the office. But this suits me fine, as I still haven't a clue how I'm going to broach the subject of him and Sandra.

Friday morning, however, finds him sitting in his car outside my flat. We're off to the Boat Show, as Nick – or rather 'the company' – has decided to buy a boat. While this kind of rash corporate expenditure would normally be something I'd resist in the strongest terms, we've already checked with Mark that we can (unlike the monkey business) offset part of the costs against tax – and although I don't know my port from my, er, fortified wine, I actually quite like the idea of sailing around at the Inland Revenue's expense. Besides, the Boat Show is taking place just round the corner, and it would be rude not to at least explore the possibility.

Nick revs the Ferrari's engine impatiently as I lock my front door and walk over to where he's double-parked. I had suggested on the phone yesterday that perhaps we could walk there, but he'd just given me a lecture about why the internal combustion engine had been invented, so I jump into the passenger seat, and he screeches off before I've even closed my door properly. He's looking tired and a little harassed, and I notice that he hasn't shaved for a few days as he's sporting a patchy growth on his chin.

'Hello, mate,' I say. 'What's new?'

'Well, they've managed to clone a sheep . . .' replies Nick.

'Heavy night?' I ask, as he struggles to conceal a yawn.

'Sorry, mate. Up till late looking through brochures for the honeymoon,' he says, wearily. 'It's a nightmare. Just can't decide between the Maldives or Zanzibar.'

'Gosh, it must be tough being you,' I tell him. 'Nice beard, by the way. Razor broken?'

'Fuck off,' he says. 'It's not a beard. It's designer stubble.'

'Well, you need to get a better designer. Who was it – Stevie Wonder?'

It takes us a quarter of an hour to negotiate the rush-hour traffic and cover the mile or so from my flat to Earl's Court, during which time I fill Nick in about my encounter with Charlie. He listens patiently, then slowly shakes his head. 'Wuss!'

Nick roars into the underground car park, leaving the Ferrari parked across two spaces to avoid those annoying door dings, and we make our way into the hall, brandishing our complimentary tickets. He's already decided on the type of boat he wants: something that's big enough to entertain people on without ever actually having to leave the safety of the marina, and, of course, the plushest most expensive one in its class, but he's decided to go to this stand last so he can be fawned over by lots of other manufacturers beforehand.

We wander round for a while, looking as much at the bikini-clad girls draped over the stands as the boats themselves, and chatting to the odd exhibitor whenever Nick sees something that takes his fancy. After an hour or so I tell him that there's only so much sales talk I can stomach, and head off in search of a coffee.

I walk through the luxury yacht section and soon find a cafeteria near the entrance. Ordering an espresso, I sit down at a corner table and flick through the exhibition programme. It's good coffee, so I get a refill and gaze around at the boats, some of them bigger than my flat. The multi-millionaires' playthings that cost more per metre than most people earn in a lifetime look a little odd displayed out of the water, and I marvel silently at the money that's floating round this part of the exhibition.

As with women's breasts, one espresso's never enough and three's too many, and as I still have half an hour to kill before I'm due to meet Nick again I decide to drool at the yachts instead.

It's a higher class of demonstrator girl here too. Off come the bikinis and on go the business suits, and as I walk round the various stands I'm somewhat shocked to see Charlie. This must have been the other job she mentioned – I hadn't asked her what it was – and I suppose, on balance, that I'm pleased to see she's not half naked and draped over a speedboat, but looking very respectable, standing in front of a large blue and white motor cruiser that's probably twice as big as and at least ten times more expensive than my parents' house.

The boat is propped up on a huge trailer adorned with white and blue flags. Up on the deck a man and a woman are sitting opposite a smug-looking salesman, who seems to be in the process of accepting a cheque from the male half of the couple, a short, bald, tanned chap in his sixties, whilst his platinum-blonde wife, who can't be much more than my age, pouts her surgically enhanced lips in her husband's direction.

Charlie hasn't seen me, so I decide to spectate for a few minutes while considering my approach. As she hands out leaflets and chats pleasantly to passers-by, a couple of middle-aged businessmen in ill-fitting suits walk towards her. I say walk, but it's actually more of a stumble, as they've obviously spent the best part of the morning in the hospitality section, and I can almost smell their beer breath from where I'm standing, or rather lurking, behind a small speedboat named, I note with amusement, the *Penetrator*. Charlie sees them, and in a split second sizes them up, but doesn't miss a beat, greeting them with a beaming smile, and handing each of them a brochure. I see the fatter one of them feign interest in the boat, whereas the other, skinnier man seems more interested in Charlie's curves than those of the sleek cruiser.

I move a little closer, banging my left shin painfully

on the *Penetrator*'s propeller, managing to stay just out of Charlie's line of sight, but near enough to listen in on their conversation. It's clear she's a little uncomfortable, particularly as the drunker of the two (although it's a close-run thing) seems to be edging towards her.

'So, sweetheart,' asks fat drunk man, pointing unsteadily at the boat behind Charlie, 'what does it cost to get on board one of these?'

'Well,' replies Charlie, 'if you'd like a price list I'll just—'

'And what does it cost to get on board you?' leers the other one, putting a sweaty hand round her waist and pulling her towards him. She tries politely to remove his arm but he's got quite a firm grip.

I've seen enough, and hurry over, fighting my first urge, which is to lay the guy straight out. I hurriedly decide on Plan B.

'Hello, darling. Sorry I'm late,' I announce in a loud voice, leaning towards her and kissing her full on the lips. Unsurprisingly, she looks surprised.

I turn back to Laurel and Hardy. 'Excuse me, gents. Can I just borrow my wife for a moment?' Without waiting for an answer, I take Charlie by the hand and lead her away. Thin drunk man's expression changes from a leer to a frown, and he removes his hand sheepishly from Charlie's waist. I'm probably a good six inches taller than him, and he's plainly not stupidly drunk, so he doesn't say a word. Charlie still hasn't spoken either, and for a moment I'm worried she hasn't recognized me.

'Are you okay?' I ask her, when we're out of earshot.

She breaks into a smile. 'Shining armour suits you.'

I look back at the two men, and, hoping Charlie can't see my face, give them my best 'fuck off' glare, which actually just consists of me scowling at them and mouthing 'fuck off' slowly and deliberately. Fortunately, they fuck off.

'Sorry if I came over a bit forward there,' I say, turning back to Charlie. 'I just thought they might be bothering you.'

'Yes,' she says, 'they were. How lucky that you happened to be passing just at the right time,' she adds, raising one eyebrow.

'Oh no, I was watching you from over . . . I mean, I didn't—' I want to say that I didn't want to interrupt her at work but she cuts me off before I can explain.

'Well, whatever you're doing here, I'm glad you are,' she says. 'But what are you doing here?'

'Oh, the company has . . . well, Nick's thinking of . . .' Damn. Why can't I string a sentence together when I'm around her? 'We're thinking of buying a boat. Maybe. For the business.'

'Wow!' says Charlie. 'I wish I'd taken that job after all. Anyway, you've come to the right place.'

Charlie glances back towards her stand, where some other potential customers have arrived. Fortunately, they appear sober.

'Adam,' she says, 'I have to get back to work now, but . . .' she pauses, and then she reaches up and kisses me quickly. 'Thanks.'

I don't say a word, but feel myself wanting to kiss her again. All I can say is, 'You're welcome,' as I stand there and watch her walk away. But just before she reaches the stand she turns round, takes her mobile phone out of her pocket, points to it and mouths something, which I hope is 'Call me'. I grin and nod like an idiot.

Realizing that I'm due to meet Nick soon, I stroll back towards the main hall, and suddenly remember that I have my mobile on me. Scrolling through the received calls section I find when Charlie phoned earlier in the week, hoping it doesn't say 'number withheld'. It doesn't, and before I lose my nerve I press the dial button. After two rings she answers.

'Just wanted to check those guys had gone,' I say.

'Yes, thanks.'

'And . . . I wondered if you needed an escort home?'

'No thanks, I've got my Fiesta.'

'No, I mean—'

She cuts me off with a laugh. 'I know what you mean. Duh! But if you're calling to ask me out, then I'd love to, and I'm free for dinner tonight.'

I'm slightly taken aback. 'Tonight? As in this evening?'

'Sounds good. Pick me up at eight? You've got my address on my CV, I think?'

'Er, okay.' Duh indeed! And I'm the one who's supposed to be good with words.

The rest of the conversation is a bit of a blur, punctuated by mostly monosyllabic responses on my part, but we eventually decide on this new restaurant she's heard of, and I tell her that I'll book a table and see her later. More than a little elated by the time the call ends, I head off like an excited five-year-old to tell Nick.

I spot him over at the other side of the building, engaged in conversation with a bored-looking sales-girl on a stand selling jet skis. I text a rude message to his mobile, and he excuses himself and comes over to where I'm standing. I can't seem to stop grinning, and tell him what I've been up to as we head off to find HMS *Please Yourself*.

'Wuss,' he repeats.

An hour later, clutching an armful of brochures and slightly drunk on complimentary champagne, Nick leaves the salesman with a promise that we'll 'think about it'. We retrieve the Ferrari, paying the ransom to get it out of the car park, and head off back towards the King's Road.

The lunchtime rush hour has just started, which isn't such a problem as we're not going anywhere in particular – some days Nick just likes to drive up and down the King's Road in his Ferrari. Unfortunately, there seem to be a lot of people just driving up and down the King's Road in their Ferraris today. We consider (for about half a nanosecond) going into work, but instead decide to head up into town for, in Nick's words, a 'spot' of shopping. What exactly constitutes a 'spot' of anything, I wonder idly, although I manage to stop myself from asking whether he's ever suggested 'a spot of sex' to Sandra.

We come to a temporary halt just opposite

McDonalds, where a group of shoppers are taking their time on the zebra crossing in front of us.

'Get out of the way, poor people,' Nick shouts at them.

I shrink in my seat, worried that the roof is down and they can probably hear him, but then realize that he's revving the engine so loudly that it's doubtful anybody can hear anything within thirty feet of the car.

We speed along Sloane Street and pull up at a set of traffic lights, where an old Fiat Punto edges up next to us. The driver glances at Nick and starts to gun his engine, edging forwards as he waits for the lights to change. Nick takes up the challenge and does the same, blipping the Ferrari's throttle to produce a glorious sound from the twin exhausts. I look across at him and let out an exaggerated sigh.

'What?' he asks me, without turning his attention from the lights. They change to amber and then green, and he floors the accelerator. The Ferrari leaps forward, leaving the Fiat some way behind. That is, until we reach the backed-up traffic a hundred yards further up the road.

'Yes!' cries Nick, slowing back down to a sensible speed. The Fiat idles up alongside us, its driver refusing to make eye contact.

'Can I ask you a question?' I ask Nick.

'Sure,' he replies.

'What's the point in proving that a Ferrari is faster than a Fiat? Didn't you know that when you bought it?'

Nick thinks about this quickly and grins at me. 'Mate,' he says, jabbing a thumb in the direction of the defeated Fiat driver, 'I'm not proving it to myself. I'm proving it to them.'

We're aiming for Selfridges, and after a white-knuckle journey up Park Lane, where the West End's entire fleet of black cabs seems to be trying to play dodgems with us, we manage to find a parking meter just off Oxford Street, and head on into the store.

I love Selfridges, in particular the home entertainment department. You know those people who always choose to have their ashes scattered in a special place where they've spent many a happy hour? I'll have mine scattered here, somewhere between the hi-fis and the flat-screen televisions.

Taking the escalator down, we head through the bookshop and follow the sound of music until we're standing in the middle of my spiritual home. Nick heads off to check out the newest mobile phones on offer, and I browse through the racks of CDs, occasionally picking up and replacing items where the cover has caught my eye. A bored-looking assistant comes over and asks with zero enthusiasm if he can help me; when I tell him I'm 'just looking' he sighs and drifts away. I suddenly feel guilty, so buy an album to make him feel better. If he does, he doesn't let on.

I stroll on towards the Bang & Olufsen section and gaze adoringly at the latest Danish minimalist miracles that look too pretty to actually play music on, one of which currently occupies pride of place in my front room.

'Afternoon, Mr Bailey,' says a voice from behind me. Danny, the over-anxious sales assistant who sold me my hi-fi, steps out from behind the tallest but thinnest speakers I've ever seen and shakes my hand.

'Hello, Danny,' I reply. 'What's new?' Sometimes I'm really hilarious without even trying, as Danny's syco- phantic laughter tells me is the case today.

'Well, we've got these new remote-controlled rotating televisions,' he says, all but rubbing his hands together.

'Great. Rotating, eh?' I ask him, not wanting to add the obvious *why?* Fortunately, Danny's just bursting to tell me.

'Yes,' he says, picking up a handset the size of a NASA console and aiming it at a futuristic-looking set in the corner. 'It means that you can watch it . . .' – he pauses for effect – 'from anywhere in the room.'

We stand there as the screen swivels to face us, and I look at Danny as he beams like someone who's just shown me the cure for cancer. I'm about to tell him that I have my own favourite chair that I always sit in to watch TV from, thus rendering this inno- vation useless, but stop myself when I realize firstly how disappointed he might get, and secondly how sad that makes me sound. I eventually walk away clutching a glossy brochure that it would have seemed churlish not to take, collect Nick, and we head back upstairs and into the men's clothing section, where, astoundingly, the amount of money I spend on a shirt to wear on my date with Charlie shocks even him.

'Blimey,' he says, taking it from me and looking at the price tag. 'I hope she's going to be worth it.'

I snatch the bag back from him. 'Yes. Well. I'm quite keen on this one.'

'Ha!' he scoffs, as we head out of Selfridges and back towards the car. 'You're keen on them all when you first meet them. But all too soon they achieve beautiful-but-unsuitable status, simply because they, I don't know, write *X*mas instead of *Christ*mas in their cards.' Nick despairs sometimes.

'Ouch! That's a little harsh . . .'

'But true. What was that one's name again?'

I think back, trying to remember the Xmas girl. 'Er, Liz, I think. But that wasn't the only reason we split up.'

'Well, what else was there?'

'Er . . .' I can't actually recall. But there must have been something. Mustn't there?

'I rest my case,' sighs Nick, shaking his head. 'You're obsessed with the details. The small print, if you like. You can't just enjoy the bigger picture. You'll go out with Charlie for a few weeks and then dump her, not because there's any real problem, but because she breaks one of your precious rules.'

'That's not true,' I reply. 'I have a feeling she's—'

'Different?' interrupts Nick. 'I've heard you say that before.'

I'm getting all defensive now. 'No. I was going to say . . .' I hurriedly try and think of something else, as 'different' is exactly what I was going to say. Unfortunately, 'special' is the word I come up with.

Nick just mimes sticking his fingers down his throat.

We drive back into Chelsea and park outside Bar Rosa. Nick asks me if I'm coming in for a 'spot' of lunch, and it occurs to me that now might be a good time to try to talk to him about Sandra, but then he says that she might be joining us, so I make my excuses, telling him that I have to go home and get ready for my date with Charlie.

Nick rolls his eyes. 'And her having a boy's name isn't a problem this time?'

Ah. Charlie. Or is it Charley? Does that count, I wonder, when it's spelt with 'ie' instead of 'ey'? Or vice-versa?

The funny thing is, it hadn't even occurred to me.

Chapter 8

Charlie loves fish. This is unfortunate, because over the years I've come to realize that if you can't drown it, I can't eat it. She particularly adores sushi, and if you think about it, for anyone like me who can't stomach fish in its cooked and prepared form, where at least it can be disguised by a combination of sauces and flavours, the prospect of munching on raw mouthfuls of the stuff is pretty nauseating.

We're sitting in one of London's newest and therefore trendiest seafood eateries, Catch Twenty-Two. The restaurant is located on the twenty-second floor of one of the capital's tallest hotels, affording us a fantastic view of the London skyline. I can't work out whether they decided on a name for the place before picking which floor to put it on, or whether they'd built it on this floor before picking the name . . . oh, never mind.

We're here because Charlie's read about this place, and apparently it's the restaurant of the moment. I'm slightly suspicious of this because not only have I managed to get a table at short notice, but the place is only half full at nine o'clock on a Friday evening.

It's one of those establishments where the waiters and waitresses all look like catwalk models, dressed head to toe in this year's black, which seems for once to actually *be* black. Even the toilets are a work of art, decorated in some Japanese minimalist style, with shimmering waterfalls to provide encouragement if you're having a problem going. Once you've washed your hands, smartly attired attendants hand out origami'd hand towels in exchange for a tip in the requisite saucer, which seems only to be filled with pound coins. Whatever happened to spending a penny?

Anyway, it's our first date, and it's going pretty well. I've opted for the standard non-fish dish on the menu at every seafood restaurant, but it's actually a pretty good steak, and the waiter didn't give me too pitying a look when I ordered it. The only slight blip for me is when Charlie tells me how nice her tuna is and that I really should try some. All my life, despite me telling people who obviously like fish, because they've ordered it, that I don't like fish, which should be obvious because I haven't ordered it despite being in a venue that has every variety, they've tried to make me try theirs. Usually I hear the tempting line 'Go on – it doesn't really taste like fish.' Well then, what's the point? I don't like fish, so you're saying that I should try your fish because it doesn't actually taste like fish. And tuna is the favourite one for this – apparently when cooked well it tastes like steak. Well, I've actually got steak, thanks all the same.

But Charlie seems to be enjoying herself, and, in a moment of unusual selflessness, I realize that I am, too,

and for that very reason. This takes me aback, so much
so that I agree to try her fish.

Once I've returned from the toilet, where I'm so
embarrassed after throwing up in the unfortunately
minimalist sink that I feel I have to tip the attendant
five pounds, Charlie tells me more about herself, in
particular her part-time job as a model. And not just
any model, catwalk or catalogue, but actually a specialist
hand model. Any time a company needs someone with
particularly nice hands, for example for a washing-up
liquid commercial, or a jewellery ad, Charlie's up for
the job. They'll normally film the rest of the ad with
the regular actress, but when it comes to the close-
up of someone holding the product, or luxuriously
washing their hands as if on the brink of orgasm, they
call in Charlie.

She's actually been the hands for a number of television ads, she tells me, including the latest one for
that flaky chocolate bar that always gets consumed as
if the actress is performing oral sex rather than simply
eating chocolate. When Charlie tells me that this
involved her standing close behind another woman
suggestively feeding her chocolate for the best part of
an afternoon I have to stop myself from asking for an
invite to her next shoot.

'Can I see?' I ask, and use this as an excuse to lean
over and take her hand, ostensibly to inspect it more
closely, although again I find myself not wanting to
let it go.

She tells me that she has to wear gloves a lot to
protect her 'assets', and a broken nail for her can actually

be a real disaster. I'm amused when she gets all embarrassed telling me that work of this type is known in
the advertising world as a 'hand job', and when I
mention that we've got whole websites dedicated to
that sort of thing, she removes her hand from mine
with an exaggerated sigh.

We find ourselves talking in that easy way that lets
you know you have a connection, and somehow the
food and the wine seem secondary to the conversation. She laughs when I remind her not to let her
dinner get cold, because it's sushi, so of course it's cold
anyway, and not for the first time since we met I find
myself noticing my awkwardness around her.

'Can I ask you a question?' says Charlie, once the
waiter has cleared our plates.

'You just did.'

Charlie kicks me gently under the table. 'If we
hadn't bumped into each other at the boat show this
morning, would you ever have asked me out?'

'Well, technically, it was you that asked me
out . . .'

'You know what I mean. It's just that . . . I felt we
had an attraction when we met at the interview, and
then when I phoned you to tell you that I'd got the
other job I hoped you might . . . but, nothing. I
thought you must have been married or something.'
There's suddenly a strange expression on her face.
'You're not, are you?'

'Oh no,' I say, perhaps a little too quickly, then hope
I haven't conveyed any reluctance or aversion with my
answer. 'I mean, no. I haven't . . . Not yet. You? Married?

Ever been?' I ask her, forcing her to rearrange my words before they make any sense.

She shakes her head. 'No.'

'Engaged?'

'Once. A long time ago.'

'What happened? The engagement, I mean.'

Charlie shrugs. 'What normally happens, I guess. He proposed, gave me a ring . . .' she says, with a smile.

'No, I meant why didn't you go through with it. Or was it his decision?' I regret asking as soon as the words have left my mouth, particularly when her smile fades.

'It was just . . . not right, I suppose,' she says, wistfully. 'And when we found out we couldn't . . .' She stops talking and takes a large gulp of wine as her eyes seem to mist over a little.

I suddenly feel bad, like I may have overstepped the mark. 'Do you mind talking about this? We can change the subject if you like.'

Charlie takes a deep breath and continues. 'No, that's okay. I was quite a bit younger, and, well, he was older than me, and seemed so certain of what he wanted out of life, and what he wanted for me too . . .' She pauses as the waiter refills her glass. 'Plus he kept talking about marriage as a partnership, an arrangement, a . . .'

'Compromise?'

'Yes,' she nods, 'a compromise. All very impersonal words, you know, like it was something you had to work at. And at the time I thought that sounded like the most unsentimental thing I'd ever heard. I'd always believed in this spark, this feeling when you met that you just knew you should be together, and that everything else would sort of fall into place around that. Sure you'd have bad times, but I suppose I kind of naively thought that the minute you had to "work" at it the battle was sort of lost.'

I don't say anything as what she's just said sinks in. As she waits for me to respond, I realize that now would be a good time to come up with something deep and meaningful to signify that I agree with her.

'I agree with you,' I say.

'Plus,' she continues, a half-smile on her face, 'there was the name issue.'

I frown. 'Name issue?'

'Yes. Looking back, I think he only wanted to marry me because he was so into motorbikes.'

I'm completely lost now. 'Motorbikes?'

'Well, his surname was . . . Davidson.'

'Davidson?'

'Yeah. So I'd have been . . . ?'

'Charlie Davidson!' I laugh.

She smiles again. 'Exactly!'

I find myself repeating 'Charlie Bailey' in my head a couple of times to check that it doesn't sound ridiculous, and it's both reassuring and worrying to find out that it doesn't. I decide to impart some of my wedding wisdom.

'You know,' I tell her, recycling my own enlightenment from the other night, 'a friend once told me, on the eve of his wedding, that your partner should be someone who brings out the best in you. Someone who you always want to impress. Who inspires you, if you like.'

Charlie looks as if she's absorbing this for a moment. 'Hmmm. I see what he means. Does he feel that about his wife?'

I nod. 'Yeah, he did. Until they got divorced last year!'

Her face drops. 'Oh no. Really?'

'No – not really. One child already, another on the way.'

Charlie fixes me with a steady gaze. 'And what about you, Adam? What are your views on marriage?'

Oh my god. That question. What am I going to say? What's the politically correct response here? Normally, I'd give some glib response, but that hardly seems appropriate given Charlie's recent admission. I swallow hard, and reach for my glass of water.

'Er . . .'

'Don't worry,' she says, resting her hand on mine. 'I'm not going to hold you to your answer.'

'Well . . . I think it's a fine idea in principle, as long as both parties are sure they're going to be together for the rest of their lives.'

'Ah-ha!' she announces. 'Therein lies the flaw in your theory. How can anyone ever be sure of that?'

I sit back in my chair, being careful not to remove my hand from underneath Charlie's. 'Exactly! But I'm not just talking about the love and starry-eyed commitment stuff. A lot of people get together simply because they can't be bothered to look for anyone else any more.'

'You old romantic!'

'I'm serious. Look at my best friend Nick, for example. He's about to get married for a number of reasons, but I don't think love would make the top three.'

Charlie's eyes widen. 'Are you kidding?'

I shake my head. 'Nope. And it was his fiancée who proposed. Not him. He just kind of went along with it because he thought it was the thing to do.'

'You're joking. Have you told him what a bad idea that is?'

'Well, I've been trying to, in a roundabout sort of way . . .'

Charlie lets go of my hand. 'How "roundabout"?'

I realize that it's probably more of a U-turn than a roundabout. 'Well, you have to understand that men find talking about this sort of thing difficult.'

'Why?' asks Charlie, amazed. 'Women do it all the time.'

This I know – I've read their magazines. I decide to try and condense Mark's theory and explain.

'Well, it's like this, really. Man is traditionally the hunter-gatherer. He's not biologically designed for monogamy. And, so, if he decides that he's found a female of the species that he wants to commit to for the rest of his life, and asks her to marry him, thus going against all those millions of years of genetic programming . . . Well, who are we to tell him he's got it wrong, I suppose? The bottom line is this. You can say what you like about your mates. But commenting about your mate's choice of *mate* . . .'

Charlie sits there silently for a few moments, as if she's carefully considering all I've just said, then raises her eyes to the ceiling and shakes her head.

'Rubbish!' she says. 'And anyway – I thought you said she asked him?'

'Er, yeah . . .'

'Well surely that makes it all right for you to say something?'

'Well, okay, he might not have asked her directly, but the fact that he agreed . . .' I start to protest, weakly, but Charlie folds her arms and fixes me with a stern expression.

'But you do think he's doing the wrong thing?'

'Big time.'

'And this is your best friend?'

I refill our wine glasses. 'Yup.'

'And if you were in the same situation, wouldn't you want your best friend to tell you?'

For a moment I find myself wishing that Mark were here, so he could hear this. 'Well, I don't think I'd allow myself to make that sort of mistake . . . Ouch!' Charlie kicks me again, much harder this time, before I can say 'a second time', which is probably just as well. I don't really want to go down that road this evening.

I reach down to rub my shin. 'What was that for?'

'Don't be so . . . so self-smug.'

'Self-smug? What does that mean?'

'Just that it's easy to sit here and be black and white about other people's emotional issues. Don't assume that if you ever find yourself in the same sort of situation you'll still be able to apply such clinical judgement.'

'Ouch, for different reasons.'

She looks at me seriously. 'Adam, you've got to tell him. It could be the biggest mistake he'll ever make.'

'But how? You can't just go up to your best friend and tell him that the woman he's marrying is a complete bitch who's going to ruin his life.'

'Well, if *you* can't, who can?'

I surreptitiously move my legs out of Charlie's range. 'You? I'll pay!'

'That's not funny. Talk to him. Tell him. Or at least think of something to show him the error of his ways.'

I hold my hands up in defeat. 'Okay, okay.'

'Soon!'

'I promise.'

'Good.'

Fortunately, just then the waiter arrives with the dessert menu, which I'm pleased to see contains no fish dishes. Charlie *ums* and *ahs* for a while until I offer to share something with her, and she chooses ice cream, which we eat in silence for no other reason than the fact that Charlie is demolishing her half at an impressive rate.

'Sorry,' she says, noticing my amused expression, and adding, 'I love ice cream,' rather unnecessarily. She scoops up the last spoonful and holds it up to my mouth with a mischievous smile. I open wide and she feeds it to me, pausing only to dab a little on the tip of my nose.

We order coffee – she even manages to pronounce

espresso properly – and talk for a while, oblivious to
the fact that we're the last people in the restaurant.
On my way to the gent's I suddenly catch sight of
the waiter yawning in the corner and realize that,
unfortunately, it's time to go.

When I come back from the toilet, having refused
to give the surly attendant any more money, I ask
Charlie if she's ready.

'Yes,' she replies. 'That was lovely.'

'I'll just get the Old Bill then,' I say, at the same
time realizing just how little my little joke is, and I
summon the waiter over. He looks at me with a smirk.

'It's okay, sir, your wife has already paid,' he says.

'My, er . . .' I'm at a loss for words on two counts,
and don't quite know what to do. I look at Charlie,
who's grinning sheepishly.

'It's a thank you for rescuing me earlier.'

'But . . .'

'No buts. You were a real gentleman then, so be a
gentleman now and don't argue.'

The waiter is still hovering. I can tell he's amused
by my discomfort, and he raises one eyebrow before
strolling away nonchalantly.

We leave the restaurant and walk to where I've
parked the Impresser – I had no qualms about driving
this evening, and I've been careful about how much
wine I've had – and I blip the remote and open
Charlie's door for her. I drive her home and double
park outside her building, my engine running, and the
Impresser ticking over quietly too. And when I thank
her for a great evening, and find myself nervously

asking if I can see her again, she leans across and answers me with one of those kisses that is too short to be an invitation upstairs but too long to be a no. She gets out of the car and I watch to make sure she gets into her flat safely, waiting a few extra seconds until a light comes on upstairs.

On the way back to my flat I take a diversion down Nick's road, Charlie's words ringing in my ears. The Ferrari is parked outside his building, but it's late, and Sandra's bound to be there too, so I decide not to go up. Charlie's right, of course. I do need to have that conversation with him soon, or at least work out a way to get him thinking about things a little more seriously than he seems to be doing.

When I get back home, my answerphone light is flashing. Rushing over to the machine I stab at the button, hoping it'll be Charlie, but instead Mark's voice comes booming out, wondering whether his, sorry, *Cosmo*'s theory is true. There's a second message, from my mother, chastising me for not telling her that Nick's getting married. Apparently Nick's mum had gone round to tell her the 'good' news this morning, and she's decided to take the opportunity to launch into one of her 'When are you going to think about settling down' speeches. My mother loves answerphones, because it's the one chance she gets to talk and talk without being interrupted by my father. I listen as far as the point when she starts lecturing me about the stag night, telling me that she hopes we're not going to end up in one of those clubs with those 'laptop dancers', before the tape runs out.

Smiling, I hit 'delete' and stroll through to the kitchen. Laptop dancers! I haven't even thought about the stag night, as I've been kind of hoping things won't get that far. But then I stop dead. That gives me an idea . . .

Chapter 9

Draining his glass, Nick burps loudly and slams it back down on the table, causing a few of the tattooed drinkers near us to swivel their skin-heads around to look in our direction — a remarkable feat considering most of them seem to have no necks. Fortunately, when they see there's no trouble they resume talking to their husbands and boyfriends.

The pub is one of those places where the ceiling, walls and floor are all the same dark brown colour, more a result of years of cigarette smoke rising up and beer dripping down than the application of any decorator's brush. It stands alone at the end of the Fulham Road, a beacon of resistance against the spritzer and sun-dried tomato set, sticking two nicotine-stained fingers defiantly up at the gentrification of the surrounding streets.

It's Wednesday evening, and we're off to see Fulham play Manchester United. Like so many other non-Mancunians, Nick has recently converted to Unitedism, and has managed to get us tickets at the last minute thanks to his new invitation only — as he takes great pride in explaining — credit card. It was

136 *Matt Dunn*

this or front-row seats for a Mick Jagger concert in Hyde Park, apparently, but Nick had quickly decided on the football.

'If I want to see a bunch of old stones in a field, I'll just head down to Salisbury Plain,' he'd said.

Like every drinking establishment near the ground this evening, our pub is packed with football supporters, all standing round drinking in groups of three or four, waiting to make their way down to the ground in time for kick-off. Even though we're only a mile or so down the road, we're feeling a bit out of our 'patch' here, and we've tried to roughen our accents accordingly. Worryingly, we're the only drinkers to have bothered with a table, which I'm sure marks us out as soft Chelsea nancy boys.

We're waiting for the constantly late Mark, and meanwhile I'm telling Nick about my night out with Charlie. He, of course, is only interested in whether I slept with her or not, and when I answer in the negative, he just laughs.

'Loser!' he says. 'And speaking of losers . . .'

I follow his gaze to where Mark has just appeared through the pub doorway. He's still wearing his suit, having come straight from the office, and is somewhat self-consciously looking around, trying to spot us. I wave him over to the table.

'Sorry, boys . . .' Mark starts to explain, but Nick cuts him off with a shake of his head, not wanting to get into another discussion about the intricacies of West London's bus routes. It's Mark's round, we decide democratically – and mainly due to his lateness – so he goes off to get the drinks, and I follow to give him a hand. We get served surprisingly quickly given the amount of people crammed together at the bar, and I look around surreptitiously to check we haven't pushed in front of some thirsty hooligan looking for a pre-match scrap.

There's still half an hour before the game starts, so Mark orders us two pints each, mainly because he doesn't fancy a return trip to the bar. When he tries to pay with a fifty-pound note, the mountainous barmaid, who has run out of fivers, tells him to sit down and she'll bring his change over to the table. He looks uneasy at the thought of leaving so much of his money in someone else's hands, but is even more uncomfortable at the thought of waiting at the bar on his own, so he sits back down with us and settles for glancing anxiously in her direction every few minutes.

She does as good a job of ignoring him now as she did in serving him earlier, and we've nearly finished our drinks by the time she appears with a cheerful 'I bet you thought I'd forgotten you, love.' As she's about to give him his change, she suddenly scrunches up her face, takes a deep breath and lets out a massive sneeze, which she just about manages to cover with her hand. The hand still holding Mark's money.

'Ooh! Bless me!' she cries, handing Mark back the now soggy notes, and he can't help grimacing as he takes them. We watch in horror as she waddles back behind the bar, pausing only to wipe her hand on a tea towel, which she then uses to dry the clean glasses from the dishwasher.

Mark removes a packet of tissues from his inside pocket and carefully cleans each note before putting them back in his wallet.

'Wow,' he says. 'She must be really hot stuff between the sheets.' Nick and I shudder simultaneously. 'Speaking of which . . .' he continues, looking at me and raising one eyebrow, but before I can answer Nick leans across the table, pulling up his cuff to expose his watch and tapping the dial.

I peer closely at the gleaming lump of metal fastened round Nick's wrist. 'Are you telling us we should get a move on, or showing off yet another new and ridiculously expensive watch?'

Nick shakes his head disdainfully. 'Much as I'd like to sit here discussing your sexual exploits . . .'

'I *would* actually like to sit here discussing Adam's sexual exploits,' interjects Mark. 'I am a married man you know. The last woman I slept with will probably be the last woman I ever sleep with, if you see what I mean, so hearing about Adam's adventures is the closest I have to any sort of varied sex life.'

Nick ignores him and stands up. 'Time, gentlemen, please,' he announces, and strolls out through the doorway. As Mark heads for the toilets, his bladder struggling with the early drinking pace, I follow Nick outside, where he's doing a bad job of trying to look inconspicuous amongst the crowds, whose shirts proclaim their allegiance to their preferred players. By the same token, Nick's favourites would appear to be the Italian defensive pairing of Dolce & Gabbana.

After a couple of minutes, a relieved Mark emerges, and we follow the throng down towards Craven Cottage and into Fulham's ground. We squeeze through the turnstiles, find our seats in the stands (as if that makes sense) and wait for the game to start.

We're sitting right next to the pitch. Nick has as usual managed to get hold of the most expensive tickets, made a big deal about how much they would have cost, and then made an even bigger deal about refusing our offers to pay him back for them. Mark's obviously excited to be here, partly because we actually know him to be a true Fulham fan but also because, given the control Julia normally keeps on their household budget, we know this is something he wouldn't normally get a chance to do.

'Should be an enjoyable game,' he says, watching the pitch intently. I don't like to remind him that, given the respective league table positions of the two teams, it's probably only the opposition fans who are likely to 'enjoy' tonight's game.

As the Fulham players run out on to the field, the crowd erupts into song. When Mark joins in at the top of his voice, word if not note-perfect, Nick and I shrink down in our seats. Mercifully, the whistle soon blows, and Fulham immediately hoof the ball towards the United end, and straight out of play.

'Yoooouuuuu're . . . . SHIT!' shout thirty thousand voices, including Mark, as the United goalkeeper takes the kick.

'How come you know all these chants?' I ask him.

'It's hardly difficult to learn the words to "You're Shit!"' interrupts Nick. 'Observe – the cultural phenomenon that is the Fulham supporter!'

'Well, why did you bother coming then?' asks Mark. 'Why didn't you just stay at home and watch it in your posh flat on your posh flat-screen TV with your posh flat-chested girlfriend . . .' Fortunately this last part is drowned out by a chorus of 'Ooh, ah, Cantona!' as the away supporters try to rally their side with memories of past greats.

'Because I didn't want to miss seeing your face when my team stuffs yours,' replies Nick.

'I didn't realize they were *your* team,' I say to Nick. 'When did you venture into football club ownership?'

A few minutes later, United break down the wing, the ball is crossed in front of the open Fulham goal . . . and no one in a red shirt gets anywhere near it. '*Où est Cantona?*' cry the home fans in retaliation.

Mark leans across and digs Nick in the ribs. 'There's culture for you!' he says. 'Not an O-level between them but they can speak French and be ironic at the same time.'

The rest of the game goes predictably, punctuated by United's goals and our half-time visit to the bar. With ten minutes to go, and Fulham down four-nil, Andy Wilson, the Fulham striker, is substituted on for his first game since alleged treatment for schizophrenia kept him out of the team. His arrival is greeted with a chorus from the home crowd of 'There's only two Andy Wilsons'. We get up and leave before Mark can praise their knowledge of psychiatry.

We walk up the Fulham Palace Road and towards Hammersmith, where I've earmarked a couple of venues for tonight's entertainment, and by some miracle we manage to get a table straight away at one of them. It's called Lager Than Life, and is one of these themed sports bars where they always have some obscure activity — tonight it seems to be speed rock climbing — showing simultaneously on hundreds of television sets, backed by a thumping musical track that makes any conversation virtually impossible.

We sit down and order drinks, and when they arrive Mark accidentally spills a drop of beer on Nick's sleeve. He reacts angrily.

'Jesus, Mark, be careful,' he shouts, pointing to a little tag hanging off his breast pocket, where we can clearly see who made his shirt. 'This is a fucking Armani!'

'Oh sorry, Mr Designer Clothes-horse. Can't you wash these expensive clothes then?' replies Mark, sarcastically.

'Piss off, Oxfam Man!'

'Piss off yourself. At least my clothes have their labels where they should be. On the inside.'

'Yeah, ones with your name on, where your mum sewed them.'

'Children, please!' I interrupt. 'This is supposed to be an evening of celebration. As best man I have a number of important responsibilities, not the least of which is the stag night. Tonight we're going to be checking out a couple of potential venues, and I want you both to be on your best behaviour so we don't get barred from any we might like to go back to.'

'Speaking of responsibilities, how's the speech going?' asks Mark, looking at me knowingly.

'Still working on it,' I say, wondering which one he means.

'Enough wedding talk,' orders Nick. 'I get enough of that from Sandra every bloody day. I've only got a month of freedom left, so let's just have a good, old-fashioned lads' night out, shall we? Oh, and by the way,' he adds, tapping his inside pocket. 'I managed to get hold of our friend Charles, if anyone's interested later.' Since he met Sandra, Nick has started to indulge in the occasional class A entertainment, and it's clear he's brought some along for the night.

'I don't think I know Charles. Is he a friend of Sandra's?' asks Mark innocently. Short of carrying a selection of pens and a calculator in his shirt pocket, Mark often displays all the characteristics of his noble profession.

'Someone I wish she hadn't introduced him to,' I mutter. Fortunately Nick doesn't hear me above the noise of the restaurant.

Nick looks across at Mark and sighs. 'Charles. You know, weasel dust. Nose candy. Charlie. Toot. Bolivian marching powder. Coke. Cocaine, you *Muppet*.'

Mark looks a little uncomfortable. 'Don't you think your head's big enough already without taking any mind-expanding substances?'

Nick opens his mouth to reply, but luckily the waitress arrives to take our orders before he can think of anything suitably rude to say.

Even the menu has a sporting theme, although I'm

hoping that it's bad taste in name only. Mark orders
the George Best Beef, which turns out to be Irish
stew, I choose the Niki Lauda Platter, which is a barbe-
qued selection of meats, and Nick opts for the Linford
Christie Lunchbox, which appears to be little more
than a giant hot dog. More importantly, the wine list
includes nearly two hundred different beers, ranked in
an alcohol content league table kind of way. We, of
course, ignore this completely and just choose the ones
with the most amusing names.

Once we've eaten I check my watch, and it's
approaching midnight, so time to put my plan into
action. I've been careful not to drink too much – I
feel like I might need my wits about me this evening
– and so I call for the bill. After Mark has divided it
up to the nearest penny, we leave the restaurant and
head through the back streets towards a lap-dancing
bar called, imaginatively, Bazookas. 2-Tuf has recom-
mended this place – it's one of his regular haunts,
apparently, and according to him it should be perfect
for what I have in mind.

I've already let Mark in on the secret of where we're
going, but told him under no circumstances to tell
Julia, which he'd seemed only too happy to agree with.
When I tell Nick where we're headed, he breaks into
a grin.

After stumbling up a couple of dark alleys, we finally
spot a black-painted doorway down one of those side
streets you probably wouldn't want to walk down even
in broad daylight with Mike Tyson by your side. It's
illuminated by what looks like a pair of pink neon

breasts, and as we head towards the entrance someone who looks like the aforementioned Mr Tyson's bigger, meaner brother 'greets' us.

'Do you have a reservation this evening?' he asks. Or rather that's what he obviously means, because what actually comes out of his gold-toothed mouth is one word.

'Booked?'

Immediately we all feel like perverts. 'Yes,' I say, as I stuff twenty pounds into the bouncer's jacket pocket, as per 2-Tuf's advice. 'Here's our tickets.'

'This way, *gents*!' replies the bouncer, pronouncing the word as if it were an insult, and, extending an arm the size of a tree trunk, he opens the door. Inside, we're met by the manageress, a short, fat woman with a face even a dog wouldn't lick.

'Let's hope she's not one of the dancers,' whispers Mark, a little too loudly.

'Do you want a silver table or a gold table?' she asks, looking us up and down. We stare at each other blankly, until Mark speaks up.

'What's the difference?'

'Silver table has a cover charge of £100, gold table has a cover charge of £200. Gold table is right next to the stage,' she says, reeling the figures off, and indicating the only other customers, a group of Japanese businessmen, who are sat round a table which is indeed painted gold, leering at one of the 'dancers'. We watch as she artily removes her G-string, places a hand on each cheek and thrusts her naked bottom into the face of one of their party.

'Brings a whole new meaning to the phrase "ring-side seats",' smirks Nick.

Mark surveys the club. 'How much to just sit at the bar?' he asks, still wearing his accountant's hat.

The manageress frowns. 'Well, I suppose you'd just have to pay for your drinks,' she replies, hesitantly.

'Okay. We'll do that then,' he says.

'Well done, mate,' I tell him as we head towards the bar, leaving the manageress to ponder the flaw in her pricing policy.

Mark shrugs. 'Tax Rule Number One: always look for the loophole.'

I shake my head in admiration. 'You see – that's the reason you're an accountant and I'm not.'

Mark nods. 'Well, that and several years of study, I guess.'

'I'm off for a quick pick me up,' announces Nick, pointing to his nose and heading off to the toilets. Mark and I follow him, and as we push through the heavy swing door, Mark disappears into a cubicle, and I watch Nick as he removes his credit card from his wallet.

'You don't have to pay to use the toilets here, mate,' I say. 'That would be taking the piss.' I'm such a comedian.

Nick walks over to the sink and removes a small white package from his pocket. 'Watch the door,' he says, as he sprinkles the powder on to the marble surface and starts to cut and shape it into lines with the edge of the card.

I look round nervously. 'Is that why they make those

cards black – so it's easier to see what you're doing?'

Nick ignores me and concentrates on the task in hand. Rolling up a ten-pound note, he sticks one end up his nose and prepares to vacuum up the trails of powder. Mark chooses that moment to emerge from the cubicle and, catching sight of Nick, turns as white as the lines of cocaine.

'Are you mad?' he shouts. 'What if someone comes in and sees us?'

'Relax,' says Nick, as he turns to face him. 'It's not such a big deal here in the city. You suburban boys ought to get out more.' He leans back down and starts to inhale.

'Well I'm getting out of here,' replies Mark, quickly washing his hands, and then it's Nick's turn to go pale as Mark feints mischievously for the hand drier, stopping just short of pressing the button.

'Bastard!' says Nick, cupping a protective hand round the coke, looking like he's back at school and trying to prevent someone from copying his answers.

Mark and I head for the bar, where I tell him that I'll get the drinks in, seeing as he's saved us money on the table fees. On the stage in front of us, three women in various stages of undress are gyrating, dancing hardly being an appropriate description as they seem to be oblivious to any of the music being played by the DJ. I order three beers from the uninterested barman, and watch as he reaches under the counter for a couple of warm cans of lager, surreptitiously emptying them into three glasses.

'Fifteen quid, mate,' he tells me.

I can't have heard him correctly. 'What?'

'Fifteen quid.'

'Just three beers, not all your beer,' says Nick, who's arrived back from the toilets and is standing behind me, sniffing slightly.

Wordlessly, the barman shrugs and points to the price list behind the bar, which clearly shows £5 per lager. I pay up sheepishly and tell the boys to make it last. Nick just snorts and drains his beer in one.

I take a quick walk round the club, leaving Mark to guard the valuable lager, although by the looks of him he wouldn't notice anything apart from what's happening on the stage in front of him. Eventually I find who I'm looking for and, after a quick whispered conversation and a glance back in Nick's direction, I hand over a fistful of notes and head back to join my friends.

When I get back to the bar, I find the two of them engaged in conversation with a large pair of barely restrained breasts whose owner, I learn, is named Juliet.

'Well,' she says, 'it's Sharon, really. But we all get to pick our own names in here. Something a bit more alluring.'

'Quite,' says Nick, smiling lecherously.

'So, what's the deal regarding "dances"?' Mark asks, staring straight at Juliet's chest.

'Ten pounds and I'll dance topless for you here,' she explains. 'Twenty pounds and I'll dance nude for you on stage.' She's trying hard to make eye contact but she's fighting a losing battle.

'I wonder what she'll do for a fifty?' Mark whispers

to me, all sense of economy suddenly disappearing.

I hand her a twenty and tell her to take Mark off to the stage, and he follows like an eager puppy, just about managing not to trip over his tongue. She sits him down, nods to the DJ and, picking up on the beat, starts to remove her clothing, which, given how little she's wearing in the first place, doesn't take very long at all. Mark's grin becomes more lopsided, and Nick and I smirk knowingly at each other as Mark surreptitiously crosses his legs.

She's good, and we watch transfixed from the bar until she finishes her routine. Once Mark has been left in no doubt at all as to her gender, Juliet picks up her outfit, pecks him on the cheek and disappears in search of other punters. He walks back to us at the bar, moving a little awkwardly, and sits down.

Juliet looks over from the side of the stage, where one of the Japanese businessmen is wearing her breasts like earmuffs, and winks at Mark.

'I'm in there!' he observes, his tongue firmly in his cheek.

'It looked like you nearly were,' I say. 'If she'd tripped and fallen on you, we'd have had to send in a search party.'

'You should ask her for her number,' sneers Nick.

'I've already got it,' says Mark. 'It's *twenty*, as in pounds. And anyway, I think she's more up Adam's street.'

I turn round to face him. 'What are you talking about?'

'Well, her being called Juliet, and you being such a Romeo!'

I'm just about to order more drinks when Nick nudges me. I look round to see him staring at a very attractive but flat-chested dancer, who's smiling at him from across the room.

'Now she's more my type,' he says. 'Mind you, I've seen bigger tits on my bird table.'

She flicks her eyes across at me, I nod imperceptibly, and she walks purposefully towards Nick.

'Hello, big boy,' she purrs, sitting down on the stool next to him, and resting a hand on his thigh. 'I'm Destiny.'

Nick looks her up and down. 'Of course you are.'

'I thought you might like a dance,' she says, sliding her hand further up his leg.

Nick swallows hard and stands up, and she leads him off towards the stage. I follow and lean against one of the mirrored pillars opposite.

'Come on then, darling,' says Nick, holding up a twenty-pound note. 'Show me what you haven't got!' He smiles at his own joke, until he notices the steely gaze of the bouncer stood in the corner. He pays up sheepishly, and Destiny climbs up on to the stage, running through her routine with a suppleness that would put an Olympic gymnast to shame. She's just about to finish when Nick holds up another twenty, and she starts all over again, although because she's already naked Nick is treated to a strange reverse strip, where she actually gets dressed again to the music. Still, judging by the look on his face, he doesn't seem to mind.

Mark appears next to me, carrying three glasses of beer, which he places carefully on the ledge behind us.

'Who's Nick's flexible friend?'

I can't take my eyes off the stage. 'I think her name is Destiny.'

Nick watches, mesmerized, as Destiny finishes her dance; then she leans in close to him and whispers something in his ear. She indicates a door by the side of the stage, and I hold my breath, waiting to see what Nick is going to do. After a brief conversation I see her smile and shrug, and when she kisses him on the cheek and walks away a wave of relief washes over me.

Nick comes back over to where we're standing, a startled expression on his face, and Mark hands him a beer. I can't look him in the eye.

'Strangest thing . . .' he says. Fortunately I can't detect a trace of suspicion in his tone.

I keep my voice neutral. 'What's that, mate?'

'I've just been propositioned. By a lap dancer!' He shakes his head in disbelief. 'And I didn't even have to mention the Ferrari.'

Mark claps him on the back. 'Bloody hell. Good on you!'

I pick up my beer and casually take a sip. 'What did you tell her?'

Nick looks at me strangely. 'I told her I was getting married in a month, of course.'

With frightening speed, my relief turns to guilt, and I feel a sudden need to get out of this place. Fortunately, Mark yawns loudly and looks at his watch.

'Guys,' he says, 'it's almost two o'clock. Some of us have proper jobs to go to in the morning.'

Nick takes a last lingering look round. Fortunately, Destiny is nowhere to be seen. 'Time to go?' he says to me.

I'm feeling terrible. What was I expecting? Did I think he could be swayed from the path so easily? Nick never goes into anything half-heartedly, so why should marriage be any different? Of course, I hadn't wanted Nick to disappear with some lap dancer – it was supposed to be more of an experiment, to test his resolve and to see just how committed he was to this wedding lark. But what was I thinking? That engineering a date with Destiny would somehow help Nick to see his own future more clearly?

I nod. 'Yes,' I say. 'I've seen enough.'

By some stroke of luck we manage to flag down a cab to take Mark back to Ealing. Nick has left the Ferrari on a meter down near Hammersmith Bridge and doesn't want to leave it there overnight, and, although he's had too much to drink, decides he'll drive it home. I try and talk him out of it but he's insistent, so I volunteer to keep him company and we head off towards the river.

He's parked it under a street lamp on the side next to the Thames, and I'm standing on the pavement, waiting for him to find his keys. As he's searching in his pockets for the bunch, we hear a gruff voice from the shadows behind us.

'Give me your car keys!'

Nick freezes, his mouth dropping open in astonishment as he looks over my left shoulder. Instinctively I turn round, and see a small, scruffily dressed figure emerging from behind a phone box. He's wearing one of those Gap sweatshirts with the hood up so it's hard to see his face, and he wouldn't be particularly threatening if it wasn't for the gun he's holding.

'Pardon?' Sometimes I can be too polite.

'Give me your fucking car keys. Now.' I'm not sure what the word 'brandishing' actually means, but I'm pretty sure he's brandishing the gun in my direction. I look back at Nick, who's gone white, even in the yellow glow of the street lamp.

'Nick, give me the car keys,' I order, and wordlessly he passes them across the top of the car to me. My mind is doing that sort of calculation that I always wondered if it would do if I was ever in this situation. Is it a real gun? If it is, is it loaded? Is the guy a good shot? Should I try and jump him? Have I got enough milk at home for breakfast in the morning? And then I suddenly have one of those rare moments of inspiration, or foolhardiness, depending on what happens afterwards, of course.

'I just want to get my house key off here – is that okay?' I ask the gunman, taking a key off the bunch Nick has given me.

'No, that's not okay. Just give me the FUCKING KEYS!' he shouts back, moving menacingly towards me.

'You want the fucking keys? You get the FUCKING KEYS,' I yell, and throw the remaining bunch as far as I can into the Thames. The three of us turn and watch them splash into the water, the Ferrari logo on the leather key fob glinting as it disappears into the murky depths.

'You bastard! What did you do that for?' This comes from Nick, not the robber, who's standing there, speechless.

'What are you going to do now?' I ask the gunman. 'Ever tried to hotwire a Ferrari? They don't start at the best of times.'

He looks from the car to me, turns to stare at the rapidly disappearing ripples in the Thames, then back at the car again. The gun hangs limply by his side.

'Fuck,' he says, to no one in particular.

I hold my breath as he raises the gun, but it's only to scratch the side of his head with the barrel. He looks at Nick and me, then turns and jogs casually off towards Putney Bridge. I have an insane urge to chase him, but suddenly my knees buckle and I sit down hard on the wing of the Ferrari.

'Careful. You'll dent it,' says Nick, coming round to my side of the car to stand on the pavement in front of me.

I start to snigger, and then the two of us erupt into a tirade of laughter, so hard that we almost can't breathe.

'Christ, I think I almost wet myself,' he says, the colour returning to his cheeks. 'Course, now we're buggered. How are we going to get the car home?'

'By driving it?' When I show him the Ferrari key, which was the one I'd taken off the bunch, Nick's mouth drops open. 'Trouble is, you're going to have to get a new set of office keys cut, though.'

If I was worried about Nick being over the limit earlier, he certainly looks stone-cold sober now. As he starts the car I'm suddenly reminded of Charlie's words, and so I decide it's now or never.

'So, mate, did you have a good time this evening?'

Nick looks at me strangely. 'What, up until the time you nearly got us shot and my car stolen?'

'Er, yeah. Up until that time. You know – just the three of us. Out with the lads. Just like old times. Young, free and single.' I'm speaking in clichés, I realize.

'Yeah,' he says. 'We must go to places like that more often. Especially now that I'm going to have the old ball-and-chain back at home.'

'How are you feeling about the whole wedding thing?' I ask him. 'Nervous?' *Please say yes*, I'm thinking.

'No,' says Nick. 'Looking forward to it. Big party, expensive presents, three weeks in the Maldives. What is there to be nervous about?'

I glance across at him to try and gauge his mood, but I can't see any trace of doubt, and I'm feeling much too ashamed about my behaviour earlier this evening to try and instil some. And whilst he may not be concerned, I certainly am, and what's worrying me the most is the fact that at no point has he ever mentioned the words 'love' and 'Sandra' in the same sentence.

Later, after we've reported the incident to the police, who despite the gun had seemed as interested as if we were reporting someone dropping litter – 'You mean nothing was actually stolen, sir?' – and virtually told Nick it was his fault for having such a desirable car, Nick tells me he owes me a drink.

'A measly drink for saving your Ferrari? You tightwad!'

'It's the least I can do.'

'Yeah – it probably is.'

Nick looks hurt. 'Sorry, mate. Packet of crisps as well?'

'Cheese and onion?'

'Done!'

It's nudging three o'clock by the time we pull up outside Nick's flat, the Ferrari obscenely loud in the pre-dawn stillness. As I look up at his window, it may be my imagination, but I'm sure I see his bedroom curtains twitch, and Sandra's face scowling down.

Chapter 10

Having a conscience is a good thing. Trouble is, mine is of the 'guilty' variety at the moment. So even though Nick is steaming ahead with his wedding plans, all I can do is watch helplessly from the sidelines. Besides, I've got something else, or rather some*one* else, on my mind.

Relationships are a bit like new cars. They need a gentle running-in period if you're to get the best out of them, and going flat out from the start can only lead to problems further down the road. So even though I'm straining at the handbrake, I make myself take things slowly with Charlie. Yes, I'd left her a message on the Saturday to say thanks for the previous evening. Then, as per my normal *modus operandi* to keep her keen, I'd sent her flowers on the Monday, and when she'd called to say how lovely they were we'd met up for a coffee and a chat. And whilst this might not seem like taking things particularly slowly, by the time we meet up again, on the following Saturday, I'm desperate to see her.

In an attempt to show off my arty side (or rather, give the pretence of having one) I decide to take her out for the afternoon, and so we're off to see an exhibition at the Royal Academy. I actually called in the previous day and became a member (a 'friend' of the Royal Academy, they call it), to make it look like I'm a regular visitor. How sad and shallow is that?

Unfortunately, I got no further than the membership booth, and therefore neglected to check what the show actually contained. Instead of 'the work of Young British Artists' being what I thought would be a wonderful collection of watercolours and still life paintings, it turns out not to be quite what I was expecting, as lifelike models of children with genitals for faces, sculptures made from the artist's own blood, and dissected farmyard animals line the walls. We turn a corner and I nearly trip over a tent-like arrangement embroidered with the names of all the people that had slept with the 'artist' creator. To make matters worse she had, like me, actually been born in Margate, a fact that Charlie reads out to me with glee.

I usher Charlie quickly away from it then peer inside, surreptitiously checking the tent for my name while running through my memory for any half-Turkish arty types I might have 'known' at school. When Charlie looks questioningly at what I'm doing, I hope she doesn't think I'm a pervert.

'You pervert,' she says, as we walk quickly through the gallery, but fortunately with an amused look on her face.

We don't linger at the exhibition, but stroll instead down Piccadilly towards the Ritz, where I treat us both to afternoon tea. As we sit down in the faded splendour of the hotel, I notice that we're surrounded by a curious mix, predominantly American tourists in garishly checked trousers, obviously bought from those tartan-only shops you see in this part of London. Also, the place is full of little old ladies taking tea whilst chattering to each other, all looking well over a hundred years old, about four feet tall and dressed up in full winter clothing despite the spring heat outside, with those flattened fox stoles around their necks, their glazed faces snarling menacingly at us.

After we've parted with the best part of forty pounds for a pot of tea, sandwiches with their crusts removed and a plate of fairy cakes, we stroll down through Green Park and sit on the grass opposite Buckingham Palace, watching the tourists annoy the sentries. We play the celebrity lookalike game for a while, where you point out someone in a crowd who you think looks like a famous person and then get awarded marks out of ten, where ten is if it's actually the celebrity themselves. It takes Charlie a while to get the hang of this game because she keeps pointing out people I don't know, like Mr Wilson, who turns out to be her old geography teacher, but eventually she wins due to someone who if it wasn't that chap from *University Challenge* it was his twin brother.

We talk about past relationships, mine being a somewhat edited version, and I find myself feeling slightly jealous whenever Charlie mentions anyone with any more than a passing reference. We're lying on the grass now, looking up at the sky.

'So, Adam,' she asks me. 'What are your plans for the future?'

I ponder this for a moment or two. 'Probably just to see as much of it as possible, I guess.'

'You know,' she says, as we watch a party of Japanese tourists politely take turns to photograph a squirrel on the grass nearby, 'it's actually quite refreshing to meet someone who has a bit more of a relaxed attitude to life, career, that sort of thing. A lot of the guys I meet seem to be obsessed with the idea of conforming to this male stereotype, where it's all work, work, work. You know, put enough hours in at the office and they can change the world, or something.'

I give a short laugh. 'No danger of that from me. I know I'm never going to make the world a better place. Besides, there's too much pressure on men today. Thanks to magazines like bloody *Cosmopolitan*, women expect to march down the aisle with this fantasy male – six feet tall, with a six-pack, earning a six figure salary—'

'Six-six-six?' interrupts Charlie. 'All sounds a bit sinister to me.'

'At the same time, you've got to be the perfect father, and . . . I don't know, hung like a donkey, maybe.'

'Speaking of which, what about your friend Nick?' she asks me.

'I have no idea how he's "hung",' I tell her.

Charlie digs me in the ribs. 'No, I mean, have you spoken to him yet? About the wedding?'

'I've tried.' I sigh. 'I've even attempted to show him

the error of his ways,' although I don't elaborate on this, as I don't particularly want to explain to Charlie about my failed lap dancing bar attempt. 'But he seems determined to act like an ostrich and just deal with any consequences if and when they arise.'

'Ostrich?' she looks at me quizzically.

'You know. Burying his head in the sand and letting it all go on around him. What he fails to realize is that adopting that particular position leaves his arse in the air to be kicked.'

We stare at the clouds forming shapes above us for a while.

'But,' I continue, 'aside from actually sitting him down and being rude about Sandra in front of him, which I'm worried will damage our friendship, I don't know what else to do.'

Charlie sighs. 'Well you'd better think of something, otherwise it's going to get to that embarrassing part when the vicar says, "If anyone here knows just cause why these two shouldn't be married . . . " and you then have to speak up in front of everyone, not just him.'

She's too good at this argument stuff, so I decide to change the subject.

'Speaking of the future, what are your plans for this evening?' I ask her.

'Oh,' she says, looking all serious.

'You haven't got a date?' I splutter, sitting up. 'Who with?'

Charlie grins. 'You, you moron. What do you fancy doing?'

I don't know why I suddenly feel the need to do this, but I take a deep breath and utter those three little words guaranteed to make a woman go weak at the knees.

'I'll cook something.'

Charlie quickly manages to hide her shock and surprise, and says that would be lovely.

We head out of the park and jump into a cab, and when I drop her off at her flat I give her my address, and she agrees to come round to my place at eight. When I get home I run upstairs and through my front door, panicking slightly when I notice the time. It's five o'clock, which gives me only three hours to prepare both the meal and, more importantly, myself.

Fortunately, I keep the place pretty tidy, so I won't have to waste time running the Hoover round. I love my flat – it's a decent-sized two-bedder on a nice quiet Chelsea street between the King's Road and the river. I bought it last year, when Mark advised Nick and me that we ought both to take a large dividend from the company profits, or face giving most of it back to the taxman.

'Spend it wisely,' Mark had said. 'Think about getting a roof over your head.' Nick had done exactly that, too, but of course his was convertible and perched on top of a red Italian sports car.

It's taken me a while to get the décor and ambience just right, using the GABI method – Get A Bloke In – for most of the hard work. I've kept it simple but classy, with white walls, stripped wooden floors and a few pieces of carefully chosen furniture.

Minimalist Chic, I think the style magazines would define it, or 'Can't afford a decent three-piece suite, son?' as my dad would say.

My proudest possession is the stereo system hanging on the wall above the fireplace. I read in one of those specialist magazines, *Woofers and Tweeters Weekly* or something similar, that good hi-fi among purists is measured by the Low Knob Ratio. That means the fewer switches and buttons the thing has the better it sounds. Well, this one should be a winner – no visible buttons at all. Just a rather phallic chrome remote control that looks more like something from an Ann Summers catalogue.

I don't entertain at home much, but when I do I usually call up one of those catering services where they make you up a gourmet dinner and deliver it on the morning of the meal. All you then have to do is transfer it to your own dishes (being careful not to leave any of the packaging lying round), follow the relatively simple reheating instructions, and *voilà* – a perfect meal for two with just a swipe of the credit card. But for Charlie I'm heading into relatively uncharted territory and actually making something from scratch. This means that firstly I have to get hold of a recipe, and I call my mother for help.

'Ooh, Adam's cooking,' she repeats to my father, and I hear him start to laugh in the background. Eventually I manage to get some basic instructions, and make her promise to stay in for the next few hours in case I need to call her for any emergency help. I run down to the local supermarket and buy exactly twice the necessary amount of ingredients – better safe than sorry in case I mess up first time round. I lay them out in sequence on the kitchen table, then realize I don't even own something as simple as a potato peeler so have to go back out to the shops to get one.

By seven o'clock, with Charlie due to arrive in an hour, I've produced what looks quite like the shepherd's pie my mum makes, and having double checked my instructions, don't think I've forgotten anything. There also appears to be precisely the right amount of ingredients left over to make another one, which seems to bear that out. I just have time to shower, change the duvet cover, open the wine and light a few strategically placed candles before she arrives.

I've already selected tonight's listening, and as I've never been able to find an album titled 'Music to Seduce Girls By', have pre-programmed the stereo to play the kind of artists I think would naturally feature on such a compilation. The latest (but it could be any, of course) Sade album, some Al Green, Stevie Wonder and, to apply the finishing touches, some smoochy stuff by Dina Carroll. I think twice about Barry White but then decide no, not exactly the most subtle of choices.

I do a final check round the flat, and I'm standing in the hallway, lamely watering the latest in a line of yucca plants that I've managed to slowly kill – forget green fingers, mine are more like gangrene fingers – when Charlie rings the buzzer. It's a minute to eight, and she's clutching a bottle of wine and a bouquet of what I think are chrysanthemums, which throws me a little as I've never been bought flowers before. Sade's singing in the background as we kiss hello, and I linger a little on her lips, inhaling her perfume. She's wearing a short black dress that shows her bare shoulders and, I note with pleasure, her nicely defined upper arms. I tell her dinner should be ready shortly and she follows me through to the kitchen, which I'm pleased to note has an authentic cooking aroma. If only you could buy that in bottles.

Charlie walks straight over to the bin and lifts the lid. 'Just checking!' she says, grinning at me.

I make a face of mock horror. 'What do you think of me – that I'd cheat?'

'I do hope you're not a cheater, Adam,' she replies, holding my gaze for longer than I'm comfortable with, until I have to look away. I open the wine she's brought – red, as I suppose she reasoned we weren't having fish – pour us both some, and we clink our glasses together. I just about manage to resist the urge to say 'To us' or something equally trite.

'Did you find a decent parking spot?' I enquire, as Charlie searches through my kitchen cupboards for anything that could conceivably be called a vase.

She shakes her head. 'No need. I took a cab.' I'm suddenly pleased that I've put a clean duvet cover and sheets on the bed.

Charlie eventually finds a champagne bucket, fills it with water and stands the flowers in it, arranging them neatly on the kitchen table. We move through into the lounge, and she looks around the room.

'Nice flat,' she says.

I'm just about to offer the guided tour, which normally takes all of a minute, when the timer rings in the kitchen.

'Excuse me,' I say, formally. 'Please make yourself at home. I've just got to attend to the dinner.' In reality the food's been ready and on a low heat for the last fifteen minutes, but I want to create the impression that I'm a talented chef giving the finishing touches to the meal.

'Can I give you a hand?' she asks.

'No, that's okay. You relax in here. Pick some music if you like.'

My cover is nearly blown when I'm in the kitchen removing the shepherd's pie from the oven, and checking my mum's recipe for the cooking time for broccoli, when Charlie pops her head round the door. I throw my notes into the oven to hide them, and watch as they ignite silently. Fortunately, I manage to hide this from Charlie by standing in front of the flickering glass.

'I've picked out a couple of CDs but I can't find the stereo,' she says.

'It's hanging on the wall, over the fireplace.'

'Okay,' she says, disappearing back into the lounge.

Two minutes later, she's back. 'I've found the stereo, but I can't work out how to put the CD in.'

'Just wave at it,' I tell her.

She looks puzzled. 'Pardon?'

'Wave at the front and it'll open.'

'What, from here?'

'No, I'll show you.' I take her by the hand and, walking her over to the machine, lift her arm up in front of the display and move it slowly across the cover. The glass casing slides to the left, disgorging the Sade CD into Charlie's fingers.

Charlie nods appreciatively. 'Smooth operator,' she says.

I take the CD Charlie's selected – some opera classics compilation – and slot it into the machine. The mechanism whirrs quietly and Pavarotti leaps into the room.

I tell Charlie to take a seat at the table, which I've set so we're opposite each other. Back in the kitchen I remove the warm plates from the top of the oven – unlike revenge, shepherd's pie is a dish best not served cold – and dish it up. It kind of collapses when it gets on to the plates, but still looks a little like it's supposed to, so I bring it through and triumphantly place it on the table in front of her.

'Shepherd's pie?' she asks, her face dropping.

'Er, yes. Something wrong?'

'But I'm a vegetarian. Didn't you remember?'

Oh god. 'Er, no, er . . .'

Charlie laughs. 'Only joking. You're so easy to get. This looks great, and I'm starving.' She jabs a fork in and takes a mouthful. 'Mmm, lovely. Mother's recipe?' Damn, she's good.

We make small talk through the meal, and she asks for seconds, so she's either extremely polite, extremely hungry or she genuinely likes it. I'm marvelling that despite her slim figure she seems to have a healthy appetite, which is a pleasant change from those women who are so obsessed with their weight that all they ever order is a glass of water and a crouton, which they just push round their plate all night and eventually hide under a piece of lettuce.

So far, the evening seems a success, and we're getting on so well, but for some reason I'm starting to get worried. We haven't even kissed yet, apart from the odd brief peck, and I suddenly realize what is causing my nerves. Performance anxiety.

Now, I've had sex a lot of times. With a lot of different women. That means a considerable number of 'first nights' that I've managed to negotiate successfully. And yes, there have been a few, well, several occasions where I knew that it was also going to be the last night with that particular girl, and yet I still made sure that I acquitted myself well – *ladies first*, if you know what I mean – even though I could have thought it might not have mattered. The difference is that I think it matters with Charlie.

In my experience, there are a number of ways you can tackle this first-night dilemma. By far the easiest is for the two of you just to get drunk – that way, much of the awkwardness is removed, or rather disguised. Chances are you won't remember it too clearly the next morning anyway; even if you do, if it was good then your fuddled brain will recall it being fantastic, and if it was bad you'll just put it down to the drink. The only problem with that approach is that if it was bad you won't want to try again just in case it wasn't the drink but was in fact you. Or her. Or the two of you.

Alternatively, you can try and get her drunk. Not a tactic that I'd condone, of course. On the other hand, you can both stay stone cold sober, but then you have no one to blame but yourselves if things don't come together.

Much more preferable, in my book, is if the two of you are in that halfway house between sober and drunk – merry, tipsy, call it what you like. This allows for full control of actions by both parties, with the additional benefit that both clothing and inhibitions can be removed with ease.

Anyway, we get to the stage where we've finished dinner, had coffee, and have both decided that a brandy on the sofa would be the next logical step. We haven't drunk too much – just the one bottle of wine between us, in fact – so unless we down an obscene amount of brandy we're not going to experience the 'drank too much' approach. Fortunately it's a slightly chilly evening, so I get to light the fire, which is actually a remote-controlled artistically arranged pebble-effect gas device set into the far wall, rather than actual wood – less messy and instantly adjustable. It's nudging eleven o'clock, and tomorrow's not a school day, so there's no time pressure on Charlie to go home, and, of course, being London we know she can get a cab any time she wants to, so it's not as if either of us is working to a deadline.

So, to sum up, I'm sitting on my sofa a few inches away from Charlie, the night is still young, we've eaten well (even if I do say so myself) and we're bathed in the flickering light from the fire in the corner. We're

sipping brandy, and talking about nothing in particular, and my biggest concern is, how do I initiate that
first physical contact?

I remember back to early dates as a teenager in the
cinema, and that old, corny arm round the back of
the seat trick, slowly inching it down on to her
shoulder, and then further if conditions were
favourable. Surely I can't try that approach here, I
reason. I'm a mature, responsible adult. Surely the big
thing to do would be to say something direct, with a
hint of romance thrown in, like 'I've been thinking
about kissing you all evening', which, although more
of an observation than a question, would usually
provoke some sort of answer, unless it's the dreaded
'That's nice', or similar, which then throws the ball
firmly back in my court. I'm mulling this over as
Luciano comes on again, and I get up to change the
music.

'It's okay,' says Charlie, standing up too. 'I'll do it.'

'No, that's fine, I'm there,' I tell her, picking up a
couple of CDs from the mantelpiece. 'Any requests?'

'Just the one,' she says.

I turn round to find her standing right in front of
me. I'm holding a CD in each hand, and hold them
both out towards Charlie so she can choose between
them, but instead she steps in between my outstretched
arms, puts her hands on my waist and leans forwards
and upwards to kiss me. I bend my head down and
our lips meet, her tongue poking gently into my
mouth, leaving me in no doubt that this is more than
a 'thank you for dinner' kiss. I move to take her head

in my hands, and then realize I'm still holding the two
CDs, which I have to try and transfer to one hand
and put back on the shelf behind me, all the while
trying not to break lip contact with her. We kiss like
this for a few minutes, until she pulls away, walks over
to the coffee table and picks up the two brandy glasses.

'Where's your bedroom?' she asks, and I find myself
having to think before I answer.

'Um, through there,' I reply, indicating the door at
the end of the hallway.

'Are you sure?' she asks me, a smile playing on her
lips.

'What – am I sure where my bedroom is, or am I
sure I want to do this?'

'Well, I hope the answer's yes to both of those questions,' she says, walking down the hallway and stopping by the bedroom door. 'Do you mind?'

I frown. 'Do I mind what?'

Charlie laughs and holds up the brandy glasses. 'The
door, I mean. I've got both hands full. And hopefully
not for the last time this evening.'

Later, much later (I'm adding the 'much' for effect),
I'm pleased to be able to provide Mark with several
informed proofs for his theory. We have one of those
nights where, without going into too many details,
we make love, fall asleep, and then wake up in the
middle of the night and make love again. It's a cliché,
I know, but I usually can't stand those women who
like to sleep entwined. I've researched the subject a
little, and so I'm okay with the mandatory twenty-
minute post-coital holding period, but when women

want to go to sleep in that position – no thanks. Sharp toenails, breathing directly into my face or, the worst, tickly hair all guarantee a night of no sleep for me, and even though I have a large double bed (it's 'queen' size, actually, but I don't dare mention this for fear of ridicule), if they still want to occupy the space directly next to me I can't seem to get a good night's rest.

But with Charlie I sleep, and even dream, and after we've woken up in the middle of the night for, well, *seconds*, I sleep again, soundly, until at eight o'clock the next morning the phone rings, waking us both with a start. I lie there and ignore it, until the answer-phone clicks on, and my mother's voice is piped loudly into the hallway. Like most old people, my mother gets up at the same, ridiculously early time at the weekend as she does on a weekday, and thinks that the rest of the world does too. Of course, it won't have occurred to her that Charlie might still be here.

'Adam, it's your mum.' *I know – I recognize your voice*, I always think. 'I just wanted to check that your dinner with your young lady went well, and my instructions were clear . . .'

I jump out of bed, run into the hallway and switch the volume down, and find myself blushing, not least because I'm standing in front of Charlie naked. She looks at me from the bed, bleary eyed but smiling, and stretches. I try not to stare as the duvet falls down, exposing her breasts.

'Tell your mother she's taught you well,' she says. 'The shepherd's pie, I mean!'

She surveys the room, as if seeing it for the first

time, and spots my dressing gown hanging on the back of the door. Unashamedly she throws the duvet off and gets up, walks over to the door, and pulls on the towelling robe. I'm always amazed by that morning-after bathroom embarrassment, where someone who you've spent the previous evening exploring inside and out should then feel awkward about a three-yard walk to the bathroom unless they're completely covered from head to foot in the same sheet that was discarded with such relish the night before. With Charlie, there's none of that, and while I enjoyed the brief sight of her naked as she walked over, unabashed, to the door, if anything she looks even sexier in a robe that's too big for her.

'Coffee would be lovely,' she replies to my unasked question, and disappears into the bathroom, calling 'Can I have a shower?' back over her shoulder. I fetch a clean towel out of the hall cupboard and shyly pass it round the half-open door to her.

I pull on my boxer shorts and a T-shirt and stroll out of the bedroom with, I notice, a slight spring in my step. In the kitchen, I realize there's no breakfast food in the house and so, quickly donning a pair of jeans and a sweatshirt, I run down to the corner store and pick up an assortment of croissants, pastries and some fresh milk.

I know that I've got about fifteen minutes before Charlie will emerge from the bathroom, so I'm back and ready with a pot of steaming coffee and warmed pastries by the time she appears in the kitchen, freshly scrubbed, and still wearing my robe, I'm pleased to note.

We sit eating breakfast, perhaps a little uncomfort-ably, but this is more as a result of those stupid designer stools I bought that aren't quite big enough in the seat and have a too-low foot rest, than the previous evening's activities. We're not saying much as we sip our coffee, but then Charlie breaks the silence.

'Thanks for a lovely evening.'

'Thank *you*.'

'Oh, and thank your mum for a great shepherd's pie recipe. Maybe I'll get to try the original one day?'

'That sounds like this was more than a one-night stand?'

'Well, that depends on one thing.'

'What's that?'

Charlie grins. 'You asking me out again, of course!'

'So,' I say, standing up to clear the table once we've finished our croissants. 'What do you normally like to do on a Sunday morning?'

She gives me a playful look. 'Stay in bed.'

'Sounds perfect,' I reply, and lead her by the hand back into the bedroom.

That night, I meet Nick in Bar Rosa. 'I don't need to ask you how your evening went,' he says, as I yawn for the thirtieth time. 'No disasters with the cooking, I take it?'

'Nope – thanks, Mum,' I say.

'And how was Charlie?'

'Fine, once she'd got something warm inside her.'

Nick grimaces. 'Oh please. Spare me the details.'

'Spare me no details,' calls Rudy, who's been eaves-dropping from behind the bar.

'So, when are you seeing her again?' Nick asks me.

'Er . . .' I suddenly realize that I haven't arranged anything, and feel a momentary panic.

Nick raises one eyebrow. 'Oh yes? Do I detect a little problem creeping in?'

'No, I just want to take things . . . steadily.'

Nick looks at me disdainfully. 'What was it this time? The way she holds her fork? Does she snore? Or wasn't she very—'

I cut him off. 'No. Nothing like that. It's just that . . .' How do I explain that it's quite the opposite, and rather that it's because I don't want to muck it up that I'm not rushing in? I'm considering my answer, but Nick interprets my hesitation as confirmation.

'You see!' he announces. 'I was right. That's the end of her after . . .' he looks at his watch, 'what, two weeks? Next please!'

I bristle slightly. 'Oh, I'm sorry. And if I was working to your timetable, I suppose Charlie would have moved in by now.'

Nick glares. 'You know what your problem is? Or rather, *who* your problem is?'

I feel myself start to tense up. 'Why don't you tell me.'

'That one who left you. What was her name again?'

I can't bring myself to mention it. 'I know who you mean.'

'Yeah, well. Since *her*, you've been scared to let yourself get involved with anyone. Even when there's absolutely nothing wrong with them.'

I stare at him, open mouthed. 'That's not true. I . . .'

'Okay. I'll give you an example. What was the name of that girl you met last year?'

'Can you be more specific?'

'The one you met at the gym.'

'Again, can you be more specific?'

'The one with the huge breasts?'

'I need a little bit more to go on than that . . .'

'You know, the lawyer,' says Nick.

'Mandy.'

'Mandy. That's right. Like a photo-finish in a Zeppelin race, if I remember correctly. You went out with her for a while, didn't you?'

I have to think about this for a few moments. 'Yeah, about a month, I think.'

'Blessed-in-the-chest Mandy,' sighs Nick. 'What was wrong with her, for example? We had high hopes with that one.'

I shrug. 'Much as I'm enjoying this trip down Mammary Lane, I can't remember.'

But, of course, I can. I remember them all, however short lived, and I remember Mandy particularly. Lovely girl, very bright, we got on extremely well, but in the end it was the sex that was the problem. You know that phrase that men always get insecure about and women always joke about: 'size matters'? For me, with women, *sighs* matter. With some of the women I've slept with, orgasm has been almost a religious experience: 'Oh God, oh God,' and so on. Others come in the affirmative: 'Yes, yes, yes,' while some are in denial: 'No, no, no.' You understand what I mean. But with Mandy, it was worse. You know that sensation when you take a mouthful of food that's too hot, but you're in much too polite company to spit it back on your plate, so you have to make an 'O' with your mouth and do that sort of chimpanzee puffing and blowing in an attempt to get as quick a passage of air passing over it as possible in order to try and cool it down? That was the noise she made in bed. I kept getting visions of Cheetah in those old black and white Tarzan films flashing through my head every time we slept together, and knew it could never last.

Nick laughs. 'It's lucky that not everyone responds to being dumped like you did.'

I'm getting irritated now. 'How do you mean?'

'By becoming a serial shagger for the rest of their lives.'

'Bollocks!'

'Bollocks yourself, Adam. Ever since she-whose-name-we-dare-not-speak left you, you've been treating relationships like . . .' he searches for an example, 'like those little pots of tester paint that you can buy from the DIY store. All you ever do is paint a small corner of your room, just to see how it looks, and then quickly decide you don't like the colour, because it's not as good as the original.'

'That's not true. I . . .'

Nick rolls his eyes. 'Don't you get it? Sometimes you've just got to go ahead and paint the entire room. See what it looks like after you've lived with it for a while.'

I suddenly sense an opportunity to turn the

conversation round: a chance to tell Nick what I really think about what he's doing.

'Yes, but . . . how can this approach guarantee that you're going to be happy with this woman for the rest of your life? I mean, especially if you've not known her for that long.' This is the best I can do, and, although it's clumsy, it seems to do the trick.

'Because how else can you find out what—' Nick's face darkens. 'Hold on, who exactly are we talking about here?'

I struggle to keep the metaphor going. 'It's just that . . . Sandra . . . Well, you're painting the entire house, aren't you? And you've . . .' What's my killer line? Got too small a brush? I run out of steam. '. . . bought gloss by mistake?'

It's Nick's turn to get annoyed. 'What are you trying to say?'

'I think you can do better than Sandra.' There.

'What's wrong with her?' he asks me, his voice just about managing to stay level.

'Well, she's . . . not very friendly, is she?'

He looks at me crossly. 'Is that the best you can do? Besides, you've hardly given her a chance to be.'

'But that's because . . .' I stop myself because he's actually correct on that point. 'Don't you worry even a little that she might not be *the one* for you?'

'Jesus, Adam. Just because we don't all have your . . .' He pauses, trying to find the right word.

'Standards?' I reply, a little too quickly.

Nick grabs his keys from the table and stands up angrily. 'No, I was actually going to say "idiosyncrasies", but I was worried that you wouldn't know what it meant.'

'But shouldn't you at least wait until you're sure?'

'What – and be alone for the rest of my life like you? No thanks! Because *un*like you, I'm not scared to put my money where my mouth is. If you'd been in a proper relationship for more than five minutes you'd know what I'm talking about.' He looks at me pityingly and shakes his head. 'And you've got the nerve to try and give *me* advice?'

My window of opportunity is closing rapidly, I realize, but before I can say anything more Nick slams it firmly shut. And on my fingers.

'Oh yes. Something you might want to think about before you hand out any more marriage guidance,' he says, just before he makes for the door. 'At least mine didn't run a mile when I asked her.'

Chapter 11

Great. Less than four weeks to go until the big day, and I've blown my best and only chance of talking Nick out of it, particularly because he's not even speaking to me at the moment. By Monday evening, I decide that I can't face any more of his barely polite grunting in the office, and some R&R away from it all in Snowdonia seems a good idea. When I call Charlie, she answers after the third ring.

'What are you doing for the next couple of days?' I ask her.

'Er, nothing. I've got to work on Friday, but . . . Why?' she says, drawing out the last word.

'I thought I'd take you away somewhere. Dirty weekend and all that.'

I hear her laugh down the phone. 'A dirty weekend – and in the middle of the week, too! Where are we going?'

'It's a surprise.'

'Will I need my passport?'

I try and remember whether there's border control on the Severn Bridge. 'Er, no.' I suddenly feel cheap.

'Oh. A posh frock for the evening?'

'I was thinking more like hiking boots and water-proofs . . .'

There's a slight pause before she answers. 'Oh. Lovely.' But I can hear the disappointment in her voice, and have to think on my feet.

'Only kidding. Posh frock would be good.' I tell her. Damn.

'Sounds great,' she says, sounding much happier all of a sudden.

My next call is to the B&B I'd booked in North Wales to cancel, and then, in a moment of inspiration, I ring the Grand Hotel in Brighton. Being my old 'stamping ground', I reason, it will be a good excuse to show Charlie where I spent some of my formative years. I'm worried they won't have a room at such short notice, but fortunately they have a suite with a sea view that the receptionist describes as 'stunning', and although the price is pretty stunning, too, I just grit my teeth and book it anyway.

The next afternoon, when I pick her up as arranged, Charlie seems to have packed for two weeks rather than two days, and I almost give myself a hernia as I struggle to carry her luggage down the stairs and squeeze her bags into the Impresser's boot next to my small holdall. Heading out of the capital, we join the thousands of other Londoners intent on spending three hours in their cars driving at five miles an hour through the biggest car park in the world – the M25. My turbocharged engine sits there in danger of overheating, but thanks to the automatic climate control, which I always think is an interesting concept in England, we don't.

As we near Gatwick Airport, Charlie pretends to get all excited, and asks me if this is our exit, telling me she's brought her passport just in case. I take the off-ramp just to see her jaw drop in amazement, and then rejoin the motorway straight away without saying a word.

A few miles further on the traffic lessens, as does the ache in my shoulder from where she's punched me. With a growl of relief the Impresser surges forward as I finally manage to change out of second gear, and we're soon up to warp speed. As we drive, I tell Charlie about my conversation with Nick.

'*I think you can do better than Sandra*?' she repeats, incredulous at my lack of sensitivity. 'And you're surprised he reacted in the way he did?'

'Maybe I'm getting it all wrong,' I say, as if thinking out loud. 'Perhaps I should just let him get on with it. Maybe I'm too close to it all. I need an independent opinion. Someone who doesn't know either of them . . .' I stop speaking and stare at the road ahead.

Out of the corner of my eye, I see Charlie look at me and shake her head. 'Okay,' she sighs. 'But it'll cost you.'

I grin back at her. 'It's a deal.'

'I haven't told you what I want yet,' says Charlie, resting a hand on the top of my thigh, causing me to swerve slightly towards the central reservation. She removes her hand quickly. 'But getting us to wherever we're going in one piece would be a start.'

By eight o'clock, we're driving along Brighton seafront. I've told Charlie that I want to show her the town where I went to college, and this desire to share my past with her seems to have scored me several Brownie points. When we pull up outside the Grand Hotel, a name of which nowadays, judging by the faded exterior, only the 'hotel' half is actually true, her eyes light up. We're met by the liveried doorman, who opens Charlie's door and summons the porter for our luggage. The porter winces as he tries to lift her bags, making the same face as I did when I'd heard the price of the room.

We check in, and follow the porter to our room. The interior is quite magnificent, although in an ever-so-slightly-tatty kind of way, and our room does have a sea view, but of course by now it's too dark to see anything. The porter makes a great play of showing us the bathroom, which I'm sure we'd never have found without his expert guidance, and then hovers by the door. I reach in my pocket where I've previously made sure I had a couple of pound coins, and give them to him, at which point he finally passes over the key.

Charlie starts to unpack, and I see her hanging up a very sexy little black dress, so I call down to reception and book dinner in the hotel restaurant for tomorrow night. We're both a little peckish, so we decide to go for a walk along the seafront for fish and chips, or rather fish and chips for Charlie and something land-reared and chips for me, which we eat off little polystyrene trays with wooden chip forks. I make a face when Charlie smothers hers in salt and vinegar, but she has the last laugh when I spill ketchup down the front of my shirt while trying to open the little sachet with my teeth.

It's a beautiful sea-breezy evening, still quite warm, and we stroll along the seafront hand in hand, dodging the joggers, roller-skaters, and kids on those ridiculous small silver scooters. We walk along the pier, eating our chips and gazing out to the sea, framed by the noise and flashing lights of the amusement arcade. When we've finished, we go in and play one of those video games where you both have steering wheels and can race along the Grand Prix circuit side by side. I decide to let Charlie win, but then my male pride gets the better of me and I try to just pip her at the line, not reckoning on her last-minute turn of speed.

Once Charlie eventually stops celebrating her victory, we find a quiet bench and sit, holding hands and staring back at the Brighton skyline, which is reflected off the ink-black sea. With a shudder that I barely manage to conceal, I realize that we're right next to the spot from where I threw the ring, just a few short years ago, although right now it seems like a lifetime away. I realize that I'm experiencing a strange mix of emotions, which seems to be contentment and excitement at the same time, and I'm trying to work out how this can be when Charlie suddenly breaks the silence.

'Adam,' she says, and immediately I know there's a big issue coming. People never start a question with your name unless they want a serious answer.

'Yup?'

'Do you want children? Eventually. A family?'

Now this is a conversation I've had before. Many times, actually. And in my head, it always goes something like this:

Them: 'Do you want kids?'

Me: 'No, I'll never be able to be a father, actually.'

Them, sympathetically: 'Oh dear. Why not?'

Me: 'Because I'm too selfish.'

It's not that I don't like kids, you understand. It's just that I don't know what to do with them, particularly if they're babies or toddlers. Once they reach their teens I'm a little more comfortable – they can either start to have proper conversations and are more interested in adult-type things, or they're not interested in talking or doing anything at all, which also suits me fine.

I'm the sort of person to whom people learn not to hand their newborn babies. I look so awkward trying to carry the things and just about know which way up to hold them. Whilst someone else might be happy to make faces, and play aeroplanes, and do all those ridiculous things you see people do with babies, my only concern is to not be the one who drops it, which I'm pretty sure would be a bad thing to do. So whilst I haven't completely ruled out the possibility of being a father sometime later in life, my answer now, if you pressed me, would be a resounding no. Probably.

But what do I say to Charlie, on this lovely spring evening, sat here on the pier, hand in hand? How do I give an answer that combines vagueness with an appreciation of the complexities of the human reproductive urge, the ever changing direction that one's life takes, the desire to extend one's dynasty through the ages? How can I deflect the line of questioning whilst leaving the door open for further debate at a future moment in time?

I've got it. 'Don't know,' I say. 'You?'

She ignores my skilful conversational parry, and when she doesn't answer, I look across at her. She's staring up at the sky, and I think I can see a tear welling.

'Why not?' she asks, eventually.

'Er, I think I'd be lousy at it,' I say, which I know is a better answer than the 'I'm too selfish' one. Charlie tries to reassure me, but then she hasn't seen me with India yet.

'How about you?' I ask, again.

Charlie lets go of my hand, and there are definite tears in her eyes now. 'I can't,' she sniffs, as the tears start their journey downwards.

Now, I can't handle women crying, and usually go to extreme lengths to avoid witnessing this spectacle. Usually these lengths have involved use of the telephone, rather than face to face situations, for the imparting of bad news ('you're dumped') or discussion of sensitive issues ('why you are dumped'). But here, tonight, I have Charlie sat right in front of me, eyes leaking like a faulty tap, and it's melting me inside.

I pass her a napkin, which I pinched from the chip shop earlier. 'Why not?' I say, stupidly. 'Don't you like kids?'

'I love them, you idiot,' she says, between sobs. 'I

can't have them. Physically, I mean. I had an illness when I was a kid and they had to operate, and it means I was okay, but I'll probably never be able to get pregnant . . .'

Charlie stops speaking but keeps staring at me, and I realize that this is what she was about to say when we were talking about her engagement. This is why they broke up. Because she couldn't have children.

'It's a big deal for . . . some people.' She sniffs. 'And I just wanted to tell you before we, *if* we . . .' she blinks away her tears for a moment '. . . got serious.'

My initial thought is 'Yes!', both at the prospect of getting serious with Charlie and, admittedly, at the thought of maybe not having children, but I manage to stop myself from jumping up from the bench and punching the air. I can tell that, given the way she's looking at me, what I say next is probably the most important thing I've had to say to Charlie since I've known her. Relationships are made and lost on moments like this. All I need is one killer line to demonstrate my sensitive side, showing that I can be both strong and caring. Here it comes . . .

'Well, we could always adopt.'

We? *We?!* What was I thinking? And adoption? Talk about bulldozing over her problem. I brace myself for her reaction, but instead she leans across and gives me a long, albeit slightly snotty, kiss.

'Yes, I suppose *we* could,' she says, smiling as she wipes her eyes. I just hold her, tightly, and the moment passes.

We head back to the hotel at eleven, and the bar's

still open, so we go in and order a couple of brandies, taking them over to the large leather armchairs in front of the fireplace, which is lit despite the mild evening. Charlie decides she'd like a coffee to go with her brandy, and calls the waiter over, asking me if I'd like one too.

'Are you sure they won't stop us from sleeping?' I ask innocently, as the waiter hovers.

'I'm not planning on sleeping,' she replies, levelly. The waiter coughs and goes off to make the drinks, bringing them back with a grin a few minutes later.

We stare at the flames, not saying much, sipping our slightly-too-hot coffee. Eventually, Charlie finishes hers and looks at me. She picks up her brandy glass, swishes the golden liquid around a couple of times and then drains it in one gulp.

'Come on, lover boy!' she says, standing up and taking me by the hand. 'Bedtime!'

We have the lift to ourselves, but there's not that many floors to go so instead we hurry along to the room. I fumble with the key, and once inside we make for the bed and kiss for a while, until I pull away reluctantly.

'Wait a sec,' I say, getting up and heading towards the bathroom. 'I need to, you know, put something on.'

Charlie grins. 'What – like the radio?'

But when I emerge from the bathroom a couple of moments later, it's with a look of disbelief. 'You're not going to believe this,' I tell her. 'I forgot to bring any condoms.'

Charlie looks up at me breathlessly from where she's lying. 'That doesn't matter. Remember, I'm hardly likely to get pregnant, am I?' she says, and I worry for a moment that she might start crying again with this subject raised. Fortunately she's more interested in raising something else.

I can't recall the last time I had sex without using a condom. In fact, I can't remember *ever* having had sex without a condom. I've usually been so worried about unwanted pregnancies that I've always been extra careful, and bought the thickest, most unbreakable brand you can find. I don't go with these people who use all sorts of other methods: withdrawal, time of cycle, or even the pill. In my view, unprotected sex is like playing Russian Roulette with an automatic pistol. Every shot is live — it's just whether you're aiming at the target when the gun goes off.

It takes me just a couple of minutes — an embarrassingly quick couple of minutes — to realize that, for all these years, sex with a condom has been the equivalent (not that I've ever actually done it) of feeling somebody up wearing rubber gloves. But fortunately the novelty factor is so, well, stimulating that it's not long until I'm able to try again. As we eventually drift off to sleep, I find myself thinking that we might see precious little of Brighton this weekend.

Breakfast is served until ten a.m., so we get there at around five minutes to. I'm sure hotel staff all over the world hate those people who come down just before the breakfast session ends and then linger for a hour in the room over their toast and coffee. I order

my favourite full English breakfast, without fish or
tomato, and Charlie has kippers. Fortunately, she
doesn't ask me to try them. After breakfast Charlie
decides she wants to buy a new pair of shoes, and
when she asks me whether I'd mind coming with her
I don't have to think twice.

I love shopping with women, not least because it
gives me a legitimate reason to hang around various
women's clothes shops and leer at the assistants. Plus,
I'm perversely fascinated by the differences in the male
and female approach to shopping.

A woman, for example, will buy anything if it's on
offer, even if she doesn't need it, whereas a man will
pay whatever he has to if it's for something he wants.
If, on the other hand, a woman is looking for something
specific, then, conversely, this brings in something called
the uncertainty quotient. She might be shopping for,
say, a pair of shoes, but whilst out may suddenly decide
to get a skirt to go with them. She may have chosen
the shoes, been quite happy with her selection, but
she won't buy them yet, or, if she does, keeps the
receipt handy, because she: a) might find the exact
skirt to go with them, but this is of course most rare
and unlikely; b) might find a skirt she likes that doesn't
go with the shoes she's bought, and therefore will buy
the skirt but then need to exchange the shoes, or
indeed find another pair; c) might find another pair
of shoes she likes better anyway on the way to buy
the skirt; or d) confuses herself so much that she ends
up buying nothing. A man, on the other hand, may
be looking for, say, a blue shirt, and might be happy

to spend, for example, fifty pounds. The first shirt he finds that fits, is blue and costs around fifty pounds, he'll buy.

If you're shopping with a girlfriend, there are a number of cardinal rules that apply. Firstly, and it is probably blindingly obvious, but when you're asked for your opinion, they NEVER, I repeat, NEVER, look fat. Secondly, if they show an iota of preference for one item when comparing two things which, to you, look identical, agree with them whole-heartedly. Believe me, it saves an awful lot of time.

You'll also never want her to actually buy anything revealing. Nothing she wore that attracted you when you originally saw her will you ever want her to wear again, particularly if she's going out without you. There's no way you want her to be leched at by other men like you do at other women out with their boyfriends. The bottom line is this: Men don't notice what a woman is wearing – just how little.

We end up spending the whole day strolling around the shops, pausing for lunch in a little café in The Lanes, that warren of old streets in the centre of the town. We visit probably every shop in Brighton that sells shoes, some of them more than once. By late afternoon, when it's me who's in need of some new shoes to replace the ones I've worn out, Charlie has narrowed her choice down to two pairs, but can't decide between them. I can't tell the difference, and when I suggest that she buy both Charlie looks at me as if the idea is preposterous. True to form, she ends up buying neither.

Eventually we head back to the hotel and get changed for dinner, which takes longer than expected, as we're still in that early phase of the relationship where any incidence of joint undressing develops into something else. We're twenty minutes late by the time we get to our table in the hotel's posh restaurant, but the waiter doesn't seem to mind, and Charlie looks fabulous, which, on reflection, is possibly why the waiter doesn't seem to mind. I'm wearing a suit and tie, which is unusual for me, and as I catch sight of the two of us in the mirrored hallway I'm struck by what a good-looking couple we are. I don't mean that we're both attractive people, more that we look good *together*.

It's one of those traditional restaurants where the menu Charlie gets doesn't have any prices on it. We have a gin and tonic while we choose, share a bottle of wine with our food, and then cognac to finish, and by the time we're ready to go I'm feeling a little light-headed.

We're on our way to the bar when we hear music coming from somewhere beneath us, and follow the sounds to the nightclub in the hotel's basement, where Charlie decides she'd like a dance.

I'm not a great fan of dancing. In my opinion, there are only four reasons to go out to a nightclub. One, you're a student and aged under twenty-two. Two, you're aged between twenty-two and thirty and have run out of drugs. Three, you're a professional dancer and need to practise. Four, you're in a group of lads so drunk that you think a club is a mystical place where women will find your beer-fuelled dancing so sexy that they'll all want to take you home.

But if you can't avoid it, never enter a club sober. You'll be self-conscious of your dancing, you'll resent the prices you have to pay for drinks, which you'll put down somewhere only to find them gone when you try and locate them again, and you certainly won't like the music, which will be so loud that any hopes you have of conducting any type of conversation will be drowned out completely.

My deliberations are cut short as Charlie drags me by the hand through the door and straight on to the dance floor. Standing there, slightly drunk, I suddenly realize that I've forgotten how to dance. It's debatable whether I ever knew anything more than the standard left step feet together right step feet together move that most guys get away with, but I thought I had a little more rhythm than this. However, here I am, on the dance floor with Charlie, the DJ is doing his best to get everyone moving with a selection of seventies and eighties numbers, and I'm suddenly feeling so awkward and uncoordinated that I have this overwhelming urge to sit down.

If you're a man, chances are no one has ever taught you how to dance properly. You've either got it or you haven't, and as I look around me I suddenly think there might be a market opportunity here, one that I must discuss with Mark, as it's plainly obvious that most of the men here, including me, haven't. When you're a kid you dance a certain way, and then you become a teenager and you dance in a different way, and then when you're an adult you seem to lose all coordination and dance like one of those *Thunderbirds* puppets.

Surely people would pay to learn the proper, or rather, appropriate moves? When you're slow dancing, for example, and you've finally managed to convince a member of the opposite sex to sway unsteadily around the floor with you, think how much better it would be if someone had told you beforehand that you shouldn't be singing along to 'Lady In Red' into her ear. At the other end of the scale, Nick and I hadn't dared 'dance' at the Uzi Street concert – instead, we'd looked on in amazement as most of 2-Tuf's moves made him look like he was ruffling the hair of two small boys.

It doesn't help that Charlie is moving around like she's made of liquid, eyes half shut as she feels the music and shimmies around me. Catching sight of myself in one of the mirrored walls, I realize that I look like I'm dancing to a completely different beat, as if I'm wearing my own set of personal stereo headphones and ignoring the huge speakers in front of me – which, ironically, are blasting out Sister Sledge's 'He's The Greatest Dancer'. I last a couple more numbers, and then self-consciousness defeats me.

'Upstairs?' I yell at Charlie, as the Village People extol a life on the ocean wave.

'I love you,' she shouts, over the music.

'Pardon?'

'I'd love to,' she repeats, and I feel stupid. But later, lying with Charlie asleep in my arms, and listening to the faint sound of waves breaking on the beach below our window, I find myself wishing that I hadn't misheard.

All too soon it's Thursday morning, and after we've just about made it downstairs in time for breakfast again, it's time to check out. I try and keep a straight face when I see how much the bill is – I can see now why the hotel is called the Grand, as I've been charged as much as Nick paid for his monkey – and politely decline Charlie's offer to pay half.

On the way back home we take a detour past Beachy Head, the venue for so many of my college bonding, or rather bingeing sessions with the boys. We drive along the road that runs parallel to the crumbling chalk edge, and park near to where the cliff is highest. Charlie's never been here before.

'Wow,' she says, taking in the stunning scenery. 'It's quite spectacular. I'm not surprised that this is where all the suicides come.'

We walk up the grassy slope and towards the abrupt drop, where a number of people are stood gawping at the view or lying on their stomachs and wriggling forward to look over the edge. Charlie grabs my hand for support and leans gingerly over, gasping when she sees the crashing waves so far below. As we turn and head back to the car, she rubs her fingers and makes a face.

'Ow!' she says. 'You needn't have held on to me so tightly.'

Didn't know I had been.

Chapter 12

When I call in at the office that afternoon, Nick and I act as if nothing ever happened. He makes a big show of asking how things are going with Charlie, and I pretend to be interested in the wedding plans. When he tells me he's booked the registry office, and I express my surprise at Sandra not wanting a church wedding, he even makes some joke about her having an aversion to crosses and holy ground, which I accept as his clumsy attempt at an apology.

On the Friday we sign up a number of new sites, including one called Anal Accountants, which features photographs of naked women (who I assume are accountants, due to the fact that they're wearing glasses) playing hide the calculator, which we email to Mark at his office. Charlie films a commercial for hand cream, and that night I get to experience first hand just how good the product actually is.

By Saturday, and with less than three weeks left to convince Nick of the error of his ways, it's time to put the next phase of my plan into action. The only trouble is, I haven't thought of a 'next phase' yet. In the meantime, Charlie and I have been invited, along with Nick and Sandra, round to Mark and Julia's for dinner this evening, and beforehand, so I can get my second opinion, we're driving back down to Sussex, where Nick is due to turn out for the local village cricket team.

Nick's been playing (well, appearing for, 'playing' being rather a kind description of his on-pitch antics) for the Upper Dicker (I kid you not) second eleven ever since college, and today Upper Dicker are due, Nick tells me, to play Lower Bottomley, or some such village that's probably little more than three houses, a pub and a post office-cum-newsagents-cum-video-rental shop. It's a pre-season friendly, Nick tells me, although I can't ever recall hearing about an *un*friendly. Even so, he's assured me it should be exciting.

'Will there be a streaker, then?' I'd asked.

I'm no cricket fan – all those 'silly mid ons' and 'leftfielders' – although the idea of a short slip does interest me. Also, what's the point of a game where there never seems to be a clear winner or loser unless one team has absolutely been pulverized? It seems to be good enough for a draw even if one team's score gets within fifty runs or so of the other, as long as the light is fading or, in that strange mid-match tradition, it's time for tea. Well, I'm more of a coffee man myself, but it's a nice sunny day, and the chance to lounge around on the grass with Charlie whilst taking the piss out of Nick is too good to pass up.

Although the four of us would all fit comfortably in my car, Nick's driving down with Sandra separately. He always takes the Ferrari to Sussex – I suspect to remind his team-mates, most of whom are middle-management and lucky if they can afford the leather-seat option on their company Ford Mondeo, just how rich and successful he is now. This means that I'll have to take his cricket gear in the back of the Impresser, because with Sandra occupying the passenger seat of Nick's car, his boot is hardly big enough to hold his protective cup, let alone his Harrods-issue whites, pads and bats. Yes, *bats*, as in the plural.

We rendezvous outside my flat, where I introduce a slightly nervous Charlie to a leering Nick, who, true to form, sneaks a peek down her top as he kisses her hello. Sandra is a little cool, shaking Charlie rather formally by the hand, but fortunately doesn't seem to be suffering from foot-in-mouth disease, probably due to my reminding Nick last night to ask her to be nice.

Setting off from London, I try hard not to lose sight of the gleaming red sports car as it swerves danger-ously round buses and taxis. Once out on the motorway we maintain a steady hundred in the outside lane, until we hit the winding lanes of Sussex, where I manage to overtake and pull away, much to Nick's annoyance. Normally he'd give chase, but I know that Sandra's constant nagging at Nick to slow down can only count in my favour; and, in fact, by the time Nick and Sandra eventually arrive at the village green, Charlie and I are already out of the car and waiting next to the pavilion.

Nick parks a safe distance away from the pitch – a lesson he learnt after a previous game where the less-than-sporting opposition kept trying to aim their shots towards his prominent bonnet. We walk over to meet them.

'What kept you?' I ask him. He just glances in Sandra's direction and raises his eyebrows.

We stroll back towards to the pavilion, the two girls chatting away in front. They're obviously talking about the wedding, and when a beaming Sandra shows off her ring Charlie can't stop her eyes from widening. Nick nudges me, a proud look on his face.

Upper Dicker are fielding first, and as Nick heads off to get changed Charlie turns to Sandra and holds up the picnic rug, which we've retrieved from the Impresser's boot.

'Where shall we all sit?'

Sandra waits until Nick is out of earshot. 'Oh, actually, I think I'll wait in the car. Cricket's not really my thing,' she replies, adding, 'If you don't mind, that is?' as an afterthought.

'We don't normally see her out in daylight,' I whisper, as she heads back towards Nick's car and sits sideways on in the passenger seat with the door open, facing the pitch, thus ensuring no one forgets that she owns a Ferrari by proxy. Charlie and I find a spot on the grass, stretch out and watch as the spectacle unfolds in front of us. As Nick takes up position on the field, I see him looking smug as a group of spectators cluster round his car – and of course the pretending-to-be-blasé Sandra – more intent on its shiny curves than what's happening on the pitch.

The first half of the game passes without incident. Nick misses a couple of easy catches and manages to

trip over a couple of times when running after the
ball, which we cheer and clap accordingly. After a
couple of hours, Lower Bottomley declare at two
hundred for six, whatever that means, and we amble
towards the clubhouse, where the other players' girlfriends and wives are passing round sandwiches and
tea. Sandra has elected to stay in the car, where her
mobile phone seems to be glued to her ear.

Then it's Nick's team's turn to bat. Nick is 'in at
number ten', which, when I get this translated by one
of his team-mates, means that he's not quite the worst
batsman on the team, but almost, so we wait with him
in the clubhouse, smiling patiently as he gives us his
'expert' commentary on how the game is progressing.
When the Upper, er, Dickerians are nearly all out, he
removes the whitest pads you've ever seen from his
bag and makes quite a show of strapping them on, as
if his life depends on them fitting properly. He picks
up one bat, and then the other, and then the first one
again, which he informs me is 'state of the art titanium cored', as he goes through an elaborate series of
warm-up strokes. The bats used by the other players
are somewhat scuffed and imprinted with various red
marks where they've made contact with the leather
cricket ball. Both of Nick's, despite not being that
new, are unmarked.

With just a few runs needed for victory, Nick finally
gets his chance, and, striding confidently to the crease,
he calls for his position from the umpire. He's a
formidable sight, towering over the wicket, concen-
tration etched on his face, and I'm sure the combined

whiteness of his outfit and the reflection off his pristine bat must be dazzling the opposition.

Glaring menacingly at Nick, the bowler rubs the ball against his groin for a little longer than is perhaps necessary. He starts his run-up from fifteen yards, gathering speed as he nears the wicket, and then unleashes his delivery. It's a short ball, and it leaps up tantalizingly, just asking to be thwacked over the boundary. Nick decides to hit out, and is – missing the ball, over-balancing and colliding with his own stumps. Charlie and I applaud politely as he trudges back towards the pavilion, as dejected a sight as I've ever seen, surrounded by the celebrating opposition.

In the pub afterwards, we commiserate with him.

'Bad bounce,' he claims. 'That pitch is awful. I don't know how they can still use it.'

'Didn't seem to affect the other batsmen,' I mutter. Nick throws me a withering glance.

We chat about work for a while, Sandra's only contribution being a disdainful 'So you're a model?' aimed at Charlie, pronouncing the word 'model' like she is saying 'drug dealer' or 'paedophile'.

'Yes. Mostly exhibition work, with the odd commercial now and then,' replies Charlie, pleasantly. 'In fact, I filmed a hand job this week,' she adds, reddening when she realizes what she's just said.

Nick splutters into his pint. 'What did you say?' he asks, incredulously.

Charlie tries to explain, but only succeeds in making it worse for herself. 'That's what we call them. Hand jobs. You know – just using my hands on someone else.'

Nick cuts her off. 'We've got—'

'I know,' says Charlie, patting him on the back of the hand. 'Whole websites dedicated to just that.'

Charlie and Nick are getting along well, which pleases me, and watching Charlie banter with my oldest friend brings a strange feeling of pride. Nick, as usual, is trying his best to flirt a little, but he's so bad at this that I'm not at all offended, and instead take it as a sign of his approval. Sandra is sitting on the periphery, not really making an effort to join in, despite Charlie's valiant attempts to include her. Eventually, I notice our glasses are empty, and stand up.

'Whose round is it?' I ask. 'Sandra?' in the vague hope that she might actually get up and put her hand in her pocket for once.

'No, nothing for me, thanks,' she replies, without a trace of irony.

Charlie stands up next to me. 'Must be my shout,' she says. 'Same again, Nick?'

Before Nick can answer, Sandra announces that, actually, she has a headache and would rather go home and lie down.

'But what about dinner at Mark's?' pleads Nick.

'Well, we'll just have to cancel,' she says, a little acidly. 'I'm sure Adam won't mind telling them I wasn't feeling very well. I wouldn't be much company anyway.' *No change there then*, I think.

'Anyway,' she adds, getting up from the table. 'We've got things to do. You'll have plenty of time for your little friends after we're married.'

Biting my tongue, I try unsuccessfully to catch Nick's

eye. Even Charlie can't believe what she's hearing as she stares quietly into her glass.

We head outside and wave them off, a dejected-looking Nick roaring out of the car park, Sandra not bothering to look at us from the passenger seat. I'm disappointed that Mark and Julia will have gone to such an effort for them not to show up, and slightly worried that I'm not going to get the opportunity to expose Sandra's shortcomings in front of everybody, but at the same time quietly pleased to see the back of her.

Once they've gone, Charlie shakes her head in disbelief.

'So, that was the infamous Sandra,' she says, as we walk back towards the car.

'Yup.'

Charlie stops and turns to face me. 'If you don't tell him, I will.'

I look at her earnestly. 'I might hold you to that.'

'It's just that Nick's so . . . so . . .' Her voice tails off.

I laugh. 'Yes. Most people struggle for an adjective to describe him. There are plenty of nouns, on the other hand.'

'And, well, Sandra. She's just . . .' Again, Charlie struggles to finish her sentence.

'So not Nick?'

Charlie nods. 'How can he not see that?'

I shrug, and open Charlie's door for her. 'Therein lies my problem.'

We take a leisurely drive back towards London,

phoning ahead to explain Nick and Sandra's no-show, and it's early evening by the time we reach Mark's place. Parking next to the people carrier, but well away from the trees, therefore avoiding the risk of bird droppings, I retrieve a bottle of wine from the boot and, kissing Charlie on the way past, go to ring the doorbell. Mark has heard the car and beats me to it, opening the door with a broad smile on his face. I've already briefed him on the conversational topics he and Julia are not allowed to cover tonight, which primarily include my ex-girlfriends, and Julia's theories about why there are so many of them.

'Mark – Charlie, Charlie – Mark,' I say.

Mark offers his hand to Charlie, and she grabs it and kisses him on the cheek. He smiles back at her, embarrassed, and ushers us in, clapping me on the back while raising both eyebrows and nodding as I pass him.

We walk into their front room, and Julia appears, my goddaughter India peeking shyly out from behind Julia's legs. India is hiding from me because last time I saw her she'd proudly told me how one of her milk teeth had fallen out.

'And I put it under my pillow and the fairies came and took it and left me twenty pence,' she'd told me proudly, in that way kids have of talking without any punctuation.

'Twenty pence?' I'd said, whispering 'tight git' to Mark. 'Well, you'd better be careful you don't ever fall asleep with your head under your pillow,' I'd told her, 'or the fairies will come and take *all* your teeth out.'

Mark told me later it had been a week before India was sleeping properly again.

Julia shakes Charlie's hand a little formally.

'And who's this?' says Charlie, bending down to smile at India.

'I'm India,' she lisps.

'What a pretty name,' says Charlie, putting a hand on India's cheek.

India gives Charlie a gap-toothed grin. 'It's where I was conceived,' she says.

Julia and Mark look at each other, and then at me accusingly. 'I don't know who told her that,' says Julia.

'Not guilty,' I say, holding both hands up.

'But it's true, isn't it, Mummy?' asks India.

'Yes dear,' says Julia, blushing slightly.

'India, do you know what "conceived" means?' I say.

Julia shoots me a murderous glance, but India just shakes her head and runs out of the room, fortunately not asking me to explain.

'Seriously, though, what a beautiful name,' says Charlie. 'I love it when people's names actually mean something significant. Whereabouts in India were you, if it's not an indelicate question?'

'Goa,' laughs Julia. 'But we didn't think we could quite call her that.'

I smirk. 'Quite. Not the best name for a girl.'

'Lucky though,' says Mark. 'We were in Phuket the week before.'

Julia turns back to Charlie. 'So, you're the one who's finally tamed our Adam?' she asks. 'We were worried

he'd never go out with someone for more than *oof*!'
The 'oof' comes from Mark elbowing her sharply in
the ribs. Charlie turns to look at me quizzically, but
fortunately just then we hear a bark, and Max bounds
into the room, his tail wagging excitedly, and sticks
his nose straight into Charlie's crotch.

'Oh I am sorry,' says Julia, grabbing him by the
collar and pulling him away. 'He always likes to stick
his nose somewhere smelly.' Her expression changes
as she realizes what she's just said. 'Er, I mean . . .'

'Drinks?' says Mark, trying to save his wife's embarrassment.

'So, Charlie,' asks Julia, once Max is safely shut in
the garden. 'What was it about Adam that made you
go out with him?'

'He asked me. Eventually,' replies Charlie, still
smarting a little.

'I hear you're a model,' says Mark, trying to steer
the conversation back to a civil level. 'Have you done
anything I'd have seen?'

'No dear, I don't let you read those kind of magazines,' says Julia, rubbing her ribs. 'Only joking,' she
says to Charlie, a slightly false smile playing on her
lips. I can see the two girls are locking horns, and I
worry it'll be a long evening. What is it about good-
looking women that they feel threatened when
someone else attractive comes on the scene?

Charlie turns back to Mark. 'Adverts mostly,' she
replies. 'Have you seen that latest camcorder one?' She
goes on to describe some television advert that finishes
with the camcorder cradled in a pair of gold-painted

hands. 'But you wouldn't recognize me – it's only my hands you see.'

Mark is fascinated, much to Julia's annoyance.

'Really? How did you get into doing all these, what do you call them?'

'Hand assignments,' I interrupt, tactfully.

'Well basically, the rest of me wasn't up to scratch,' laughs Charlie, before Julia can reply. 'Adam tells me you're a top-notch accountant,' she says, changing the subject. 'Do you do models?'

'In his dreams,' I reply, and we all laugh, except Julia, who stands up and makes some comment about checking on the dinner.

'I'll give you a hand,' I say, and follow her out of the lounge.

'Not bad,' she says, when I join her in the kitchen. 'Attractive and smart.'

'You think?'

'Yes. I'm sure she'll soon see through you then,' she replies, kissing me on the cheek to show me she's joking.

'Well, you ought to be nice to her then, as you might be seeing more of her.'

I'm serious as I say this to Julia. Her expression visibly softens, and she regards me for a minute from the other side of the kitchen.

'Point taken,' she says.

'Anyway. Can I help with anything?' I ask, out of politeness.

'No thanks. I just need to put the timer on for the vegetables. You'd better go and rescue Charlie before

Mark sends her to sleep with talk of tax returns.'

When I walk back into the lounge, Mark is indeed talking to Charlie about her tax return. To her credit, her eyes haven't yet glazed over.

'I always wondered why they called it a tax return,' I interrupt, sitting down next to Charlie. 'It's not as if you ever actually get any tax returned, is it?' I'm rather pleased with my little joke.

'That's because I make sure you hardly pay any in the first place,' Mark replies indignantly. Just then, India runs back into the room with a mischievous smile on her face.

'Uncle Adam,' she says, grabbing hold of my shirt to climb up on to my lap, painfully removing a number of chest hairs. 'Will you come and tuck me in?' She's obviously been put up to this by Julia.

'Of course, sweetheart,' I tell her, and picking her up awkwardly I carry her out into the hallway. Charlie watches me with a smile.

'Don't forget to say goodnight to Uncle Adam's . . . friend Charlie,' Mark tells her.

India wriggles out of my arms, runs over and gives Charlie a hug. 'G'night, Charlie,' she says. 'Are you going to be my new auntie?' I grab her, quick-ening my pace out of the room before Charlie can answer.

Once I've put India to bed I head back downstairs. 'Out of the mouths of babes, eh?' I say, joining them at the table.

Charlie turns to Julia. 'Oh, congratulations, by the way,' she says. 'I hear you're expecting?'

Julia and Mark both beam proudly. 'That's right,' says Julia. 'Due in October.'

'How lovely,' says Charlie. 'It'll be nice for India to have a little brother or sister.'

Mark grins proudly. 'Oh yes. We can't wait.'

'We'd wanted one sooner,' says Julia, 'but we just couldn't seem to get pregnant.'

This is true. Mark used to turn up at Bar Rosa looking exhausted when they were, to use that wonderful phrase, trying for a baby.

'Surely that just means you have sex as often as possible?' I'd asked him.

'If only it were that simple' he'd replied, stifling a yawn as he'd described how he was called to perform on certain dates, at certain exact times, day and night, and then the minute he'd done his duty (which with Mark probably was little more than a minute), Julia would push him off and sit with her legs above her head for the next half-hour.

'Still, at least you don't have to cuddle her afterwards,' had been Nick's typically sensitive observation.

I'm a bit worried about where this conversation might be going, so I blurt out the first thing that comes into my head. 'Julia had India naturally. No drugs, or anything.'

Charlie makes a face. 'Didn't that hurt?'

Julia nods. 'God, yes!'

'And you're going to do it the same way this time?' Charlie asks, in amazement.

'Oh yes. I think it's an important part of the bonding process. And anyway, it's a bit like having a tattoo.

Hurts like hell, but when you see the end result you forget all about the pain.'

'I see what you mean,' says Charlie. 'She's a real cutie.'

'Do you want kids?' Julia asks.

I see a flicker pass across Charlie's face. 'Oh yes,' she says, looking down at her wine glass. 'One day.'

I change the subject rapidly, cursing myself for not having briefed Mark and Julia about this. 'Shame old Nick let us down this evening.'

Mark looks at the date on his watch. 'Well, they've probably got a lot to sort out. How long is it to go now?'

'Two weeks six days,' I mumble. 'Roughly.'

'Will we be seeing you at the wedding, Charlie?' asks Julia, brightly.

Charlie looks across at me awkwardly, but before she can answer Mark sticks his oar in.

'Not if Adam's got anything to do with it,' he says. 'Oh no, sorry, Charlie, I didn't mean that how it sounded . . .'

Julia looks at me accusingly. 'You're not still on this crazy sabotage mission?'

'Thanks, *mate*,' I say, glaring at Mark. 'No, I . . . I just want him to be sure he's doing the right thing, that's all. That he's marrying her for the right reasons, you know. Love, and all that stuff.'

Mark laughs. 'Adam, you don't get it, do you? In the real world, you don't get married to a girl you fall in love with. You're lucky if you can find one who's not a nightmare!'

Julia reaches across and pinches him. 'Well, I'm pleased that he's getting married. It's about time that Nick had a bit of good luck where women are concerned.'

Charlie is, I notice, staying diplomatically quiet.

I exhale loudly. 'He'll need all the luck in the world if he marries Sandra.'

Julia rolls her eyes. 'Sandra's not that bad. And, anyway, it's nice that he's met someone else. I felt so sorry for him after his last girlfriend dumped him.'

'Oh no,' says Charlie. 'What happened?'

Mark and I look at each other guiltily, and tell the story between us. 'Well, we were going on a golfing weekend . . .'

'And he was packing . . .'

'And she noticed that he was taking a packet of condoms . . .'

'So she chucked him.'

'I've always thought that was a bit harsh,' says Julia. 'I mean, it's not as if he'd actually done anything . . .'

Mark shrugs. 'If he'd packed a swimming costume you'd have assumed he was intending to go swimming . . .' Charlie covers her mouth with her hand but I can tell she's trying not to laugh.

The kitchen timer chooses that moment to let us know the vegetables are ready, and as Mark and Julia disappear off to sort out the mangetout, I lean across and give Charlie's hand a supportive squeeze.

During dinner I try unsuccessfully to get the conversation back on to Nick's impending doom, but by dessert the only thing that's clear is that Mark and

Julia are unfortunately singing from the same hymn sheet. I'm also a little worried about the impression that my anti-marriage rants are having on Charlie, and it's a relief when, by midnight, we're all struggling to conceal our yawns, and decide to head off for bed.

Julia thoughtfully has put Charlie and me in different rooms – her idea of a joke – but I make sure Charlie knows which door is mine before she heads off to use the bathroom. Charlie is taking her time, so I get under the covers and switch the light off.

After a few minutes I hear the door open and shut again, and footsteps coming towards my bed. Suddenly I hear a request that I wasn't expecting.

'Can you read me a story, Uncle Adam? I can't sleep.'

I click the light on and smile at India, who's lying drowsily next to me, clutching a large cuddly dinosaur and her *Bumper Book of Bedtime Tales*.

I'm halfway through a story about a family of crocodiles, where quite implausibly (although I don't point this out to India) the baby crocodile is a vegetarian, and India's eyes are just about shutting, when Charlie opens the door and tiptoes in, smiling at the scene in front of her. I get out of bed, thankful that I'd kept my boxer shorts on, and carry India back to her room, Charlie following with the book and dinosaur. She stands at the door and watches as I tuck India in, and then giggles quietly as I shut the door behind me, pick her up and carry her into my room.

'Will you tell *me* a story, Uncle Adam?' says Charlie,

pushing me down on to the bed and jumping on top of me.

'Sure,' I say. 'Are you sitting comfortably?'

Charlie wriggles on my lap for a few seconds. 'No, actually . . .'

Chapter 13

Tuesday, April 29. Over halfway through my six-week spoiling period, and I don't seem to be any closer to an end game. This situation isn't helped by the fact that Nick's rarely in the office, as Sandra constantly has him out running one errand or another. I know as best man I should be offering to help, particularly because he's looking so stressed at the moment, but I'm afraid I just can't raise any enthusiasm where this wedding is concerned. Besides, someone's got to run the show in his absence.

Since 'running the show' at PleazeYourself only involves logging on to the Internet for a couple of hours each day, I still have plenty of spare time to see Charlie, and today, with my mother and father coming up to London, I decide to take the risky step of introducing them.

It's been a while since I've taken a girlfriend to meet my parents, partly because I don't think they approve of my serial dating, but also because I've found that, despite full briefings beforehand, they always call the new one by the previous girlfriend's name. 'So, which one are you again, dear?' isn't the best conversation starter.

I did once try going out with girls with the same name successively to see if this was any easier for them, but for some reason they found this more confusing, so in the end I decided that keeping them apart was the best policy. Plus, whenever I did take them home, my mother would insist on producing one of her most cherished possessions – an age-yellowed cutting with my photograph from the local paper just after I was born, when I won that year's Bonny Baby competition.

I love my parents to bits, and as they get older I try and spend more and more time with them. It's not because I feel guilty and don't think they've got much time left, but rather that I really enjoy their company. They've never burdened me with expectations, or pressurized me into being anything else but happy. I remember when I was seventeen and they paid for me to take my first driving lessons and then I failed my test. I was almost in tears when I told them, and apologized for letting them down.

'You didn't let us down, son,' came the reply. 'We didn't think you'd pass anyway.'

My dad was an English teacher at one of the local secondary schools – I guess you'd call it a comprehensive now – for nearly twenty years, and even though he retired ages ago he still gets stopped all the time on the street by his ex-pupils wanting to say hello and let him know what they are doing. No one ever has a bad word to say about my dad, and it's clear to me that he touched a number of lives over the years. He's always been my hero, and the only time I've ever seen him cry was when I told him that. You know people sometimes use that phrase 'He's turning into his father' like it's a bad thing, as if you should be a new, improved version? Well, my dad's a pretty cool guy despite his advancing years, and he still has all his hair, so if I eventually turn out like him I won't complain.

My mother is one of those hardy Scottish women who doesn't seem to have aged at all over the last couple of decades, and looks like she's going to live for ever. She and my dad have been married for over forty years now, and I can't remember the last time I saw them have an argument. Oh, they have words every now and again, but it's usually over some triviality like my father's constant watching of sport on television, or my mother's habit of confusing minor details.

They're up in London today to take a 'flight' on the London Eye, here on one of their regular bowling club trips. They took up bowls a couple of years ago, when my father was recovering from a minor heart operation, and my mother, normally the most reluctant of sports followers, became hooked, particularly because she kept beating my dad (the results of their matches is now a taboo subject round the dinner table at home). They play at least three times a week, and also have these regular coach social outings from Margate, so I often arrange to meet up with them for lunch, as they quite like the variety of cuisines that London has to offer. Back in Margate I don't think they're spoilt for choice, unless you count the hundred and one burger joints that line the seafront. I've agreed with Charlie that she should join us afterwards for a drink. That way she'll avoid having to make small talk during the interminably long time it takes my parents to eat.

Despite being somewhat long in the tooth for all this modern technology, my father has bought himself a mobile phone 'for emergencies', which my mother insists he brings whenever they come up to town 'just in case'. I'm running a little early, so I decide to give them a ring to see where they are, but I call the number twice and it just rings without an answer. This means I've got some time to kill, and as I walk along the King's Road I get the foolish notion to buy Charlie a present.

This is made slightly tricky by the fact that we've only been together for a few weeks, and therefore we're in that grey area where I don't really know her well enough to get anything too personal, yet something bland and neutral might suggest that I'm not very interested, or not very thoughtful, or both.

Women and men are worlds apart when it comes to presents. Women can go into one of those gift shops that men avoid like the plague, full of various made-to-look-old items and smelly things. They'll find something like a scented candle that even unlit smells like toilet cleaner and buy it because they think it's romantic to sit around in the darkness with stinking, flickering flames. Alternatively, they'll get one of those tiny decorated boxes that's too small to ever hold anything useful and is therefore useless, plus a card with some hideously abstract glitter-encrusted front and twee message, even when they don't yet know who they're going to give it to.

Yet for men, present shopping for women is a mine-field. Clothes? She'll never wear them and oh-so-sweetly ask for the receipt so she can change them 'for a slightly different colour', then swap them for another handbag or yet another pair of shoes, because 'they didn't have my size'. Jewellery? It can never be silver, and to guarantee this she may even tell you she's allergic to the cheaper of the precious metals. No woman I've ever met has been allergic to either gold or platinum.

There's always lingerie, but this can't be bought too early on in the relationship. The correct size is of paramount importance, the only guarantee of which is to rifle through her underwear drawer when she's not looking to check, and if you get caught . . . Then you have the problem of type. A red silk stocking and suspender set may get your pulse racing, but she'll think it means you don't find her sexy enough as is. Similarly, get her anything too plain and she'll think you don't find her sexy at all.

But worst of all, how do you sign the card that goes with it? Love from? With love? All my love? These may mean all the same (i.e. nothing) to you, but women can extract whole relationship judgements from your choice of these little words. After twenty minutes of these issues buzzing round my head, I still haven't bought Charlie a thing. I'm starting to get desperate, until I suddenly remember that you can circumvent the whole present-getting problem by buying flowers.

When I come out of the florists it's one o'clock, so I head towards the restaurant, trying my parents again on the mobile to let them know I'm on my way. Today we're trying something a little different, and have arranged to meet at a new Lebanese place called Beirut Brasserie, in Knightsbridge. There's still no answer from their phone, so I go in, find my table, order a beer and wait for them. I've made sure I've got a window seat, and ten minutes later, when I'm just starting to get a little worried, I spot them outside, double checking the directions I sent them to ensure that they are actually at the right place. My mother has a clutch of Harrods bags with her, which explains their lateness and my father's somewhat pained expression, although knowing him he'll have set himself up in a chair in the books section and waited until my mother had exhausted her pension money, which in Harrods probably didn't take her long.

I tap on the glass and wave, gesturing for them to come in. I can almost hear her say 'Come along, David', as he limps along behind her, his recent knee replacement still not quite healed. My mother bustles over to the table and gives me a kiss, followed shortly afterwards by my father, who I greet with a sort of half hug, half handshake. We're not big on physical displays of affection, my family, and my dad and I are at that funny stage where we're not quite sure what the correct greeting procedure should be.

'Oh, they're lovely. You shouldn't have,' says my

mother, picking up the bunch of flowers and smelling them. I don't have the heart to tell her that I didn't.

'This looks nice,' she says, sitting down and surveying the room. 'But I'm surprised to see a male waiter.'

I frown. 'Why?'

'You know, in a . . .' she lowers her voice to a whisper '. . . lesbian restaurant.'

I look at her for a second. 'Lebanese, Mum.'

'Well, however you pronounce it,' she says, picking up the menu. My father just rolls his eyes, making that face that says 'Women, eh?'

I order a port and lemon for my mother, which I have to explain to the waiter how to make, and a bottle of red wine for my father. When the waiter pours him a little to taste he sniffs, sips and rolls it around his mouth for so long that I'm worried he'll spit it out rather than swallow it.

My father does this every time, as he makes his own wine and always likes to compare his to any he has when he's out. It's not as if he crushes his own grapes, but he is rather handy with those packet kits you buy from Boots. He's filled their airing cupboard and spare bedroom with all sorts of tubes, bottles and filtration systems, meaning that nowadays a night in my parents' house is always accompanied by a vibrant soundtrack of bubbling and fizzing.

He does a pretty good job; the white certainly is a 'cheeky little number' and the red has the same effect as Ribena mixed with vodka. Over the years he's perfected the amount of sugar he needs to add to get just the right alcoholic kick, which is a good few percentage points above the norm. In fact, Dad's home-made wine has such a following amongst my friends that he always gives me a couple of bottles to take back to London, and I'm guaranteed a visit from the boys once I'm back to 'help' me drink it. After what seems like an eternity, he finally nods his approval at the waiter. 'Not bad,' he pronounces.

Over lunch, I try and explain my dilemma surrounding Nick, hoping that by some miracle they might come up with a solution. My father is one of those people who will always offer advice, whatever the subject, and although I normally just smile and nod when he's handing out his pearls of wisdom, for once I'm genuinely interested to see whether he has any good suggestions. That I'm desperate enough to ask for their help shows that I'm at my wits' end, but although my parents have known Nick for as long as I have – and therefore know what he's like – they are also big fans of marriage, and are starting to despair that they'll never go to another wedding given my relationship history. They've also never met Sandra, and quite frankly I don't have the energy to respond to my mother's 'She can't be that bad' comment. When, as usual, my mother turns the conversation round to why I'm not married yet, I find myself switching off, and it's a relief when, catching sight of Charlie on the street outside, I work frantically to change the subject.

As she walks over to the table, all smiles, my father struggles to stand up, his knee having stiffened since he sat down.

'Charlie – my parents, my parents – Charlie,' I say, emphasizing her name at each opportunity.

'How lovely to meet you, Charlie,' says my mum. 'Adam, why don't you call that lovely Somalian chap over and get Charlie a drink.'

Charlie, my father and I exchange glances until I finally cotton on. 'Mum, it's *sommelier*.'

'That's what I said, dear,' she replies, and turns back to Charlie.

I order some more drinks and then take a back seat as Charlie charms them. The only hiccup is when I excuse myself to take a phone call, and return to find my mother showing Charlie the Bonny Baby clipping that she's actually brought with her. I really must destroy that one day.

'Nice photo,' grins Charlie.

'Mum,' I manage, in a voice that suggests my mother has just knitted me a particularly embarrassing jumper. 'Don't forget that I'm the one who'll be picking your rest home.'

An hour or so later we usher them outside and into a cab, and as we say our goodbyes Charlie promises that, yes, she will come down and visit them soon. I remember that I couldn't reach them on their mobile phone earlier, and wonder whether my mother has accidentally switched the ringer off, but when she gets the phone out to check we find that she's actually brought their home cordless phone by mistake.

I pay the driver, sending them back off towards the Eye, and Charlie and I take a leisurely walk back towards my office. I leave her shopping on the King's Road, stroll into reception and smile at Becky.

'Any messages, gorgeous?'

Becky blushes. 'Just the one,' she replies. 'Sandra phoned — Nick's had a breakdown. She's got to go out so can you go right over?'

'Wh-what?' I can't believe what I've just heard.

'That's what she said,' says Becky, reading from a little yellow tear-off memo pad. 'Nick's had a break-down.'

'When did she call?' I ask, anxiously. 'Why isn't she with him?'

Becky doesn't seem at all flustered by this. 'Oh, about ten minutes ago. She mentioned something about a hair appointment, so can you go round and sort Nick out.'

Sort Nick out? Bloody Sandra. If only I'd been a little more helpful, or said something earlier, or had her killed . . .

Mind racing, I rush outside and grab a cab round to Nick's flat, where I'm a little surprised to find him waiting outside, sat disconsolately on the bonnet of the Ferrari.

'Mate!' I shout. 'Are you okay?'

'No I'm not okay,' he fumes. 'Bloody car won't start. Again.'

Ah-ha. That kind of a breakdown.

'Would you believe the AA didn't have any replace-ment fan belts for a Ferrari?' he continues, although he seems strangely proud about this inconvenience. 'Can you give me a lift down to the dealership? I want to shout at them, and that's best done face to face.'

Nick knows nothing about cars. He'd even phoned the AA when he couldn't find the engine one day. 'Have you tried looking in the boot, sir?' the exasperated AA mechanic had asked him. 'These are rear-engined cars, you know.'

We walk round to my flat to pick up the Impresser, and I drive us through Chelsea and over Wandsworth Bridge. The showroom is just across the river, and I park carefully between approximately a quarter of a million pounds of Italian engineering. As Nick climbs out of the car he bangs his door, or rather my door, if you see what I mean, into the wing of the adjacent Ferrari, taking an inch of its gleaming red paintwork off in the process.

'Be careful,' I tell him.

He surveys the damaged wing. 'It's just a little scratch, mate. Probably come off with a bit of polish.'

'No, I meant *my* car. And, anyway, that's probably about two-of-your-monkeys' worth of damage you've just done there.'

Nick looks at the dent, shrugs and walks off into the dealership. I follow him in past a beautiful black Ferrari with the word 'wanker' neatly scratched on to the bonnet.

Beyond the heavy glass doors, the dealership has an air of sanctity – red thick pile carpets emblazoned with the prancing horse logo, plush leather armchairs, which exhale as you sink into their embrace, and a coffee machine which serves only the finest Italian blends. The place is a shrine for the worship of all things Italian.

'No wonder it costs so much for a replacement windscreen wiper blade,' I mutter to Nick, while helping myself to a large espresso.

'Good afternoon, Siignor Morgan,' says an instantly materializing sales assistant, wearing a name badge that identifies him as Paolo, and talking in an accent that wouldn't be out of place coming from the villain in a Bond movie. 'And 'ow are you today?' I'm not making this up. This is how he speaks.

'I'd be much better if I could have driven here in my fucking car that I paid you a hundred grand for less than a year ago, rather than some cheap Japanese piece of crap,' replies Nick. 'No offence, mate,' he says to me.

Paolo from Roma becomes Paul from Romford.

'I'm, er, I mean, Ey yam zorry to 'ear zat,' continues Paolo. 'What seems to be ze trouble?'

'Ze trouble is ze fucking fan belt. Eet has fucking overheated. Again,' replies Nick, mimicking Paolo's accent expertly.

Paolo sighs and looks to the heavens. 'The Ferrari – eet ees like a beautiful woman, no?'

'No,' Nick replies.

'Well, it is like Sandra,' I say.

Nick turns and frowns at me. 'How do you mean?'

'Well, you spend a lot of money on it and all it does is sit there.'

Scowling, Nick turns back to Paolo. 'So, *Paolo*,' he continues, 'when can you get me a mechanic out to fix the bloody thing? I think you know the address.'

'Well, Meester Morgan, I will check but our customer serveece technicians, they are very busy.'

'That's because your fucking cars always break down,' says Nick, getting angrier.

'Zey are not really meant for London driving. Eet ees all these stop and start.'

'Well, it *has* stopped and I want you to start it again. Today.'

Eventually, Paolo agrees to send an engineer out that afternoon. I finish my coffee and we get back into my Japanese piece of crap, which starts, as ever, first time. As we drive off, I look in my rear-view mirror and see the owner returning to the Ferrari that Nick has dented. He gets into his car, starts the engine, then gets out again as the dent registers. As his face goes through a mixture of confusion and anger, I put my foot down.

As we head back into Chelsea I'm suddenly conscious that I'm running out of opportunities, so ask Nick if he wants to come for a drink, but he cries off, explaining that he wants to be there when the mechanic arrives. I drop him off outside his flat, and look at my watch. It's nearly five o'clock, so I head on over to Bar Rosa, park outside and stroll in, saying hello to Pritchard, who is sitting at a table chatting to a good-looking, young chap. Rudy is keeping an eye on them from the bar, so I sit down right in front of him to purposely obscure his vision.

'Checking up on Pritchard?' I ask him.

'Get out of the way,' he says, moving a couple of feet to his left. 'New chef interview. Anyway – where have you been for the last few days?'

'I've been out . . .' I start to say, and then change my mind '. . . working.'

Rudy squeezes my bicep. 'Working out, more likely,' he scoffs. 'Oh – hold on. What's that smell?' He breathes in deeply. 'Reminds me of that cheap nineteen seventies perfume. What was it called?'

I sniff, but can't smell anything. 'What are you talking about?'

He grins. 'I remember now. *Charlie*, isn't it?'

'Ha ha. Good one, Rudy,' I reply, my voice as sarcastic as I can make it. 'You've been talking to Nick, I take it?'

'Might have been.'

Pritchard walks past me and back behind the bar. 'I hear you've been, what is it you Cockneys say, *feeling a proper Charlie*?' he says, high-fiveing Rudy, and heading off towards the kitchen.

I shake my head. 'Christ. Not you as well.'

Rudy turns back to me. 'So, when do we get to meet the girl who's charmed our Adam?'

'Maybe I'll bring her in here one day,' I say, 'when I feel confident enough that you two won't scare her off.'

'First Nick and now you,' says Rudy. He puts his hand up to his ear. 'What's that ringing sound?'

Normally I'd find this kind of thing amusing. But with time running out where Nick's concerned, the only bells I can hear ringing are alarms.

Rudy walks off, singing 'Love Is In The Air'. I pick up a pistachio from the bowl on the bar, take aim and throw it at him.

And miss.

Chapter 14

By Thursday I'm bored of sitting in the office on my own. I last until late morning, then stroll home, switch on the lunchtime news and wait for the weather report. Some chap wearing a standard-issue weatherman jacket – in one of those particular pastel hues that doesn't match his trousers – proceeds to tell me how the weather is at the moment. 'Well, that's saved me looking out of the window,' I say to him, and then realize I'm talking to the television. I'm not due to see Charlie until this evening, but I decide to phone her anyway.

'Busy?'

'I was,' she says, 'but I'll drop everything if you like . . .'

I resist the juicy bait she's dangled in front of me by asking whether she's had lunch yet. She hasn't, and when I suggest a picnic in the country I can hear the delight in her voice.

I stroll round to my local Sainsbury's to stock up on food and the primary ingredient of all successful picnics – a chilled bottle of Chardonnay – and then, picking Charlie up on the way, head out of London on the A3. When, twenty minutes later, we arrive at

Richmond Park, she seems a little surprised, but this is as country as I'm prepared to get. After all, the Impresser might have four wheel drive but surely that's to keep me on the road rather than to take me off it, and also I'd have to wash the car afterwards. With Charlie sitting by my side, I can think of better things to do with my time.

I'm an experienced picnicker. I've got all the gear: waterproof zip-away rug, collapsible wine glasses, bottle chiller, Frisbee, although I stop short at plastic cutlery. I leave the Impresser across two spaces in the car park, copying Nick's trick, and we head off towards the ponds, Charlie holding my right hand, whilst my left struggles to keep a grip on the heavy, industrial-sized cool box that I need to transport all of the above.

It's not your usual English spring day – the sun is shining, there's not a cloud in the sky – and the park is full of people walking their dogs, and mothers with children learning to ride their stabilizered bikes. We walk over to the larger of the two ponds, find a sunny bench overlooking the water, and watch the swans, geese and ducks vying for scraps at the water's edge, until the incessant noise from the Heathrow-bound planes overhead gets too annoying.

Finding a quieter spot away from the path, I spread out the rug, and Charlie sits down next to me, laying out the various foods as I open the wine and pour us each a glass. We're just about to start eating when a huge wasp flies by and starts buzzing round my face. I try to swat it away, and only succeed in hitting myself painfully on the nose.

'Just ignore it,' says Charlie, as my eyes water.

'Ignore it? This huge buzzing stingy thing?' Wasps aren't my favourite creature on God's earth. When I eventually manage to trap it in my glass and take great pleasure in trying to drown it, Charlie just rolls her eyes.

Once we've finished eating, we just sit quietly side by side, basking in the early afternoon warmth, and sip our drinks. *This is perfect*, I find myself thinking, and, for a minute, manage to forget all about Nick and Sandra. That is, until Charlie turns to face me.

'So, how's it going with you-know-who?' she asks. 'Have you had *the chat* with him yet?'

'Er, sort of.'

She looks at me enquiringly. 'Sort of? You don't exactly have a lot of time left, you know.'

'Well, it's not for want of trying. I keep hinting about Sandra but he never seems to take the bait.'

Charlie looks to the heavens. 'Have you ever thought of just sitting down and talking it over with him *without* insulting his fiancée? Or would that be too obvious an approach?'

'It's not quite as simple as that . . .' I start to explain, but Charlie cuts me off with a poke in the ribs.

'Do you know what I don't understand?' she says.

'Einstein's theory of relativity? The offside rule?'

She pokes me again, but harder this time. 'No. Why you men can't ever talk to each other about anything more serious than sport or cars.'

I think about trying to rephrase Mark's explanation from a couple of weeks ago in Bar Rosa, but I'm not sure I can. Besides, Charlie didn't buy it before, and, to be honest, neither did I. 'You know,' I suggest, 'it's all that stuff about *Men Are From Mars, Women Are From*—'

'Twix?' interrupts Charlie. 'Don't be ridiculous. And anyway,' she continues, 'how are you going to feel when it's five years down the line, they've got a couple of kids, Nick's miserable and you could have prevented all this with one simple question?'

I refill our glasses, being careful to remove all traces of pickled wasp from mine. 'Blimey! The thought of Nick as a dad! Do they make baby seats for Ferraris, I wonder?'

I'm chuckling to myself at the vision when Charlie suddenly looks at me, slightly more seriously than I'm used to.

'And how will you feel when your best friend is involved in a series of affairs?'

'He should be so lucky,' I say, adding, 'and, anyway, Nick's not like that.' Charlie gives me a withering glance. I decide not to tell her that I've tested this out recently.

'He may not be now,' she says, 'but in my experience, once a guy decides to make an honest woman of someone, it can make a dishonest man of him.'

'In your experience?'

'Let's just say that I have . . . a friend who's been through similar circumstances,' she says, cryptically. 'It's the worst feeling in the world. The lying, the suspicion . . .' Charlie swallows hard, and when I see the look on her face I decide not to pursue this line.

'Maybe . . .' I say, trying to convince myself, '. . . maybe Sandra is right for him. Maybe she'll keep him on his toes and that's the best way to be . . .'

Charlie snorts. 'Adam, Sandra's horrible. Nick may think she's what he wants, but no one deserves to end up with someone like her. I've only met her once and I can tell that already. And besides, do you really want to see him in one of those IKEA marriages?'

'IKEA marriages? What are you talking about?'

'Where it looks nice in the catalogue, and initially fits together perfectly, but a few years down the line it starts to come apart, and you find yourself thinking that a couple of extra "screws" might make it steady again . . .'

This is one of the worst metaphors I've ever heard. And three guesses where she got it from – bloody *Cosmo*. I decide to change the subject in the best way I know how – by rolling on top of Charlie and kissing her hungrily. After a few minutes she removes my hand from inside her top.

'Not here,' she says. 'It's a little bit public for my liking.'

I ignore her and put my hand back where it was, only to remove it again quickly as a group of school-children appear on the path.

'See,' says Charlie, sitting up and straightening her clothing.

'Spoilsport,' I say. 'We'd have heard them coming.'

Charlie gives me a mischievous look.

We drain our glasses, pack the cool box up and carry it back to the car. On an alcohol-inspired whim, we hire roller-blades from the hut near the car park, which seems like a great idea until I try and stand up in them and fall flat on my backside. I try again, and fall straight back down, and it's not just a little collapse-type fall, but a heavy slam-type fall. I'd always wondered why they rented them out along with the knee and elbow pads, but within seconds I've found out exactly why.

I'm a little embarrassed when I have to hand my roller-blades back to the pimply kid in the hire shop a mere fifteen minutes later, mumbling something about having a meeting I'd forgotten I have to go to. I retire hurt to a nearby bench and watch Charlie as she finds her feet, or rather wheels. She's obviously done this before, and I look on in admiration as she glides up and down the path in front of me, looking quite sexy in a semi-bondage kind of way with her gloves, pads and helmet, almost like an extra from *Rollerball*.

Charlie skates on for a while, and I walk with her, dragging her by the hand up some of the small inclines where the path weaves through the trees. We continue on round the corner and unexpectedly come across a mother deer and her fawn on the grass in front of us. The fawn is clearly only a few hours old and still struggling to stand, and its mother watches us warily as we approach. I feel Charlie's hand tighten on mine and so I smile at her, and it's that moment that I think, yeah, there are worse situations to be in than having a family and a life partner, but then I catch sight of a girl sunbathing on the grass nearby, and am snapped back to reality.

'Come on, skate-boy. Race you back to the car,' shouts Charlie, and she speeds off back towards the car park, leaving me to follow sheepishly on foot.

Later, when I've driven her home, I walk her to her door and ask if I can come in, but she tells me that I have to go round and have it out with Nick. 'Now!' she says, slapping me playfully on the behind.

'Yes, miss!'

Charlie hands me my phone – she'd kept it in her bag so I didn't break it when I fell over, and I switch it on, find Nick's number on the speed dial, and then stop myself.

'I need to think of what I should say . . .' I tell her, standing there like an idiot with the phone to my mouth.

Charlie gets exasperated with me. 'Adam! It's not a mission to the moon you're planning. Don't think – just go round there and talk to him.'

Just then, my mobile rings, making me jump, and I stab the answer button, to hear, coincidentally, Nick's voice, asking if I want to come to Bar Rosa for a drink.

'I'm meeting Mark there later,' he tells me. 'Thought you might want to come and stop him boring me with his latest get-rich-quick schemes.'

'Call you straight back,' I say, and I ask Charlie if she wants to come along. She'll be able to meet Pritchard and Rudy, I tell her.

She thinks about this for a second. 'And Nick's going to be there too, is he?'

I nod, naively.

'Then I'd love to,' says Charlie. 'I can make sure the two of you have that talk.'

I make a face, and then ring Nick back. 'Do you mind if I bring Charlie?'

'Not at all,' he replies, slightly surprised. 'Do you want some money towards it? Make sure you get the good stuff—'

'No,' I interrupt him. 'I mean my Charlie. Not Sandra's.'

'Ah, oh, yeah. Of course. See you later,' he says.

Charlie looks at me sweetly. '*My* Charlie?' she says, raising one eyebrow.

When we arrive at Bar Rosa, Mark is indeed holding forth in front of a glazed-looking Nick, who looks incredibly relieved as we walk in. He jumps off his stool and kisses Charlie hello and, as usual, peers down her blouse as he does so.

'Hi, Mark,' she says, as Mark turns round in his chair. He stands up and holds his hand out to her, which she ignores and instead gives him a big kiss on the cheek. He can't stop himself from raising his hand to wipe where she's left an imprint of lipstick.

'I'll get the drinks in,' announces Nick, heading off to the bar before anyone can tell him what they want. Sure enough, he arrives back with a grinning Rudy, who's carrying a bottle of Moët, Pritchard looming behind him.

'Champagne? Is Sandra here?' I ask, causing Nick to glower.

Placing the bottle on the table, Rudy beams at Charlie. 'And who is this lovely creature?'

'It's Mark,' I reply, as Charlie blushes. 'I thought you knew . . . Oh, sorry. You mean Charlie?'

I do the introductions, and Pritchard clasps Charlie in a big hug. 'Pleased to meet you both,' she says, as Rudy takes her hand and kisses it.

Pritchard pops the champagne open and pours everyone a glass, including himself and Rudy. We all squeeze round one of the barrels, and Rudy announces a toast.

I glance round suspiciously. 'What are we drinking to?'

'Oh, nothing special,' says Rudy, as the others all avoid my gaze. 'It's just nice to finally meet you, Charlie,' he says, holding up his glass.

'Likewise,' she says. 'I've heard so much about you.'

'Most of it under-exaggerated, I'm sure,' laughs Rudy.

'So,' says Pritchard. 'Tell us all about yourself. I hear you're a model?'

'Catwalk or catalogue?' asks Rudy.

Out of the corner of my eye I see Nick about to open his mouth. I silence him with a look as Charlie talks a little about her work, although she's clearly embarrassed about being the centre of attention.

'Any family? Brothers or sisters?' says Pritchard.

'Brothers in particular?' asks Rudy, raising one eyebrow.

Charlie nods. 'Just the one. A brother, I mean. He's a writer. You might even have heard of him?'

'What's his name?' asks Mark.

'Richard. Richard Evans,' replies Charlie. 'I think his book is called *French Letters* or something.'

'We know it,' chorus Pritchard and Rudy. '*A Queer In Provence*. It's fabulous!'

Nick almost spits his champagne back into his glass. 'What did you say?' he splutters.

'*French Letters — A Queer In Provence*,' repeats Pritchard. 'It's about this gay guy who goes and lives in a small French village for a year . . .'

'. . . and how the locals react to his lifestyle,' adds Rudy. 'It's hilarious.'

'You should read it,' recommends Pritchard. 'I think I've got a copy upstairs if you want.'

'No thanks. It's hardly my idea of bedtime reading,' says Nick, indignantly. 'So, your brother, Dick . . .' he asks, turning back to Charlie.

'Richard. Not Dick. He doesn't like Dick,' she interrupts, innocently.

Nick lets out a loud snort. 'That's not what it sounds like!'

Charlie blushes, and I suddenly feel a little pissed off at Nick, even though I have to fight not to smile.

Charlie ignores him, and turns back to Pritchard and Rudy. 'He's coming over to visit soon. You should meet him.' She glances back at Nick. 'He's a bit like Nick really.'

'Like me?' says Nick, slightly taken aback.

She smiles. 'Yes. Except he's good looking, charming and has a great sense of humour.'

'Ha! She got you!' says Mark, laughing. Nick just sulks and pretends to be interested in something floating in his glass.

'Seriously though,' continues Charlie. 'I'll bring him in to meet you guys, if you like.'

'When's he here?' I ask.

'Oh – he normally just turns up out of the blue,' she replies. 'But I'll be sure he comes in and says hello. I'll get him to bring some signed copies of the book along.'

'Yes please,' says Pritchard.

'Yes please,' says Rudy.

'No thanks!' exclaims Nick. I nudge him under the table, and he looks at me sharply. Sometimes I think he forgets who owns the bar where he's drinking.

'Maybe you should read it,' suggests Mark. 'It might help you get in touch with your feminine side.'

Nick slams his glass down loudly. 'What would I want to do that for, Mr Cosmo? It's feminine *in*sides I want to get in touch with, and I don't think that's going to be helped by reading some French fairy story.' He turns to Pritchard and Rudy. 'No offence.'

'I've often thought that I should write a book about the time I spent in Ireland when I was younger,' says Rudy.

'Really? What would you call it?' says Mark.

Rudy frowns. 'What is it the Irish say – *Looking for the Craic*?'

'Except in your case, you'd spell it C-R-A-C-K,' says Pritchard, causing them both to dissolve into laughter.

Mark looks at the two of them disdainfully. 'Move over Little and Large – there's a new comedy double act in town.'

The evening rush is just about to start, so Rudy

returns to the bar, where some other customers have been waiting impatiently for a while, and Pritchard heads off to the kitchen. Once we've finished the bottle, which given Nick's capacity for champagne doesn't take that long, I join Rudy at the bar to order another.

'She's lovely,' he says to me.

'I know,' I reply, looking proudly back towards the table, where Charlie is talking animatedly, Nick and Mark listening intently to her every word. Or rather, Mark is listening intently and Nick is still trying to look down her top.

I head back over and squeeze in between Nick and Charlie. Pritchard brings us over some complimentary tapas, and as Charlie pops an olive into her mouth, Nick suddenly leans over.

'Have you ever tried these with pepper?' he asks her. 'They're delicious!'

Charlie says she hasn't, and so Nick picks up the pepper pot and shakes a much too generous helping on to the plate. I look at him curiously, and too late realize what he's playing at, as the cloud of pepper causes Charlie to sneeze. He and Mark sit there transfixed as she sneezes. Eleven times. A record since I've known her.

'Excuse me!' says Charlie.

'Er, bless you!' says a wide-eyed Mark. Nick just sits there, leering.

'I'm sorry about Nick,' I tell her. 'He was dropped on his head as a child and he has these funny turns every now and again.'

'Do you know,' says Charlie, recovering her composure, 'the sneeze is the second most pleasurable bodily
function, apparently?'

'Oh yes?' says Nick. 'And what's the first?' He looks
at her, raising one eyebrow.

'Shopping!' she laughs. I almost expect to see Nick
nodding in agreement.

The four of us chat for a while, Charlie gamely
trading lines with Nick, as Pritchard and Rudy maintain a steady supply of food and drink from the bar.
When, eventually, Mark looks at his watch and
announces that he has to go, surprisingly, Charlie does
the same. I get up to leave with her but she puts a
hand on my shoulder.

'Oh, that's okay, Adam, I'll just get a cab. You stay
here and keep Nick company.'

I don't get it for a moment, and then realize she's
leaving me to have *the chat*.

'Give me a call,' she says, kissing me goodbye.

I watch as she flags down a cab outside and gets
in, then walk back over to where Nick is sitting,
wondering how I'm going to start the conversation.
Fortunately, he does it for me.

'You'll be next,' he says, when I get back to the
table.

I look at him strangely. 'What are you talking about?'

'You and Charlie. You won't be long.'

'I don't think so,' I scoff.

Nick regards me suspiciously over the top of his
glass. 'What have you got against marriage, anyway?'

I take a deep breath, determined not to let this

opportunity slide. 'Well, for one thing, over half of all marriages end in divorce nowadays, so what's the point of getting into something that will statistically only help to improve the standard of living of lawyers?'

Nick sits back in his chair. 'Blimey! What's turned you into Mr Cynical all of a sudden?'

'It's just . . .' I take a deeper breath. 'Marriage isn't something you can just try for a while and then discard. It's not like buying a car that you can then trade in for a newer model whenever you feel like it.'

'Isn't it?' he says, and I think he's joking, but then I see he's not. 'How else do you know whether you're going to like it or not? Sure, you can try an extended test drive, but sometimes you've just got to go for it.'

Cars. Excellent. One subject we can talk about. I decide to keep the analogy going, in the hope it won't make me sound like I'm being nasty. 'But what if, for example, I'd driven . . .' I correct myself quickly, 'I mean, read a review of the car you were planning to buy, and knew that it wasn't the right . . . model for you?'

His face darkens, and for some reason I'm suddenly reminded of a piece of advice my father always used to give me – *never return to a lit firework*.

'What do you mean?'

'Say, for example, there were certain problems, in terms of . . . economy, or . . . reliability, that you might not be aware of.' I'm clutching at straws now.

Nick puts his glass down and stares at me. 'What exactly are you saying, Adam?'

'Well, we think—'

'We?' he interrupts. 'Who is "we", exactly? You and Charlie? Little Miss Perfect? Or am I going to have to have this same chat with Mark?'

I realize I'm getting in deeper water without a paddle, or whatever the phrase is, so I try a different tack. 'We . . . I mean, I'm worried that Sandra's motives may not be as . . . heartfelt as they should.'

Nick snorts. 'What are you saying? That she's only marrying me for my money? Thanks very much!'

This is exactly what I'm saying. I think Sandra's philosophy is something along the lines of 'If it ain't broke, marry it'. But I realize that this is actually a grave insult to Nick, suggesting he has no other qualities apart from the size of his bank balance.

'No, I just . . . I haven't ever heard either of you say that you're in love,' I counter.

Nick shrugs. 'Maybe so. But when was the last time any of us ever admitted that we loved anybody? Except for Mark of course, but he cries at films.'

'But you've always said that you'd never get married unless you really loved the person.'

'I say a lot of things. And I also reserve the right to change my mind.'

'But . . .'

Nick swallows hard. 'Mate,' he tells me, 'it's all right for you. Any time you feel like it you can go out and find yourself somebody to, for want of a better word, shag. You see someone you like and off you go, like some kind of meat-seeking missile, knowing that your odds of success are pretty good. But the rest of us, well, quite frankly we have to take any opportunity we can, and when we finally find someone who agrees to have us, well . . .' He pauses and takes a long gulp of champagne. 'Life's all about making choices. Are you a lager drinker or a bitter drinker? Do you like Dairy Milk or Galaxy? Do you stay single for ever, or . . . Well, let's just say I've made my choice.'

I'm thinking about my response to this, wondering whether I should mention Guinness, or Bournville. I want to tell him that these things aren't mutually exclusive, but then Nick looks at me and sighs heavily.

'Let's just say that I've failed in too many relation-ships in the past to want to go through it all again. I'm sick of them always ending so badly.'

'Nick, every relationship you have is going to end badly except for the last one. Or, to put it another way, everyone fails at every relationship except one. Look how many I've "failed" at, for example. Don't let your poor track record stop you from trying to find *the one*.'

Nick sighs wearily. 'It's not my "poor track record", to use your delightful phrase, that I'm worried about. It's just that I'm tired of going through the same process, and it all leading to nothing. Sandra and I, we're . . .' He searches for the right phrase. 'We're *ready*, you know? And sometimes in life you just have to decide on a course of action and follow it through. If it goes wrong, well at least you've had the courage of your convictions and tried it. And, anyway, what's the worst that could happen? It doesn't work out and we get divorced. Big deal.'

It's now that I should deliver the killer blow and

hit Nick in his most sensitive spot – his wallet – by adding 'and she takes half your money', but for some reason I can't bring myself to do it. All I can manage is 'That's the best reason for getting married I've ever heard.'

Nick ignores me. 'Anyway,' he continues, 'Sandra thinks you're jealous because you're worried that she's stealing your best friend, or some bollocks like that.'

When I don't reply, his expression suddenly changes to one of concern. 'You're not, are you?'

'No!' I reply, perhaps a little too loudly. 'No. I . . .' I look round to check that no one's in earshot. They're not, but I lower my voice anyway. 'I just worry about you, that's all.'

'Ha!' exclaims Nick. 'That's a good one. And I'm touched, really, but you don't have to. I know what I'm doing. I know you're not the greatest of friends with Sandra, but please try and get on with her. For me.'

I open my mouth to say something, but Nick interrupts me.

'You're going to be my best man, for Christ's sake. And as my best man, *and* my best friend, I expect you to support me.'

How can you refuse a plea like that?

Chapter 15

Well, that's that, then. I guess I just have to accept that despite my best efforts, which if I'm honest haven't been worthy of the word 'best' (and in some cases would have struggled to be called 'efforts'), Nick seems determined to soldier on with his wedding plans. And for the next few days, and for the sake of our friendship, I try as hard as I can to be enthusiastic.

So on the Saturday I spend a ridiculous afternoon in Moss Bros., where Nick tries on a succession of dress suits and top hats, and then sulks for the rest of the day when I answer his 'So, how do I look?' Sunday afternoon finds me sitting in Nick's flat, patiently writing addresses on envelopes as he and Sandra argue about whom to invite to the reception, and I cringe quietly as Sandra crosses name after name off Nick's list. On the Monday, and on Sandra's insistence, I help Nick look for horse-and-carriage hire firms to transport her, sorry, *them*, from the steps of Chelsea Town Hall to the reception venue, despite the fact that it's due to take place at Bluebird, the Conran restaurant just across the road. And on Tuesday Charlie and I even accompany them there for dinner, so Sandra can check it'll be good enough for her, sorry, *their*, guests.

In the midst of all this I also have to think about my speech, as I haven't written a word yet. I even go as far as phoning Nick's dad to ask him for any amusing family anecdotes about Nick's childhood, only to replace the phone an hour later wondering how I can possibly make any of his stories sound funny but now feeling duty-bound to include at least one.

At the same time, because I find myself spending more and more of my spare time with Charlie, I feel less and less able to criticize Nick, mainly because Charlie and I are moving at a pace that makes his and Sandra's romance look positively pedestrian. We're already at that stage in our relationship where we're not quite living together but don't spend many nights apart. As is customary, I've left a toothbrush at her place, and she's taken three out of the four shelves in my bathroom cabinet for her stuff. Charlie is happily disproving that monogamy equals monotony, and whilst neither of us have actually used the 'L' word yet, she has given me a key to her front door. I have had a spare key cut to my flat for her, too – I just haven't actually got round to giving it to her yet.

By Wednesday evening I'm exhausted by all the goings-on, so I've postponed the usual night with Mark at Bar Rosa until Friday, and am instead sitting with Charlie in her flat, watching a video, with beer and pizza for company. I used to do this regularly every Sunday round at my place with Nick and, when he could make it, Mark. It's another tradition that started back when we were at college as some sort of film appreciation evening, where Mark would try and get us to watch some obscure art-house movie he'd read about in the *Guardian*, but we'd always end up with the latest Bruce Willis action-adventure, or the next instalment in the *Rocky* series.

We'd kept it going for as long as we could, but it kind of fizzled out after Mark moved westwards. He'd decided, or rather Julia decided for him, that it was a little inconvenient – I think her word was 'selfish' – for him to travel back into London on Sunday nights 'for some silly college piss-up ritual'. Again, her words.

We've chosen a film called *Devil's Advocate*, starring Al Pacino, whom I'm a big fan of, playing a lawyer who's the devil, and Keanu Reeves, who Charlie likes, as . . . well, I won't spoil it for you if you haven't seen it yet. We're lying on Charlie's sofa, sprawled in that familiar, comfortable way, munching pizza and drinking beer from the bottle, as we sit through the obligatory twenty minutes of trailers before the film starts. Charlie wants to fast forward, but I like to watch them, as I think trailers are a great idea.

I used to wish that women would come with trailers too (and don't get me started on the value of subtitles). That way, rather than having to endure the whole full-blown relationship, you'd have a chance to assess a summary of what's in store for you. Thinking about it, that's why it's sometimes a good idea to try and sleep with a woman on the first date – that way you know if the main action sequence is any good, and what the special effects are like without having to sit through the endless dialogue to get there. Then again, trailer or no trailer, subtitles or not, my problem is that, up until now, all the endings have been the same.

We watch the video draped comfortably over each other, but have to pause it for half an hour when other events take over (we've only been dating for a few weeks, don't forget, so stuff like this still happens at impromptu moments). Then, when the film's finished, and at the risk of sounding like an old married couple, we decide that we'll have a cup of tea. I go into the kitchen and put the kettle on, but when Charlie opens the fridge she finds that there's no milk.

'Don't worry – I'm happy to have it black,' I say, generously.

'I'm not,' she replies, and before I can offer to go for her she announces that she'll get some from the corner shop, walks over and kisses me, and heads out.

I've not been in her flat alone before, and it feels a little daring, so I have a bit of a nose round, walk into the bedroom, open the wardrobe doors, that sort of thing. I don't know what I'm looking for, but I'm enjoying looking – it's as if it helps to build a picture of her apart from me, or something. She's very neat, and her bedroom's not too girly, you know, not a soft toy in sight, or any of those pathetic little troll-type dolls with the brightly coloured flyaway hair, but actually quite feminine and sophisticated, and for a moment that makes me a little panicky as I wonder whether Julia's right, and that Charlie might soon see through the 'likes' of me.

And then it happens. You know when you read those interviews with people who have climbed

Everest, and asked why they did it they say, 'Because it's there'? Well, suddenly, in Charlie's underwear drawer (which I've only opened with a mind to check her size for future purchases, you understand, rather than to try anything on), I see it – an expensive-looking leather-bound volume with, quite simply, 'Diary' written on the front. It's too ornate to be simply a planner, so I guess it must contain some of her inner thoughts and feelings.

I push the drawer shut guiltily, then open it again. Why is it in a drawer? And why her underwear drawer? Has she hidden it away from me when she knew I was coming round for the evening? Does she always keep it in here? Is she embarrassed about what she's written in there about me so she's panicked and shoved it in the first place she could think of? I pick it up, and it feels surprisingly weighty in my hand.

I know where the corner shop is, so I reckon I have about five minutes before she comes back. The devil (Al Pacino) on my left shoulder is of course saying *Go on, open it, have a read – what harm can it do?* The angel (who may or may not be Keanu) on my right is, of course, saying *Just put it back and forget you ever saw it* – which is what I do. Then take it straight out again, telling myself that Al's right. A little look won't do any harm.

This is how drug addicts start – just a tiny bit won't hurt. I know that if I even glance at the first page then I'm going to want to read the whole thing, which of course I can't do in five minutes. I also might not get a chance to see it again, because this may just have

been a temporary hiding place utilized in panic, and
next time I'm here I might find that she's put it somewhere out of my reach.

Okay then, I decide, I'll just have a little peek. As I
say, because it's there. I open the diary and turn to the
date I first met her, but stop myself just for a second.
What if I read something that I can't ignore, and then
can't possibly confront her about because she'll know
I could only have read it in her diary, or alternatively
do confront her about, which would tell her that I'd
both read her diary and been looking in her underwear drawer, neither of which I'd be keen to admit.

When I do flick through, much to my disappointment and relief at the same time (which are two
strange feelings to have concurrently), I can't find
anything too revealing. It's mostly factual stuff, times,
places, dates, work appointments – nothing much
personal at all, in fact, and I'm just about to put it
away again when I see it. Scribbled inside the back
cover is a list of signatures, like when you're buying
a new pen and you try it out several times by writing
your name on the sheet of paper they offer. The
Christian names are repeated, but randomly. Charlotte,
Charlie, C., Charlotte again, and so on, until at the
bottom, it says 'Mrs Charlotte . . .' But it's the surnames
that have been scribbled as if she's trying to get used
to them that catch my eye. And why? Because it's not
'Evans' she's been practising signing, but 'Bailey'.

By the time Charlie arrives back with the milk, my
tracks are well and truly covered, and I'm sitting in
her lounge flicking through her latest copy of *Cosmo*.

But, as fascinating as the article on *What Your Vibrator Says About You* is, I can't stop wondering what I've just seen in her diary means. Is it just some childish fun? Something that girls of all ages do? Or is it all part of some sinister plan to lure me into marriage? And later, before I finally drop off next to a soundly sleeping Charlie, I'm troubled by a much more pressing issue. What on earth do I feel about it?

The next morning my watch alarm wakes me at eight. Charlie is still comatose, so I slip out without disturbing her and sneak off to the office early, propping a note up on the kitchen table reminding her to take the video back. Such a romantic.

Nick's not in, so I decide to try and clear the backlog of work that's mounted up over the last few days, but instead spend nearly the whole morning just rewriting the front page on the website – a job that normally takes me no more than an hour. For some reason I can't seem to concentrate on what I'm doing, and I'm having a hard time getting excited about the sites that I'm supposed to be describing in such glowing terms. As I've said before, there's only so many pictures of naked women you can look at, and, although that number is pretty high, I am, I tell myself, a *creative* after all, and need to be inspired by what I'm seeing in order to come up with a suitable tag line. But in reality it's because I can't stop thinking about what I saw in Charlie's diary.

I'm deliberating over a particularly dull site of supposedly candid voyeur shots, where in actual fact the 'voyeured', if that's the right word, seems to be fully aware of the camera, because she's looking right into it, and the only way we're supposed to know they are actually voyeur shots is that the webmaster has superimposed those binocular outlines on each picture, just like they do in films. I'm snapped out of my musings by a phone call from reception.

'Delivery for you, Adam,' says Becky, in a somewhat strange voice. I don't get many deliveries at the office, so I walk down to reception, somewhat intrigued. When I get to her desk she's got a silly smile on her face, and she smirks as she produces a huge bunch of flowers from underneath her desk, along with the card, which she's opened.

'Sorry, but I didn't know who they were for,' she says, handing them over guiltily.

'Didn't the delivery driver know?'

'Oh, yes, but I thought it was strange, you getting flowers, so I just had to check. Anyway, they seem to be from one of your, you know,' she lowers her voice, despite there being no one else in earshot '. . . *gay* friends.'

Snatching the card from her hand, I take the flowers back to the office. I've seen the name Charlie on the bottom, under a tiny paragraph of writing that I'd rather be in private to read. This is the second time Charlie's bought me flowers, and again I don't quite know what to make of it, but I'm secretly flattered, particularly when I read the card and it says: 'Thanks for a lovely evening! If you've recovered in time, same again, same place, tonight?' She'd signed it not 'love', or anything like that, but 'Yours, in a number of positions, Charlie'. Probably explains why Becky was smirking.

I pick up the phone and make two calls. The first is to Charlie, and I get her message service. I'm embarrassed when I have to say 'Thanks for the flowers', and I leave a rather formal message confirming this evening. The second call I make is to Becky, on reception. I simply say, 'Charlie is a girl!' and put the phone down.

After ten more minutes of hardcore pornography I decide I need a break, and stroll out past the still-grinning Becky to my favourite coffee shop, a little Italian family-owned place just round the corner. I order an espresso, sit down at one of the outside tables and open the copy of the *Telegraph* that I've bought on the way.

Sipping my coffee, I stare at the crossword for a while, hoping that one or two of the answers might magically materialize in front of my eyes. It's one of those cryptic bastards, where I'm sure there's a knack once you learn what all the 'clever' references actually mean, but I've never really had the patience (or seen the point, to be honest). I scan through the clues a couple of times, but only manage to get two of the answers, and I'm not even sure about one of them, so I put it back down untouched. I always think it's worse to start one and only fill in a couple of clues in a pathetic attempt that others can see than to just admit defeat and not bother at all, thus escaping with your dignity intact. Pretty much my philosophy on life really.

When I look up, I see a not unattractive woman

sitting at the next table, a large cup of cappuccino in one hand and an identical copy of the *Telegraph* in the other. I don't know how I'd missed seeing her sit down – perhaps the old radar is not functioning properly, given Charlie and all that. But as I'm watching her she looks up and our eyes meet, so I quickly glance back to my paper with the sort of practised half-smile that says 'Yes, you caught me staring but it was really just an innocent scout round, kind of looking up for air if you like, and our eyes just happened to meet, but I wasn't flirting or anything . . .' Or that's what I intend it to mean, anyway.

In the video Charlie and I watched last night, Al Pacino, the devil, ends the film by saying something like 'Vanity – that's my favourite sin', and proceeds to give Keanu the opportunity to, metaphorically speaking, hang himself, by tempting him through his own egotism. And it's true, I think, that in life, just when things are going along nicely, someone, though probably not Al Pacino, always comes along and presents the opportunity to fuck it all up.

The sensible thing would be to look away and find a story in the paper that was the most interesting, absorbing thing I've ever read, or pretend that I am stuck on a particularly difficult anagram or something. Not meet her gaze again and smile, which is, stupidly, what I do.

It's kind of like when you walk past a swimming pool whilst fully dressed. You've no intention of actually diving in there and then, but you still might perhaps kneel down and dip a finger in the water, just to see

how warm it is. For us men, if you're in a relationship the same feeling applies when you meet someone
else you're attracted to. It's sort of testing that you can
pull without actually going through with it.

Normally you can tell, even if it's just a quick interaction in a shop, a couple of words of jokey banter
perhaps. You can walk away, head held high, knowing
that if you'd wanted to you could probably have
extended the conversation a little, maybe even
suggested a drink, or at least have left with that prized
possession – her number. Indifference is the defining
factor. If you can remain fairly impartial, or even un-
involved, then chances are things won't go any further,
and you'll escape with your ego massaged slightly but
no real harm done. The problem is when you're so
used to working on automatic, or haven't properly
disengaged autopilot, and so of course I can't help but
look back up half a second later, and, of course, she's
still looking at me.

But what happens next surprises me, as she picks
up her coffee, walks over and sits down at my table.
As she puts her cup down next to mine, I can't stop
myself checking her hand for a wedding ring.

'I hope you don't mind,' she says, 'but don't I know
you from somewhere?'

Oh please, I think, is this how corny it sounds when
we men use the line? But of course I'm flattered, and
this gives me the opportunity to look at her more
fully in an attempt to try and place her. 'I don't think
so,' I reply, just about managing to stop myself from
adding 'I'm sure I would remember.'

'Yes,' she continues, 'from the gym? I teach aerobics there. Haven't you been to one of my classes?'

Now, you'll know that whenever a girl comes over and introduces herself as an aerobics instructor, her attractiveness increases by a factor of around fifty. It's one of those handful of careers that can seriously elevate a woman's appeal, along with masseuse, nurse and, of course, porn star, but then how many porn stars do you actually ever meet in real life? Not nearly enough, probably.

'Er, no. Aerobics isn't really my thing,' I say, worried that she's caught me sneakily watching through the studio doorway. Truth is I have tried one class, but even hiding at the back hadn't prevented me from being sniggered at by some of the regulars, who obviously knew the routines off by heart, whereas I didn't know my grapevine from, well, whatever anything else was called.

Her name is Diana, which try as I might cannot be shortened into anything remotely masculine, from what I can tell she pronounces everything correctly, and when I surreptitiously retrieve my serviette from where I've 'accidentally' dropped it under the table, I notice that her ankles are in no way fat. Everything that I'd normally look for is here, present and correct.

So here I am, with just the keeper to beat, and yet I find myself kicking the ball firmly into my own goal by telling her about my girlfriend (yes, I use that word). We have a pleasant chat over coffee, and when it's time to leave we shake hands formally, I tell her

I'll see her at the gym some time, and it doesn't even occur to me to ask for her number.

Looking back on this later, I realize that this is some sort of test that I, or maybe even Charlie, have just gone through without knowing it. Whatever, but we've both passed with flying colours.

Chapter 16

It's Friday morning, and I'm lying in my bed, Sandra standing over me with a knife in her hand, when suddenly I'm woken up by strange sounds coming from my bathroom. There's a space next to me where Charlie should be which is pretty cold, and I'm sure I can hear retching.

I get up, cursing the cheese I ate before going to bed last night, but check warily round the room for any actual signs of Sandra before sleepily making my way towards the bathroom door. I'm pleased to see it's shut; my idea of hell is being in a relationship where you're both comfortable enough to use the toilet in front of each other, and some things are better kept as a mystery. I knock, softly at first, and then louder when I get no response.

'Are you okay?' I ask through the door.

'Yes, fine,' Charlie replies, weakly. 'Hold on a minute.' When she opens the door and pokes her face through the gap, I notice that she's been crying. 'Just feeling a little sick,' she explains. 'Must have been that fish last night.'

'You see!' I say, smugly.

'I'll be out in a minute,' she says, disappearing back into the bathroom. I think about making some joke about morning sickness, but fortunately remember that this is something of a sensitive subject. Instead, I go back to bed to wait for her, and just as I realize that she didn't in fact have fish last night she comes back into the bedroom, and I see her crying for real. I get up and try to take her in my arms, but she gently pushes me away.

'What's the matter?'

'I missed my period this week,' she sobs.

I'm suddenly wide awake. 'What? Are you sure?'

'It's not the kind of thing you can ignore,' she says, dabbing at her eyes with a piece of toilet roll.

'But I thought you said—'

'I did. And now this. I was sick yesterday morning, too, after you left. And the day before. It's like I'm being cheated by getting all the symptoms but not being able to actually get pregnant.'

I have to swallow hard before asking my next question, and my voice still comes out several notes higher than it usually sounds. 'Are you sure you're not?'

'Don't you start. I can't be. Weren't you listening the other day?' She's in danger of starting to cry again.

'But sometimes these things happen. Don't you think you ought to get checked out? I mean, if you can't, and this is happening, it might be something serious.' I regret the words as soon as I say them.

Charlie looks at me, and I see that she's very pale. 'I have bought one of those pregnancy testers, but I'm too frightened to use it,' she sniffs.

'Where is it? At your flat?' I ask, hoping that it might be.

Charlie shakes her head and points at the bathroom cabinet. 'No, it's in my make-up case. In there.'

Ah. I take her by the hand and lead her back into the bathroom. 'Come on.'

'I wish I had,' says Charlie, following me through the doorway. I take her make-up case from the bathroom cabinet and remove the small cardboard package. For something that can bring such serious news, it looks very innocuous.

'I'm scared,' she says.

Me too!

'Don't worry,' I say, placing the pregnancy testing kit into her hand. 'I'm here. I won't leave you until we know if you're pregnant.'

'So, let me just get that straight. If I am pregnant, you'll leave me?' The old Charlie surfaces for a moment, and for the first time this morning she smiles.

'Er, no, that's not what I meant. I mean I won't leave you here alone to take the test.'

She kisses me and I close the bathroom door and wait.

'Outside please, Adam,' she says.

'Oh. Sorry. Of course. I forgot that you have to, you know, pee on it.'

I walk back into the bedroom and pace around anxiously. When, after two minutes, she hasn't appeared, I knock again. 'Everything all right?'

Charlie opens the door a crack. 'I can't go.'

'Try running a tap or something.'

She pulls the door shut, and I hear the sound of the tap in the sink being turned on. Then the shower. And then (although why I got one installed I still don't know – possibly something to do with the fact that the girl in the bathroom shop was rather attractive) the bidet.

'Any joy?' I shout through the door, struggling to make myself heard above the noise of Niagara Falls.

'Yes, just a minute,' she replies impatiently. The sound of rushing water stops and Charlie emerges from the bathroom, holding the little white stick in her hand as if it's poisonous. There are two little indicator lines on the end and, even to my untrained eye, they seem to be changing colour.

'What now?' I ask her.

'We check what colour the lines go.'

'And what colour *should* they go?'

'Well, that depends on your point of view,' she says, a curious look on her face.

I'm glad one of us is finding this funny. 'If you're pregnant,' I say matter-of-factly, 'what colour will they turn?'

She studies the end of the stick intently. 'Blue, I think.'

'Are you positive?'

Charlie frowns at me patronizingly. 'Isn't that what we're trying to find out?'

'No – are you positive that they should go blue . . . oh, never mind.'

I take it from her and stare at the rapidly darkening lines as they move through various shades, inching inexorably past turquoise, indigo, navy and settling, of course, on a deep, clear, unmistakable blue. 'And would you say that this is . . . ?'

She takes it back from me and holds it up to the light. 'Er, yes.'

I retrieve the packet from where she's dropped it on the bathroom floor and remove the instructions from inside the box. The helpful little slip of paper is colour coded, and, yes, 'our' particular hue matches what it says on the box, which, I now notice, bears the brand name Clear Blue. I pass the leaflet to Charlie wordlessly, she looks at it for a moment and then passes it back to me, along with the tester stick. I'm starting to feel like I'm in a deadly serious game of hot potato.

'I guess this means . . .'

'That we've got some talking to do?' says Charlie, who's actually beginning to look a lot happier.

I make us both some tea while Charlie phones and books an appointment to go and see her doctor. When I offer to go with her she tells me that honestly, it's no problem, she'd rather go on her own, so instead we arrange to meet for lunch at a restaurant I've heard of near the surgery, which apparently serves big portions, and I make a lame joke about this being good as she might now be eating for two.

Later, when I drop her off at her flat, I wish her good luck, although I'm conscious that my idea of what would actually constitute 'good' luck would prob- ably not be the same as Charlie's as far as current developments are concerned. With nothing else to do but wait, I head on into the office and – surprise,

surprise – Nick's not in again, so I just sit quietly at my desk trying to work. But no matter how much porn I surf through, I can't really concentrate on what I'm doing, particularly when I find a site dedicated to naked pregnant women called Lactating Lovelies, which I delete in a fit of anger.

Whenever the phone goes, which is more than usual it seems, I jump, but I'm both relieved and concerned each time that it's not Charlie. It's lunchtime before she finally calls, and I head out to meet her. I think about taking the Impresser but the King's Road is jammed with traffic, so instead I set off at a brisk walk.

The restaurant is down off the end of the Fulham Road, way past all the trendy shops and bars, and I soon find myself strolling down a street where people seem to be pushing their household possessions around in old supermarket trolleys. I can hear reggae beats pumping from open windows as I pass, and the faint whiff of marijuana hangs in the air. I'm wishing I hadn't brought so much cash in my wallet, and I'm trying to make myself appear tougher by adopting what I think is a 'hard' strut, which, when I catch sight of myself reflected in a shop window, actually just makes me look like I've wet myself.

Just when the surroundings are getting so rough that they make parts of Margate look like a conservation area, I find the place – a new Italian-Jamaican fusion restaurant called Rasta Pasta. It's taken me longer than I thought to get here, and I can see an anxious-looking Charlie through the restaurant window. As I open the door my palms are sweating — I'd like to think this is from the walk, but I'm not so sure. The last time I felt this nervous was the first (and last) time I let my dad have a drive of the Impresser, but then I suppose putting someone normally used to a one litre Ford Fiesta behind the wheel of a 150 m.p.h. rally car — especially at his age — probably wasn't such a good idea. I greet Charlie with a quick kiss and sit down.

'Sorry I'm late,' I tell her.

She gives me a guilty grin. 'Shouldn't it be me who's apologizing for that?'

We study the menus silently while I think about my opening question. Should it just be 'Well?' No — probably too impersonal. What about 'How did it go?' Again, not quite the right tone. I'm mulling this over as the dreadlocked waiter arrives carrying, I notice, a large measure of Jack Daniel's, but when he places it down on the table in front of Charlie I find myself breathing a huge sigh of relief. Surely if she was pregnant she wouldn't be ordering a drink like this?

The waiter is hovering, so once I've checked it doesn't contain any cannabis, I choose the joint of lamb, smirking at my own joke, which seems lost on both the waiter and Charlie, who orders the disgusting-sounding house speciality, banana bolognese. I'm puzzled, because I suddenly remember Mark telling me about these funny food cravings that Julia has when she's pregnant, and when I remark about the whisky Charlie shakes her head slowly, and her next words knock any remnants of doubt straight out of me.

'That's for you,' she says, sliding it across the table-cloth. 'I'm pregnant. Nearly three weeks.'

I suddenly feel like I need to sit down, and then realize that I am sitting down. As Charlie reaches across the table and grabs my hand, I do a quick calculation in my head, arriving nicely back at our trip to Brighton. I stare helplessly across the table at her, not knowing what to do. Despite being thirty-one and having slept with, well, *so many* women, this is one position that, perhaps surprisingly, I've never found myself in.

For once in my life, I decide to follow one of Nick's maxims – when you don't know what to say, say nothing. Unfortunately, Charlie uncovers the flaw in this plan almost immediately.

'Aren't you going to say anything?'

Like what? I think. *Congratulations?* I take a large gulp of my drink. 'I'm sorry. It's just come as a bit of a . . .'

Charlie looks across at me sympathetically and grins. 'Surprise? But I thought you liked surprises?'

'I do like surprises. I'm just not so keen on, well, *shocks*.' I say, which wipes the smile from her face. 'Is it . . .' I struggle to find the right words.

Charlie lets go of my hand, and I see her eyes start to mist up, not for the first time today. 'Yours? How can you ask such a thing!' she says, rather too loudly for my liking given the size of the restaurant, and then bursts into tears. A couple sitting at a nearby table look at me with contempt, and the waiter scowls as he brings our food and, rather unceremoniously, plonks mine down in front of me.

'No, please let me finish,' I whisper, making a mental note not to leave such inappropriate gaps in my sentences in the future. 'I was going to say, is it going to be okay? Given your complications and all that?'

'Oh.' Charlie blows her nose loudly on her napkin. 'Sorry,' she sniffs, picking up her fork and attacking her lunch. 'Well, early days, but it seems like it should be. Though you can pat yourself on the back if you like. Apparently it's a million to one chance that . . .'

Between mouthfuls, Charlie explains some gynae-cological stuff that I would try and repeat, but seeing as men know as little about the inner biological work-ings of women as they do about what goes on inside their minds, it would be lost in translation. Suffice to say that she tells me I must be producing the Christopher Columbus of the sperm world to have been able to navigate such perilous waters.

'Actually,' continues Charlie, 'it turns out that it was always the actual conception they thought was going to be impossible, not the pregnancy itself.'

Now they tell you, I think.

I'm not feeling particularly hungry, so I try and catch the waiter's attention to order another drink. He pretends not to see me.

'Oh, Adam,' continues Charlie, her expression soft-ening, 'this must be such a shock for you. I mean, we've only known each other for a few weeks, and now we're going to get married and be a family . . .'

At the word 'married' I've obviously choked or gone

white, because she leans back in her chair and laughs, loudly enough, I hope, for the couple at the next table, who are still looking daggers at me, to hear.

'Ha! Got you! You should have seen your face!' she sniggers.

'You mean you're not . . . ?'

'Serious? No. But pregnant? Yes. And I want this baby, Adam. I really want it.' Charlie takes a sip out of my glass, grimacing slightly as she swallows, before continuing. 'Imagine if you've dreamt of something for as long as you can remember, but then you're told you can never, ever have it. It's such a disappointment to you but eventually, after you've finally resigned yourself to the fact, you suddenly hear that you can and, in fact, are.' She looks across at me, imploringly. 'What would you do?'

She's so animated now that I fear a sentence containing the word 'abortion' wouldn't be the most appropriate response. I stare down at my plate and push my untouched dinner round with my fork. 'I'd probably have it,' I mumble, like a scolded child.

Charlie gives me a concerned look and puts her hand back on top of mine, which I notice is shaking slightly. 'Adam. It's okay. You don't have to be here if you don't want to.'

It occurs to me that I'm probably not presenting the most positive front, so I try and lighten the mood a little. I look round, and notice for the first time the mural on the far wall, which shows the Jamaican and Italian flags intertwined. The colours clash almost as badly as the styles of cuisine.

'Be here? But I like this place.'

'No. Be here with me, idiot, and pretend to be interested. I know how alien this must all be to you. But I have been doing a bit of thinking about what it means, what to do, and about us.'

The way Charlie's voice quivers on the word 'us' sets the automatic commitment conversation alarm sounding deep in my brain. I look up sharply, but Charlie suddenly finds something fascinating on her plate and avoids my gaze.

'So . . . I've decided that I'm not going to impose this on you,' she continues. 'I've got some money saved, and I can still work up until he's born.' She looks back up at me and smiles bravely. 'The advantages of being a hand model, you see.'

He? I'm thinking. *Can you tell already?* 'Maybe if you'd stuck to hand jobs . . .'

Charlie scowls. 'Yes, well. As I was saying. You've been great . . . so far, and I couldn't ask for a nicer person to face this with, but you've already told me what you want out of life. I know that this wasn't in your immediate plans, so I'm giving you the freedom of choice. I won't ask you for anything, so if you decide you want to be involved, well, that's fine. If you don't, well . . .' Charlie turns her face away from me and leaves what under other circumstances I'd describe as a pregnant pause, before continuing. 'If you want to walk away, that's . . .' and I see her swallow hard before continuing '. . . fine too. All I'm asking for is a simple yes or no.'

A simple yes or no. I can't think of a *less* simple yes

or no. What is clear to me, however, is that Charlie is so happy about being pregnant that whether I said I wanted to stick around or not probably wouldn't make much difference to her at this precise moment in time.

Don't get me wrong – I know what the 'right' thing to say now is; the words that would have the crowd welling up if this scene were being played out on the silver screen. I'd take Charlie in my arms, tell her that everything will be okay, ask her to marry me, she'd tearfully accept, the music would start playing, and we'd live happily ever after. But the problem I have is that this isn't the movies. It's real life. And right now, a little bit too real.

This is one of those questions where my answer could probably change the direction of my life for ever, and not just mine, but one, no, *two* other lives as well. Lives that I've already played the most impor- tant part in changing. I haven't the heart to say no. But I haven't the guts to say yes.

I lean across the table and kiss her, but we're both conscious that it's on her forehead and not on her lips. 'We need to talk about this more,' I say. 'Once we've both had a chance to absorb what's happened.'

'I've already absorbed it,' says Charlie, quietly.

'Well I haven't,' I say, perhaps a little too abruptly, and I immediately regret it as Charlie looks a little hurt. 'I'm sorry, I mean . . . it's such a big thing. A . . .' I force the word out '. . . *baby*? I just don't know if I'm ready for it . . .'

Charlie stops me. 'Tomorrow night? Come round to mine. I'll cook us dinner and we'll have a proper chat.' She indicates my untouched plate. 'Hopefully you'll have your appetite back by then.'

I pay the bill and walk Charlie out into the street, where I flag her down a cab. Just before she gets in, she stops and turns to face me.

'Adam,' she says, forcing a smile, 'we do need to talk about this. You can't let it drag on like . . .'

I finish the sentence for her. 'Like Nick and Sandra?'

Charlie nods. 'So I'll make it easy for you. Tomorrow – if you turn up, then I'll know we've got something to talk about. If you don't . . .' Her voice tails off.

'That's very, er, fair of you,' I say.

'Well, they don't call us the fairer sex for nothing,' replies Charlie, but she's not smiling any more.

I watch her taxi until it disappears round the corner, and then walk back towards the King's Road. I think about going back to the office, but feel a bit light-headed after my liquid lunch, so instead I change direction and head down towards the river. I'm sure it must be the effect of the whisky on an empty stomach, but my route seems to be barred by screaming toddlers in bulky pushchairs pushed by harassed-looking mothers. I imagine businessmen, their expensive suits stained by baby sick, forced to drive their Porsches and Ferraris at twenty miles per hour due to the child seats in the back, nagged by fat women in the passenger seats who have never quite lost the weight they gained during pregnancy.

I find a bench overlooking the water, Charlie's words echoing round my head, and sit down to try and make some sense of it all, but after an hour or so

I've only reached one conclusion: life isn't fair. I've spent the last few weeks trying to stop my best friend from getting married for all the wrong reasons, but instead all I've managed to do is make him more determined to go through with it. And to cap it all, now Charlie's dad is going to be after me with a shotgun.

I look at my watch, and suddenly remember that I'm due to meet Mark for a drink this evening, so stand up and walk miserably back towards my second home. By the time I arrive at the bar and beckon Rudy over I'm more in need of a drink than I can ever recall.

'Mine's a large one!' I say, without a trace of a smile.

Rudy takes one look at my sullen expression. 'Jeez, Adam! I know you and Charlie are in what's called a "serious" relationship, but you don't have to take it so literally.'

When I don't respond, Rudy raises one eyebrow and pours me a whisky, which I down in one and then struggle not to bring straight back up again. I slide my glass over for a refill.

'Bit of a serious drink for this time in the after-noon,' he says, removing my glass and pouring me a coffee instead. I don't argue, and sip the steaming liquid gratefully.

'Tell me something, Rudy. Do you like kids?' I ask him.

Rudy looks at me suspiciously. 'How do you mean?'

'Have you ever thought about having them, you know, starting a family, all that stuff.'

He laughs. 'Well, seeing as Pritchard and I don't actually have a womb between us, that might be a little difficult.'

I put my cup back down on the bar. 'No, I mean, don't you sometimes wish that things could have been different, and maybe you'd followed a different route, where you'd have someone to pass the bar on to when you and Pritchard are gone?'

Rudy mulls this over. 'Hmm,' he says. 'A little Pritchard?' He seems to find the prospect highly amusing, but I decide to press on.

'Well, don't you want someone to keep you later in life, when you're a drooling wreck in a retirement home somewhere?'

'Adam — you paint such a rosy picture of old age. Besides, that's what Pritchard's for.' Rudy taps the side of his nose. 'He's younger than me, you know.'

Even in my somewhat preoccupied state, I don't have to be particularly perceptive to know he's being sarcastic. 'Seriously, Rudy. Has it never crossed your mind?'

Rudy walks round to my side of the bar and sits down. 'Why are you asking?'

I take a deep breath. 'Because . . . I'm going to be a father.' It's the first time I've uttered those words and I'm surprised at how strange they sound. Fortunately Rudy doesn't clap me on the back and order champagne for the whole bar.

'Charlie?'

'Yup.'

'Didn't your mother ever warn you how addictive

Charlie can be?' he asks. 'Perhaps you should have *just said no . . .*'

I lean heavily on the bar. 'A little late for that now.'

I explain the whole situation in great detail, although leave out the part about my mighty sperm, and tell him about her ultimatum, or so it seems to me, tomorrow night.

'So,' says Rudy. 'That doesn't leave you a lot of time. She's obviously going to want an answer of some sort.'

'I know. And I've been trying to think it through logically, but . . . A baby?' I shrug and look at him helplessly.

'Well, there's your problem,' he says, leaning back and folding his arms. 'You're looking for logical answers to a trick question. It's not really about the baby.'

I look up, confused. 'It's not?'

Rudy rolls his eyes. 'Of course not. Well, not completely. It's about you and Charlie.'

I'm no clearer. 'How do you mean?'

'What do you feel for Charlie? Forgetting the baby for a moment.'

I wish I could. 'Er, dunno. She's not bad, I guess.'

'Adam. Drop the bravado. It's me you're talking to. Do you think you and her could have any kind of future together?'

'I don't know. Perhaps. I haven't really though about it.' Just call me Mr Commitment.

'Well, you can be sure she has. Do you love her?'

I feel myself blushing. 'Er, I guess. Possibly. Yeah, maybe.'

'Have you ever told her?'

'Don't be ridic—' Rudy's steely gaze stops me mid-flip. 'No. Not in so many words.'

'Well think about it. You two have been ticking over quite nicely for a while now, but not once have you told the poor girl how you feel about her.' Rudy holds up a hand to stop my feeble protestations. 'So perhaps, even though things are going great, she's been feeling a little insecure. Possibly she's been hurt in the past – who knows? Maybe she's even aware of your reputation. And now, *this* happens, and presumably she knows that having children isn't particularly high on your list of priorities. Maybe that's why she's given you this get-out clause. At least this way she won't feel that it's *her* you're rejecting.'

I look at him, dumbfounded. 'So what do I do?'

Rudy thinks for a moment. 'Does the thought of being a father scare you?'

'God yes!'

'Good. It should. Will having this baby make her happy?'

'Oh yes.' I'm sure of that.

He stands up and leans in close to me. 'Well then, what you've really got to decide is this. How important is it to you that she's happy? And, then, how much do you want to be a part of that happiness? Once you've worked those two things out, all you have to do is tell her.'

Rudy pats me on the shoulder and heads off to serve some other customers that, as usual, he's been ignoring for the last five minutes. And as I sit there, staring into space, I realize that Charlie's happiness is probably the most important thing I can imagine. But as for the second part . . .

I order another coffee and leaf distractedly through a discarded copy of the *Evening Standard* until Mark arrives, on time for once. He nods hello to Rudy and slumps down on the bar stool next to me, yawning loudly.

'Keeping you up?' calls Rudy, sliding a beer along the bar, which Mark just about manages to grab.

'Sorry,' he says. 'India wakes me up at six o'clock every morning. I can't even remember when my last lie-in was.'

Oh great, I think to myself. 'How is my goddaughter, by the way?'

'Fine,' he says. 'A little terror sometimes, but I wouldn't change her for the world.'

'And Julia? Not giving you too much of a hard time? Particularly given the whole, you know, *pregnancy* thing.'

Mark puts down his bottle and looks at me sagely. 'You know,' he says, 'I've decided that the secret of a happy marriage is a bit like doing your tax return.'

'What's this? The Accountant's Guide to Relationships?'

'No, I'm serious. As long as you declare everything up front, you'll avoid any unexpected demands.' I smile politely at this.

We find a table, order something to eat and spend the next few minutes talking about nothing in particular. Eventually, I can't ignore it any more.

'Mark, why did you and Julia decide to start a family

as soon as you got married?' Julia had become pregnant with India on their honeymoon, and I'd never asked him why so quickly, mainly because I'd never been interested. Now, for obvious reasons, I am.

He looks up, a little surprised I guess at hearing such a question from me, and takes a large bite of his taco before answering.

'Well, to tell the truth, we hadn't quite planned on having India so quickly, and I for one had always been very careful on the withdrawals and deposits front, if you see what I mean.' I do, but I wish the image wasn't quite so vivid. 'But,' he continues, 'on our honeymoon we went for a walk along the beach one day and found a particularly sheltered stretch, and just couldn't help ourselves.'

'Didn't you have any, er, protection?'

Mark smirks. 'Sadly just a bottle of factor 25, the application of which started the whole thing off. Besides, we thought it would be okay, given the time in Julia's cycle and all that. Unpredictable things, the female reproductive organs.'

Too right, I'm thinking.

'Why do you ask?' he says. 'Feeling broody?'

'No, it's just, I mean, did you always know you wanted kids? That you'd be a good dad?'

Mark shakes his head. 'Not really. To tell the truth, I had visions of Julia and I spending a good few years together before we even broached the subject. I hadn't really thought about it until it was sort of sprung on me, if you like, and then when I saw how different Julia was when she learnt she was going to be a mum

it kind of made it all worthwhile.' He makes an embarrassed face. 'Corny, I know.'

'Different? How?'

Mark ponders this for a while. 'Happier. More . . .
radiant. And that was just while she was pregnant.' He
takes a long sip of his beer. 'Then, once India was
born, well, I know it sounds like a real cliché, but the
minute this little thing, this little part of the two of
you, sees the light of day, and looks up at you, or grabs
your finger with her tiny hand, I challenge any man
to not go through an amazing range of emotions.
Pride, protectiveness, love . . .'

'That's what Nick said he felt when he got the
Ferrari.'

Mark gives me a dirty look. 'That's one of the reasons
we made you India's godfather. So you'd at least get
to experience this and share in the development and
shaping of a new life.'

'What?' I'm a little shocked. 'Don't you think I'll
ever have kids then? Get married? Settle down?'

Mark laughs. 'Well, you've got to admit, it's a little
far from your current circumstances, isn't it?'

Little does he know. 'Er, yeah, but maybe I've just
not met the right girl yet.'

'Or maybe you have but you're just too scared to
admit it.' Mark downs the remainder of his beer. 'Are
you having one?'

I almost choke.

He holds up his empty bottle. 'I'm getting another
drink. Are you having one?'

'Oh. Er, yeah. Thanks.'

Mark orders a couple of beers and puts one down on the table in front of me. 'I'll tell you one thing, Adam. When you have children your priorities change. Really change. Suddenly you realize that you're not the most important person in the world any more, and you don't just come second, but in fact third, behind your baby and its mother.' He takes an olive from the bowl on the table and chews it thoughtfully. 'That might be quite hard for some people to take.'

'Meaning me?'

Mark nods, swallows and helps himself to another olive. 'Yeah. Don't take this the wrong way, but I look at you with your superficial life, and I see Nick with the way he just throws money at everything in the hope it will make him happy, and while I might occasionally get pissed off because I can't have a flashier car, or I get woken up by India in the middle of the night because there's a monster under her bed, I just have to look at my little daughter when she's asleep, or playing happily with Julia, and I have absolutely no doubt who's got it right.'

'In your opinion,' I say, testily.

'Yup – in my opinion. Which is all that really matters, right? "Perception is reality" and all that bollocks. Fatherhood is great. Even Julia thinks you should try it one day.'

I bang my bottle down. 'Why are people like you and Julia always trying to change other people's minds about this sort of thing? It's like when I bought the flat and you kept telling me that I could have bought a whole house out where you live for that sort of money. Why do people always have to assume you don't know facts like this. What do you think I'm going to do – slap my forehead and say "Oh no – if only I'd known, what a fool I've been"? Christ, Mark, people make choices in life and if you want to live where I live, or, more importantly, live *how* I live, then you know the price you have to pay for it. If you make a rational decision to do that then surely that's fine.'

'Steady on, mate,' says Mark, looking a little shocked at my outburst. 'And, anyway, how can not wanting children be a rational decision? It's a biological fact!'

How can tying yourself to the same woman for the rest of your life be rational? I want to ask him, but bite my tongue. Instead, I try and explain.

'What I mean is, when you tell people you don't want kids, they assume that you haven't given the decision much thought and always try and change your mind. Don't you realize, it's actually a harder decision to make not to have them than just to go along with the rest of life's lemmings and reproduce two point four of the little buggers. It's the same reaction I get when I tell people I don't like fish. They always want me to taste theirs, thinking surely theirs will be the piece of wonder fish that will suddenly convert my tastebuds, not even thinking that my opinion might be based on years of consideration and experience.'

Mark looks at me disdainfully. 'And your point is?'

'My point is that I'm fed up of other people asking me to try their fish. This desire for children? I just don't have it. Can't you just accept that, just as some of us are bad drivers, or can't cook, or have no ear for music, some of us can't get how children work?'

'They change your life . . .'

'What's wrong with my life the way it is? And don't *you* take this the wrong way, but who are you to judge me? What's so great about trying to produce a couple of smaller versions of you and Julia, who'll grow up in a world with fewer natural resources and then help to reduce these even further. You'll spend all your time and effort working to provide for these kids in the hope that by the time you're past it they'll be earning enough to support you and make sure you can afford to live out your last days in a decent manner. Why not spare yourself all the trouble and effort, keep the money you would have wasted on their education, toys and so on and buy yourself a Porsche, or even just stick it in the bank and watch it, rather than them, grow?'

Mark's a little taken aback by this. 'But think what you're missing out on—'

'No, Mark. Think what *you're* missing out on. And that's part of the problem. I think a lot of people have kids because, and don't take this at all personally, they can't think of anything else constructive to do with their lives, so they take the easy option and decide to do what everyone else does. And they don't just have the one, either – they go for two or three in the hope that at least one will turn out okay, and not become a drug addict, or a criminal, or even a lawyer. And you ask me why I don't want to get involved in this?'

Mark looks at me, open mouthed. 'Er . . .'

'Far better surely that I assume the position of dutiful godfather and play, however small, an active, positive role in India's upbringing?'

'Maybe,' concedes Mark. 'But aren't you worried that you'll get to old age and find yourself sitting there all alone, your Porsche rusting in the garage, because you're too decrepit to drive it and you've got no one to leave it to?'

'Again, I draw your attention to the benefit of godchildren.'

'But bringing a little person into the world is so rewarding.'

'Surely so is, I don't know, painting a picture, or learning a language?'

'Ye-es,' concedes Mark. 'But refresh my memory – which of those are you currently doing? And, besides, those things are rewarding for *you*. This is for someone else. You might want to think about that for a change.'

We sit in an embarrassed silence for a while, staring at our beer, while Mark finishes off the olives. 'Anyway,' he says, frowning at the empty bowl, 'why are you talking like this? Anyone would think you'd gone and got Charlie pregnant.'

When I don't contradict him, his expression changes to one of concern. 'You haven't, have you?'

I look at him helplessly. 'I don't know how it happened.'

'Well, usually, the sperm swim up the fallopian tubes . . .'

'No, I mean . . .'

'I know what you mean,' he says, smiling. 'And, at

the risk of asking a rather indelicate question, she wants to have it?'

'Oh yes.'

'And it's yours? No other shooter near her grassy knoll?'

I haven't even thought about the possibility it isn't. 'Yeah.' I grin, even though I'm not feeling particularly amused by the whole situation.

'Bit ironic, isn't it?' observes Mark, once I've finished explaining the circumstances.

'Ironic?'

'Yeah. You know – here's Julia and me, and it takes us years of trying to have another baby, and here's you, trying all your life *not* to have one, and the first time you . . . well, bingo! What are you going to do?'

'Good question. I was hoping you might be able to throw some light on the whole situation for me, but . . .' I let my voice tail off.

'Fuck, mate. Why on earth did you let me lecture you like that for the last five minutes?'

I shrug. 'I dunno. I just wanted to talk round it in an unbiased way, I suppose. Try thinking outside the box for once, if you know what I mean.'

But what was I hoping? That Mark could suddenly convince me I would, in fact, like fish? Or even that Rudy would provide me with some incredible unbiased revelation? I shake my head slowly. 'I just don't know how they work.'

'Babies or women?'

I manage a wry smile. 'Both, it seems.'

'Listen,' he says, an awkward look on his face. 'Do

you want to, you know, talk about this some more?'

I shake my head. 'Er, no, thanks. I just need to think this through on my own for a while.'

Leaving Mark to finish his beer, I head out of Bar Rosa and retrieve the Impresser from the office. But then, when I get into the car and start the engine, I just sit there, as I realize something quite important. I don't have a clue where I'm going.

Chapter 17

I find myself driving down Nick's street, and miraculously there's a space in front of his flat where the Ferrari is normally parked. I reverse the Impresser into the bay, which takes me two attempts, probably because of the beer I've already drunk this evening. I wonder if I should be driving at all, but then I needed some Dutch courage, or, given the fact that it was San Miguel we were drinking, Spanish courage, to come round to Nick's and do what I'm planning to do.

It's Charlie's fault that I'm here at all. I don't mean all this baby stuff, but the fact that with Nick's wedding happening next weekend I've decided that I just can't ignore the Sandra issue any longer. I just know it's wrong – one of those nagging doubts, like when you wake up in the middle of the night and think you might need to use the bathroom, but it's cold outside the duvet and you reckon that the effort of getting up would outweigh the slight tension in your bladder, so you lie there and convince yourself that you'll be able to go back to sleep without going, but eventually the tension gets worse and worse, and so you have to get up and go, cursing the fact that you didn't earlier . . .

Anyway, I also know that I need a plan, and, up until now, the best I have come up with just hasn't been good enough. Plan A – telling him directly – I've tried, and it doesn't seem to have worked. Plan B – getting someone else to tell him – I'd like to have tried, but, despite numerous attempts to enlist outside help, I can't seem to find any willing volunteers. So, in desperation I find myself adopting Plan Z – sleep with Sandra. And as I say, it's Charlie's idea. Well, okay, not exactly.

'So,' she'd said, a few days ago. 'Nick is sure he's doing the right thing.'

'Well, so he says.'

'In that case, why don't you go and talk to Sandra?'

'Talk to Sandra?' I'd repeated her suggestion as if she'd said 'stab yourself in the genitals'.

'Yes,' Charlie had continued. 'Sit down and actually talk to her. Surely if she can convince you that she's doing this for all the right reasons, and Nick thinks he's doing it for the right reasons too . . .'

She had a point, I suppose. Of course. Again.

But this is what actually happens. I ring the buzzer knowing, because Nick never walks anywhere, that the absence of the Ferrari means he's out. Sandra's clipped tones leap harshly from the intercom.

'Yes?'

I try and make my voice as friendly as possible, which where Sandra is concerned really just consists of me un-gritting my teeth whenever I speak to her.

'Hi, Sandra. It's Adam.'

There's a slight pause, and then, 'Nick's not here.'

I'm worried that I might lose my nerve, but I find myself asking if I can come in, and saying that it's actually her that I've come to talk to. There's another pause, for a few seconds this time, and then she buzzes me in.

I climb the stairs to the flat and knock on the door. When I get no response I knock again, louder this time, and I hear a muffled 'Hold on'. I'm just about to knock a third time when Sandra opens the door. She's wearing only a dressing gown, having just got out of the shower, she explains, as she invites me in, and clutching a half-full red wine glass that looks big enough to hold a kitten.

Sandra produces another glass for me and a fresh bottle of wine, which I open. We sit on the sofa, and I ask her how the preparations are all going. We've never really spent any time together, just the two of us, and I soon begin to realize why, as she bores me silly with a long speech about the wedding that seems to focus on how much it's all costing, rather than how much she's looking forward to the day itself. She's obviously been drinking already this evening, which I find slightly worrying, as she's more than slightly tipsy. Every time she leans forward to refill her wine glass, which is alarmingly often, I catch a glimpse down her loose-fitting robe, which she makes no attempt to tighten up.

I try, unsuccessfully, to steer the conversation round to how she actually feels about Nick, but she's more keen to tell me the price of the silver-embossed invitations. Eventually, I have to ask her outright.

'Sandra, tell me something. Are you really in love with Nick?'

Her expression changes, and she looks at me coldly. 'What's that got to do with anything?'

I put my wine glass down on the table. 'Er, everything.'

'Well let me rephrase my question,' she says. 'What's that got to do with you?'

'Same answer, I think. Nick's my oldest friend.'

Sandra smiles, but it's more the kind of smile you'd see on the face of a tax inspector or child molester.

'So you've come round here because you're worried about him?'

I'm surprised at her perceptiveness. 'Yeah.'

'Or is it that you're more worried about you?'

'Wh-what?' I stammer.

'That's it, isn't it!' she sneers. 'Typical Adam Bailey. Always Mr Considerate. You like to make out that you're thinking about other people but really you're just making sure you're okay.'

'That's not true.'

'No?' she says. 'I know what you're like, Adam. You're one of those people who always need to be in control. I've watched you. At parties you're the one who makes sure everyone's got a drink. Or if we all go out for dinner you're always the person who chooses the restaurant, or orders the wine, or divides up the bill.'

At least I then pay my share of it, I think. 'But that's not about being in control,' I tell her. 'It's called being polite. It's about being considerate, or taking responsibility for your friends.'

'That's crap,' she replies, her accent becoming less avenue and more street. 'You just can't handle the fact that, for once, Nick is doing something without you.'

I shake my head. 'You're wrong, Sandra. What I can't handle is that Nick is making the biggest mistake of his life marrying you, and he can't see it. Especially if you don't love him.'

Sandra makes a face like she's been sucking lemons. 'I see exactly where this is coming from,' she says. 'It's always been just "Nick and Adam" this, "Adam and Nick" that, living the high life and chasing round Chelsea in that car of his. Well, he's found someone else to play with now. And the Ferrari is only a two-seater.'

I find myself wondering whether Paul McCartney ever had this conversation with Yoko Ono, and I'm beginning to wish that I'd followed Paul's advice, and *let it be.*

'That's not it at all—'

'Oh yes it is,' she spits. 'For years you and Nick have been joined at the hip like Siamese twins. Well it's about time that somebody separated the pair of you.'

I'm getting angry now, and raise my voice to match hers. 'Well as long as I get the brain. I'm sure Nick can survive without it. As far as I can tell he's not used his since he started going out with you.'

Sandra glares at me. 'Do you know something? I don't care what you think, Adam. Nick and I are getting married next weekend, and there's nothing you can do about it. So what if I don't love him? At least he can afford to make me happy!'

'And that's a good enough reason to marry him, is it?' I ask, incredulously.

'It's good enough for me!'

I can't believe what I'm hearing. On the one hand, this is perfect. It proves what I've been worried about all along. But, on the other hand, what on earth am I going to do about it now?

We're standing up now, and it's in danger of turning into one of those scenes that you see in films and think 'yeah, right', when the man and the woman apparently don't like each other and are arguing and start to struggle and then the struggle turns into a kiss and the next thing you know they're at it like rabbits. So I tell her what I think, that she's only interested in Nick's money, and she says that I've never liked her and I'm more worried that she's stealing Nick away from me, and I say don't be ridiculous but start to blush because I realize that this actually is part of the problem. She starts to poke me in the chest as she gets more agitated, and I grab her hand to stop her. She struggles and tries to slap me with her other hand, so to pacify her I grab both of her wrists, and as she tries to wriggle free her robe falls open, and I see that she's not wearing any underwear and that her nipples are quite erect, despite the fact it's warm in the flat. Our faces are only inches apart and she's shouting at me, and it crosses my mind to kiss her to keep her quiet, but, like I say, that only works in the movies, and even though she does have a very nice arse – Mark is right, by the way – she is, of course, despite my repeated attempts, still my best friend's fiancée. Just at that point when I know it would be so wrong and start to move away, she leans forward and kisses me full on the lips, shrugging the robe off her shoulders.

'Sandra. No! Get off! What are you doing?' I shout, pushing her away.

'Come on, Adam,' she says, breathlessly. 'I've always fancied you. You can be my final fling. Nick will never find out.'

'Well I've never fancied you,' I reply. 'Besides, even if I did, you're getting married to my best friend . . .'

I pull back in shock and stare at her. She's breathing heavily, her face flushed, and she's making no move to pick up her robe. I'm wondering how on earth I can get out of this when suddenly Sandra glances behind me and her expression changes. I feel a hand on my shoulder spinning me round and then Nick's fist smacks into my face. It takes me by surprise more than anything, and he's not exactly the most coordinated of people so it doesn't hurt so badly, but I sit down on the sofa in astonishment, the taste of blood in my mouth. My lip is cut where Nick's signet ring has caught me – I've always said men shouldn't wear jewellery – and I put my hand up to my stinging face.

I look up at him wordlessly as he towers over me, red faced and shaking with rage. Sandra standing next to him, still naked, regards me with a look that horror writers would describe as a triumphant sneer.

'Darling, thank God you came home when you did . . .' she begins, putting one hand on Nick's arm. He shrugs her off angrily, and I'm pleased as her expression quickly changes, particularly when he calls her a slut. Nick storms out of the lounge and into the bedroom, Sandra following closely behind, and I hear raised voices and various loud thuds, which I assume to be cupboard doors opening and then banging shut, rather than any further acts of violence. Unfortunately.

I'm still sitting on the sofa like an idiot as Nick emerges from the bedroom and makes for the front door. He's clutching a holdall and refusing to make eye contact with me. Sandra follows closely behind, struggling to hang on to him with one hand whilst desperately trying to pick up her robe from the floor in front of the sofa with the other. This strikes me as ridiculous, as by now we've both seen her naked, but it seems important to her, and I smile grimly at the scene, causing my split lip to bleed even more.

The last thing I hear before the front door slams is her pleading voice, calling after Nick as he walks down the stairs.

'Nick, but it didn't mean anything!'

'You're wrong,' he shouts back up at her, his voice full of emotion. 'It means everything!'

Sandra rushes back into the room, having managed to put her robe back on, and adopts one of those comic-book hands-on-hips poses. Her eyes are ringed with red now, and she looks at me with contempt.

'Pleased with yourself?'

I stand up and childishly mimic her stance. 'Yes, actually,' I say, walking straight out of the flat.

I'm just about to get back into the Impresser when I notice Nick's car parked opposite, but he's left the roof down and I can see he's not in it, so I reckon he must have gone for a walk to cool off. Either that or, and more like Nick, he's stormed off without his car keys and doesn't want to come straight back to the flat to get them after making such a dramatic exit.

I wait for him by the Ferrari for a few minutes, replaying the scenario over and over in my head. I suppose I should be pleased at this point. This is, after all, what I've been hoping to achieve for the past few weeks. But, thinking about it, I can't imagine anyone's going to be carrying me shoulder-high down the King's Road just yet.

When there's no sign of him. I take my phone out of my pocket and, wincing when I put it against my face, try to call Nick's mobile. He doesn't answer, which I suppose isn't surprising given the fact that I can hear it ringing from inside his glove compartment. I snap my phone shut and bend over to check my reflection in the Ferrari's wing mirror. The bleeding has at least stopped, but my lower lip has swelled up so it looks like I'm in a major sulk about something.

Eventually I give up and walk back over to the Impresser, and even though I'm not supposed to see Charlie until tomorrow I decide to head round to her flat to tell her what's happened. As I drive I work out an edited version of the night's events – not including the kissing and nakedness parts of course – and I'm looking forward to some pampering as a result of my injury, suffered in no small part, as I plan to remind her, due to her advice.

It's just gone eleven o'clock by the time I squeeze the Impresser into a space across the street from

Charlie's flat, and I'm just about to get out of the car
when I see her, walking arm in arm with some chap.
He's tall, good looking – in fact much too good looking
for my liking – and strangely I realize I'm feeling a
tinge of what I can only identify as jealousy. As they
stop by the entrance and Charlie fumbles in her
handbag for her keys I shrink down in my seat, hoping
they won't see me. Probably just a neighbour, I tell
myself, as I see her hold the door open for him.

I watch them go inside, and then get out of the car
and stare up at her flat. The rest of her floor is dark,
and, sure enough, after a couple of minutes I see her
lounge light come on. But when the next light to
come on is in what I know to be her bedroom, I start
to get worried, particularly because no other lights
have come on in the building, completely blowing my
neighbour theory. I hesitate by the car for a few
moments, then walk across the street and cautiously
ring her doorbell. When there's no reply, I ring again,
longer this time, until I hear the click of the receiver
being lifted in her hallway. But then, instead of Charlie's
dulcet tones, a man's voice answers.

'Rick speaking.'

I'm not prepared for this. 'Oh. Er, hi, er, oh, I'm
sorry. I think I've rung the wrong bell,' I stammer, my
delivery not helped by my fat lip.

'No problem,' says Rick. He puts the handset down.

I stand there, stunned, until a thought occurs to me.
Maybe I did ring the wrong bell? I tentatively press
the buzzer again, making doubly sure it's Charlie's
button I'm pressing.

'Hello?' says the same voice – *Rick*'s voice – slightly less friendly now. I look up again at the flat, and sure enough the bedroom light is still on.

I start to back away from the door, and then turn and jog back across the road and quickly get into the Impresser. As I put the key in the ignition I glance back up at her bedroom window just in time to see the curtains part, and catch sight of Charlie, in her dressing gown, peering out into the night. I start the car and wheelspin off down the road.

I'm already back home by the time my mobile rings. *She must have seen me*, I think, as I angrily stab the button that diverts the call to voicemail and then turn the phone off. Almost immediately my home phone rings, and I rush to the answerphone and switch it off before it can take a message. The phone rings for a minute and then stops.

I sit down in a daze. What's going on? I've finally met the first girl I've ever really loved – yes, I do use that word in my thoughts – and I catch her doing, well, I can't even bring myself to think what she was doing. Or how she was doing it. Or how many times. Aargh!

Oh, and she's pregnant with my baby, or at least what I assumed until just now to be my baby. I suppose *this* is what you call ironic, and I'm not enjoying the feeling one bit.

Oh yes, and how could I forget? My best and oldest friend has just punched me in the face because he caught me with his naked fiancée a week before I'm due to be best man at his wedding.

Shit.

Bollocks.

What do I do now?

I pick up my mobile, switch it back on and press the message key. It clicks into voicemail, and a harsh woman's voice tells me I have no messages. I switch it off again, and throw it on to the couch.

'Bitch,' I say, meaning Charlie, not the voicemail woman.

I start pacing anxiously round the flat, wondering what my next step is going to be. How do I play this? A number of confused thoughts run round my head: I am Adam Bailey, after all. Women don't make me feel like this. Well, not since . . . Not nowadays, anyway. I'm the cold, heartless one. Love them and leave them (well, make love to them and leave them, to be accurate). Or maybe destined to die old and alone? Perhaps Nick's prediction is correct?

I shake my head to clear it. I need some time, I decide, so I walk into the kitchen and help myself to a large drink, which I take back into the front room and sip slowly, sitting there in the darkness. *Glad I found her out for what she really was before I got in too deep*, I tell myself.

Hold on, who am I trying to kid? I'm already in too deep.

It's approaching midnight when my door buzzer goes, and I just sit there and listen to it ring, three times, each ring longer than the last. After the third time, I stand up and walk towards the door, telling myself that if it rings once more I'll let her in.

But it doesn't.

Chapter 18

Pride. Noun. 1) A group of lions. 2) A stupid, misplaced feeling of self-respect and personal worth that stops men from behaving like rational human beings where relationships are concerned. So while the sensible thing would have been to call Charlie and at least hear her explanation, what I actually do is de-activate my voicemail and leave my mobile firmly switched off.

Nursing a slight hangover, I steer the Impresser down the M2 towards Margate. I don't want to be anywhere near West London at the moment, for obvious reasons, and, anyway, today's my mum's birthday. As recent developments have meant I've not been organized enough to send her a card, I'm hoping that a surprise personal appearance, backed up by a box of her favourite Black Magic chocolates and the largest bunch of flowers I could find in the motorway services, will make up for this.

I've driven down Nick's street already this morning, but the Ferrari's not there any more, and I still can't seem to get an answer from his mobile. When I call the flat, Sandra tells me she doesn't have a clue where he's gone, but leaves me in no doubt as to where I can go.

It's raining hard, and I'm driving much too fast for the conditions, impatiently flashing those cars in front of me who refuse to pull over and are quite unreasonably sticking to the speed limit. As I negotiate the Saturday morning traffic, I hold a packet of frozen peas against my face with one hand to try and reduce the swelling on my lip a little, as I don't want to turn up at my parents' house looking like I've been in a fight.

The stereo is pumping out some opera CD that I bought along with the flowers – one of those compilation albums, *Twelve Songs for a Tenor*, I think it's called, and it's pretty good, although I skip that bloody Pavarotti number that seems to be on most of these collections, and that no one can listen to any more without thinking of the World Cup football coverage. I'm not in the mood for anything upbeat given last night's developments, and so fat men singing about love, death and depression in a language I can't understand seems perfectly appropriate.

I can't stop thinking about Charlie as I drive, trying to work out a plausible explanation for the presence of another man in her flat. I suppose it could have been a friend, but the bedroom light/dressing gown scenario only suggests one kind of friend to me. And why was she so keen for me to walk away if I decided I didn't want to be involved with the baby? Perhaps Mark had a point, and maybe it isn't mine? It's getting hard to see the cars in front, and I switch the Impresser's heater on full to clear my windscreen before I realize that it's actually my eyes that have misted over.

I don't feel much better even by the time I park outside my parents' house, and, despite composing myself in the car for a few minutes before I go inside, I still have to brandish the flowers in front of me to distract their attention from my sullen expression. My mum greets me with a big sloppy kiss and a hug, then bustles off to find a vase big enough for the huge bouquet, and I'm secretly pleased when she fails and has to get two and separate the bunch. I've phoned ahead to tell them I'm taking them out to lunch, so in a change from her usual velour 'leisure' suit, she's sporting a new matching knitted skirt, jumper and jacket, which I guess is my dad's birthday present to her (which probably means that he stood by in BHS while she shopped with the joint cheque book).

I move through into the front room, where my father is sitting, also dressed up, which for him means wearing trousers with a belt rather than an elasticated waistband. My parents' dog, Patch, has had an operation on his ear, so he's wearing one of those plastic cones round his neck that's designed to stop him scratching at the scar, and he can't get used to the thing. My father is teasing him by throwing chocolate dog treats for him to catch, which, because of the collar disorienting him, he keeps missing. They land in the cone where he can't see them but can smell them, and as a result he's currently driving himself mad trying to get them out. My dad thinks this game is the most hilarious thing he's ever seen, and he's giggling so hard I worry he'll have a heart attack. He looks towards me to share his fun, but even this spectacle doesn't provoke more than half a smile from me.

'No Julie?' asks my mother, walking into the room with a vase in each hand.

'Mum, it's *Char*lie. And no. She . . . had to work today. She sends her regards.'

'Oh, that's a shame. Such a lovely girl,' says my dad. I don't comment.

'You could do a lot worse, you know,' says my mum. 'Why don't you follow Nick's example?'

'Because I don't think he's setting a very good one, for one thing. Besides, I'm not interested in getting married.' The last thing I want now is one of my mum's when-are-we-going-to-get-a-grand-child speeches.

'Oh, of course you are, dear,' she says. 'Don't be such a Palestine.'

'Mum, it's "Philistine". And anyway, I wouldn't be so sure that Nick's feeling so pro-matrimony at the moment.' Fortunately, my mother is too busy arranging her flowers to pursue this.

Not having lunch at home is quite a treat for my mum as, apart from their odd trips to London, my dad's idea of eating out is a sandwich in the garden. Gourmet restaurants being somewhat thin on the ground in Margate, unless you count the all-you-can-eat-for-five-pounds-ninety-nine carvery on the main road, we're heading out into the countryside (i.e. where the town stops and grass starts) to one of the better pubs in the area, the Badger's Arms.

I usher them out to and into the car, my dad hobbling as fast as his walking stick will let him. He loves the Impresser, and always sits proudly in the front passenger seat, relegating my mother to the back on account, he insists, of his bad knee. My mum, on the other hand, gave up driving some time in the nineteen sixties, coincidentally around the same time she met my dad, and has had her nerves frayed too many times by his recent driving performance. She's not so keen on the way I drive either, but at least restricts her comments to a nervous 'It's a very fast car isn't it, Adam', whenever I overtake anything more rapid than a milk float.

My parents always eat with metronomic precision – lunch at midday and dinner at six o'clock on the dot – so we're knocking anxiously on the pub door at one minute past twelve. I point them towards a corner table, and then go to the bar and buy a round of drinks for us all for less than the price of a pint of beer in London – the usual port and lemon for my mother, which again I have to explain how to make to the girl behind the bar, and a pint of the local bitter for my dad.

My normal rule of thumb, particularly in London, is never to eat at a restaurant that displays pictures of the food. Here we go past that, because when I pick up the menu, it actually seems to have samples of the various dishes adhering to its plastic laminated front. Fortunately, the listing is reproduced on chalkboards round the bar, so I don't have to risk food poisoning by handling the encrusted ones. My dad can't read what's on the menu because he hasn't brought his glasses with him, so I have to dictate the various choices to him, but as ever he opts for the ploughman's lunch, and, again as ever, makes the same joke about hoping the ploughman doesn't mind.

My mother, whenever she goes out to eat, chooses each meal as if she's on death row and it will be her last, and spends hours making her choice, so I've bought a packet of peanuts to keep my dad's stomach rumblings at bay. We munch through them while she debates with herself about whether to have the prawn cock-tail or the soup to start.

Eventually, with the same sort of effort as if she's answering a question on *Who Wants To Be A Millionaire?*, she opts for the prawn cocktail. Resisting the temp-tation to ask if that's her final answer, I rush to the bar to order before she catches sight of the specials board.

We proceed through our lunch with the usual family small talk – *how's work, how's the flat, what do you think about the political situation in Nicaragua* – and I wince when I re-open the cut on my lip trying to eat a larger-than-usual potato.

'Hurt your mouth, son?' asks my dad.

'I cut myself shaving,' I reply.

He looks a little confused. 'With your electric razor?'

'How's things with you?' I ask him, trying to divert the conversation away from my life, as my mother disappears to survey the choice of puddings.

'Not good,' he whispers, leaning across to me. 'Your

mother is taking a computing course.' My dad tells me this in the same tone I imagine he'll use if he ever has to tell me that she's about to go in for major surgery. Fortunately, my mother's premature arrival back at the table prevents him from going into detail.

'I thought about the spotted dick,' she tells us, 'but I've had it the last two times we've been here.' As I get up to pay the bill, she adds, as an afterthought, 'You can have too much dick.' My father and I don't dare make eye contact.

Back at home, my mother opens the box of After Eights she's been saving since Christmas, obviously having decided to keep the Black Magic for when I'm gone, and we play that game where you have to model words with bits of plasticine. My first card says 'snake' and in seconds I've rolled my plasticine into a long thin strip. My mum can't get it.

After some severe reverse cheating, where I try and ensure my mother wins (well, it is her birthday), we retire to the sofa with a glass of my dad's home-made to partake in that staple of modern family life – the television. I sit there and watch my parents drop off into a nap, barely an hour after dinner and despite the strong coffee.

As this is my parents' house, there's precious little entertainment. I flick quickly through the choice of programmes, but they only have the normal terrestrial channels, which on a Saturday afternoon provide little in the way of anything I'd be interested in. I get up and look through their video collection, but this, too, takes all of ten seconds. My father still writes the name and date of what he's taped on the side of every cassette, which means that by now there are about seven labels stuck one on top of the other, through which you can read the previous contents on the label below. When he got to the last of his labels he started writing in pencil and rubbing out the previous entry, which after about thirty uses has left the title almost indecipherable. All I can make out is 'atch of da', which I guess is last week's football, along with several gardening programmes. They do have one pre-recorded tape, *Pride and Prejudice*, but I've already had to sit through this several times, watching my mother swoon at Mr Darcy (do people still *swoon* nowadays, I wonder?), and as attractive as the prospect is of fast-forwarding to all the bodice-ripping moments, quite frankly I just can't be bothered.

Instead, I pick up the local paper and flick through, stopping as always at the property pages, which I always like to keep one eye on so I have a good idea of what to expect in the will. When I get to the 'announcements' section, I recognize various people from my schooldays, their grinning faces topped by thinning hair as they pose for their wedding snaps, caught for posterity by the paper's official photographer. Worse still, I read notices reporting their delight at the birth of their babies, and I look at them disdainfully. Or is it with a tinge of jealousy, I wonder?

I turn the page and have to stop myself from laughing out loud. It's obviously *that time* again, as there's a two-page spread featuring this year's Bonny Baby competition entries. For a moment I entertain a mad impulse to telephone them all and tell them to destroy all copies of the paper, or be haunted by their toothless mugshots for ever more, but then I realize that they are, of course, still only babies, so probably wouldn't understand.

Hearing a loud snort next to me, I look round to see my father looking startled; he's snored himself awake again. He does this a lot, but it still seems to surprise him as much as the first time. He looks at me, realizes what he's done, smiles, and is back asleep again before I even have a chance to think of anything to say.

I sit there miserably for an hour or so, and then check my watch. There's still time for me to drive back into London and meet Charlie, but I'm not in anything like the right frame of mind for that particular conversation, so instead I get up quietly and sneak into the kitchen, where I liberate another bottle of wine from the fridge and pour myself a large glass. I don't often drink on my own, but it's this or kill myself whilst watching *Little House on the Prairie*.

As I walk back into the lounge and sit down, my father snorts again and looks up. He notices my sullen expression and the large glass of wine in my hand, then glances across to check that my mother is asleep. She's sitting in her chair, her head nodding as she tries, unsuccessfully, to fight off the combined assault of two port and lemons, a large lunch and the warm room.

My dad stands up slowly, puts a finger to his lips and, picking up the bottle of wine and his glass, beckons me into his den. He pushes the door shut quietly,

leaving my mother dozing out of earshot, and, unusually perceptively, puts a reassuring hand on my shoulder.

'Women trouble, son?' he asks, and it all pours out
of me. Well, an edited version really, as I decide that
telling my mum and dad that they might be grandparents but perhaps never see their grandchild probably wouldn't do a lot for their opinion of their
favourite, albeit only, son. Particularly on my mum's
birthday.

He sits patiently as I tell him about my fears for
my future, how I have no paternal instinct and how
my friends are concerned that I'll end up alone. He
nods wisely as I explain how I still feel like a child
inside, that I'm just not ready for the responsibilities
of adulthood, and certainly not prepared for the
demands of parenthood. And, lastly, he listens carefully
while I tell him that I'm worried I might lose Charlie
because I don't know how to tell her what I feel about
her.

I finish, and gaze at him expectantly as he considers
all that I've said. The last lecture I had from my dad
was almost eighteen years ago, when he found some
pornographic magazines under my bed – they weren't
mine, of course, I was looking after them for Nick,
you understand – so I'm intrigued as to what he's
going to say.

'Son . . .' he begins, and I think, oh dear, it's going
to be serious if he starts like that, so I prepare myself
for a long tirade, lots of 'your mother and me' type
advice and examples. Instead, mercifully, he keeps it
short and sweet.

'Son, do you love Charlie?'

'Er . . .' I'm so embarrassed about this sort of questioning from my dad that I go all red and feel like I did when he discovered my, I mean, *Nick*'s copies of *Razzle*. 'Er, yeah, I think so,' I stammer.

He refills both our glasses. 'Then don't forget, the word *love* is a verb as well. And a verb is?'

'A *doing* word,' I answer, automatically.

'That's right,' he says, proudly. 'It's not just something you feel, it's something you have to *do*.'

Always the teacher, my dad, and although English was never my best subject at school, I understand exactly what he means.

I've drunk too much of my dad's home-made wine, and so, rather than drive back to London and risk my licence, I decide to stay over, reasoning that I'd better have a clear head anyway when I finally talk to Charlie. And, besides, I still don't have a clue what I'm going to say, so I keep my mobile switched off just in case. I'm in my old bedroom, but it's very different to how it used to be. Some people like to keep their kids' rooms the same as the day they left, so even if you go home to visit when you're thirty you still find yourself sleeping in the bed you had when you were fifteen, struggling to get the too-short duvet to cover your toes and your chest at the same time, whilst the model aeroplanes you made as a child still hang from the ceiling.

Not my parents. The minute I bought the flat in London they must have felt pretty sure I wasn't coming back to live with them, as they gave all my furniture

and stuff away and converted my room into a reposi-
tory for my dad's books, wine-making equipment, and
somewhere for my mother's knitting machine, which
she bought during an economy drive back in the seventies, used to make one jumper for my father that would
have been more appropriate for an orang-utan as the
sleeves were so long, and then left to gather dust, never
quite managing to throw the thing away. Thus I'm lying
in a sleeping bag on the world's most uncomfortable
sofa-bed, nursing the beginnings of my second hangover in as many days, my mind spinning with the events
of the past few days, and beginning to wish that I had
chanced the trip back to London after all.

I've just about managed to get to sleep, serenaded
by the constant bubbling of Chateau Bailey from what
looks like one of those Victorian laboratories that you
see on cheap horror films, when I'm woken by a
knock on the door. I open my eyes, struggling to clear
my head, and see two shadowy figures appear, and
when I switch the light on and sit up, blinking in the
sudden brightness, I see that it's my mother, accompanied by Nick's mum from next door. They're both
wearing their dressing gowns, and when my vision
clears I notice that Nick's mum is crying. I check my
watch and see that it's only half past three in the
morning, but I'm suddenly wide awake with the clarity
that it's going to be bad news.

'It's Nick,' she sobs.

It's a good minute before I can make any sense of
her tearful ramblings, but the words car, accident and
Beachy Head start to form an awful sentence in my

head long before she can put them in the right order. My hand goes unconsciously to my cut mouth as I recall with horror the events of Friday night, and in particular the look on Nick's face as he'd stormed out of his flat. Surely not. Not *Nick* . . .

Fighting to swallow my rising sense of panic, I usher them both from the room, telling my mum to make some tea while I get dressed. I'm downstairs before the kettle's boiled, and carry the tray through into the front room, where I manage to get the story from Nick's mum as she sips her tea, my mother's arm round her shoulders.

They'd been woken by the police, she tells us, phoning to say they'd found a burnt-out Ferrari at the bottom of the cliffs at Beachy Head. When they'd punched the registration number into their computer it had given them Nick's name at the family address, as in one of his rare cost-cutting exercises he'd registered it back at the family home in Margate. *Cheaper insurance, you see*, he'd told me.

'What on earth would he be doing down at Beachy Head at that time of the morning?' she says through her tears, but I'm glad she's phrased it rhetorically; we all know that it's the UK's most popular suicide spot. As she talks, Nick's father sits quietly with my dad in the corner. I can tell he's struggling to stay calm, and I'm feeling so guilty I can't meet his gaze.

Nick's mum has the name and phone number of the police officer at the scene, and her hand shakes as she passes it to me. I call him straight away and tell him I'm on my way down.

'When did you last see Mr Morgan?' he asks, and I tell him it had been the previous night, but again decide not to elaborate. *Need to know basis*, and all that.

I run round the house gathering my stuff together, but can't find my car keys. After enlisting everyone's help in a frantic search, they eventually turn up in the fruit bowl in the hallway.

'Where were they?' asks my father.

'Fruit bowl,' I reply.

'They're always in the last place you look,' says my mum, shaking her head resignedly.

'Mum – you always say that. Of course they're always in the last place you look. Why on earth would you keep looking for something after you've found it?' I'm a little terse, but there are times that her silly comments fail to amuse.

I leave her taking care of Nick's mum and dad, promising that I'll phone as soon as I have any news. Screeching out of the drive, and causing a few bedroom lights to come on in my parents' normally peaceful street, I gun the Impresser towards Brighton. Within minutes I'm passing the 'Thanks for visiting the Isle of Thanet' sign on my way out, and it suddenly occurs to me that I should call Sandra. She answers the phone at Nick's flat on the second ring, so I assume she's awake and aware of what's going on, although she doesn't seem to be particularly upset. She tells me that she hasn't seen Nick since Friday evening.

'If anything's happened to him, I'll never forgive . . .'

I think for a moment she's going to say *myself* . . .

'. . . you!' she shouts, and puts the phone down.

My next call, and I dial with unsteady fingers, is to Nick's mobile, but ominously all I get is a 'dead' tone. Throwing my phone on to the passenger seat, I swallow hard and put my foot down.

I make the journey with no music playing, as I want to be able to concentrate on driving fast or, more accurately, making sure I don't crash, and several times I have reason to be thankful for the Impresser's four-wheel drive as I navigate the road as if I'm playing a computer game. I manage to break my Margate to Brighton record without encountering a single police car on the way, and I'm slightly disappointed at this as for once I have a legitimate reason to be driving like a maniac.

Reaching Beachy Head just as dawn is breaking, it's easy to spot the cluster of emergency vehicles, lights flashing in the morning glow. I remember bitterly how Nick and I used to laugh when we read reports in the local paper of all those 'accidental' jumpers: dog walkers whose exuberant pets would pull them over when chasing rabbits, only for the dog to be found alive and well at the bottom guarding the mangled corpse of its owner, or intrepid kite flyers dragged over the edge by an unexpected gust. All those balmy summer evenings, Nick, Mark and me sitting up here, daring each other to get closer to the edge. And then I remember my weekend with Charlie, how I'd held on to her so tightly as we'd looked down at the three hundred foot drop, hearing the waves crashing on the rocks far below. *What a way to go,* I used to think, marvelling at the imagined thrill of such an action. Not so marvellous or thrilling now.

I drive past an ambulance, its back doors open, and force myself to look inside, but it's empty. Parking on the grass verge, with shaking hands I switch off the engine and get out. The Impresser is ticking in that over-hot way, the burning smell from the brake discs heavy in the air as I struggle to catch my breath. It seems to take a huge effort, as if I'm moving through water, for me to get out of the car and walk over to the cordoned-off cliff edge, where the winches are pulling the battered Ferrari up and on to the grass.

Nobody's stopping me, and I join the massed ranks of Sussex's emergency services as we all peer over the cliff – obviously it's not that common an event down here, a hundred grand's worth of Italian engineering ending up at the bottom of Sussex's top beauty spot, hence the good turnout. I'm still hoping that it's not his, that the police have made a mistake with the registration number, and that it's somebody else who's driven their car over the edge in a vain attempt to get a supercar to fly.

As the remains of the Ferrari swing into view I can't bring myself to look into the driver's seat. All kinds of thoughts are running through my mind, and I find myself wondering whether when someone you know, or, dare I say, *love*, dies, and they ask you to identify the body, do you agree? Would you honestly want years of happy memories to be overshadowed by one image of this person stretched out on a mortuary slab, devoid of any of the life you knew and shared? Will you forever be unable to think of anything you ever did, any time you ever shared with this person without this grotesque image leaping into your mind? Particularly if it's your fault.

I wish I'd thought about this beforehand, but then could I honestly ever have refused? Surely the 'big' thing to do is to spare Nick's parents the ordeal of having the same final, but oh so false memory of their son. And what if he's burnt? Will I recognize him? Don't cars always explode when they go over cliffs, or is that only in the movies?

As the winches grind to a halt, I suddenly catch sight of the number plate, now hanging off the distorted back bumper, and half smile as I remember how Mark and I took the piss when Nick bought the personalized registration. An instant later, I realize this proves that it is actually his car, and my smile fades abruptly. My chest tightens, and I half sit, half fall on to the soft, dewy grass, causing the waiting ambulance men to move towards me.

It's at this point I notice that there seem to be rather a large number of paramedics standing round, drinking tea from Styrofoam cups, generally not engaged in the sort of frantic action you see whenever this sort of accident is portrayed on *Casualty*. It doesn't occur to me that this might be because Nick is dead.

'Are you okay, pal?' A voice from a jump-suited figure snaps me back to reality.

'Was there . . . is he . . . did you . . . ?' I can't put a sentence together.

The paramedic shakes his head. 'Didn't find a body,

mate. Convertible, you see. Great in the hot weather, but not so good if you happen to drive off a cliff. Might have been swept out to sea or something. They normally don't find them until weeks afterwards, if at all. Friend of yours, was he?' he adds. *Was* he?

I don't answer, but get up and stagger back towards the cliff edge, past the scorched and twisted metal. Fighting waves of nausea, I look down to where I can just about make out where the car has hit the rocks below. I picture the Ferrari arcing out into thin air, wheels spinning, exhaust roaring, heading down towards the sea, then exploding in a flash bright enough to light up the whole coastline, maybe even visible from France. I stare at the edge where the car has gone over, searching for tyre tracks in the grass, any evidence that he might have tried to put his brakes on before he went over, but I can't see any traces in the lush green growth. I look back towards the water, where the tide seems to be a long way out, and I find myself remembering how my dad taught me to tell whether it's going out or coming in. Strangely, it looks to me like it's just started to come back in.

Then a thought occurs to me. Nick always hated the water. He'd never learnt to swim, reasoning that at his height most rivers or swimming pools were easily crossed with his feet still touching the bottom. I don't think he'd ever purposely have aimed to drop himself slap bang in the middle of the English Channel if he could help it, particularly given what we'd seen floating in the sea off Brighton in our years here. Then again, given the tides, and the time I'm guessing he got here, he'd have struggled to go fast enough to make the water. Even in a Ferrari.

I jump as my mobile rings. It's my mother, anxious to know what's going on, not in the least because she's been drip feeding tea to Nick's mum for the last few hours. My voice is slightly shaky and I don't quite know what to say, so I just tell her what I've seen: that, yes, it is Nick's car but, no, there's no sign of Nick, which I suppose is good news. Leaving her with the difficult job of relaying this information to Nick's mum and dad, I give my details to the policeman at the scene, then go and sit in my car and just stare at the sunrise, oblivious to the glorious day dawning in front of me.

For the second time in almost as many days I don't know what to do. It's too early to call Mark, and, besides, he'd only worry, so instead I start the Impresser and head back to London. As I drive, I can't help thinking about Charlie, and realize, rather surprisingly, how much I miss her, and even *need* her, particularly now, given what's just happened. Although I'm still angry about what I saw at her flat the other night, at the very least she deserves a chance to explain.

By the time I reach the West End, I'm almost on autopilot, and find myself driving past the end of my street and heading straight for her flat. It's still early, and I have to ring the bell several times before I hear Charlie's sleepy voice on the intercom. When she realizes it's me her tone quickly changes, but not for the better.

'Do you know what time it is?' she snaps.

I look at my watch. 'Er, yes. Hold on. It's—'

She interrupts me sharply. 'Adam! That was a rhetorical question. What do you want?'

Good point. What *do* I want? I don't know where to start. 'Er . . .'

'Adam, it's . . .' She sighs loudly. 'What *is* the time?'

'Quarter past seven,' I say, sheepishly.

'Quarter past seven on Sunday morning, and I've got to work today. What are you doing here?'

I've had a few seconds to think about it now. 'I thought we could have a talk, you know, about the other night. So I could tell you how I feel.'

Charlie's voice changes from cold to steely. 'I think you made that perfectly clear when you didn't turn up yesterday, and then refused to take my calls.'

Ah. It suddenly occurs to me that, despite all my feelings of injustice, Charlie may actually be mad at *me* for my no-show. I get a sudden feeling of déjà-vu, as if I'm standing on a cliff edge for the second time this morning.

'Charlie, about last night. Something important came up.'

I can hear the exasperation in her voice, even through the crackly loudspeaker. 'Adam, I'm having a baby. *Your* baby. What could possibly be more important?'

Despite the early hour, quite a few people are walking along the street now, and I'm starting to feel a little self-conscious, especially as Charlie's voice, amplified as it is by the intercom, seems rather loud in the morning stillness.

'Nick . . . Nick's car . . .' I try and explain, but the words stick in my throat, the image of the mangled Ferrari still painfully fresh in my mind.

'Gnaargh!' says Charlie, or something very much like that, and I'm suddenly glad that I'm not standing within striking distance. 'Nick's *car*? I'm waiting for you so we can talk about our future and instead you're off . . .' She's sounding so angry now she can't even complete the sentence, and I'm sure she's on the verge of tears. What's more, she's not the only one.

'No, you don't understand. Just give me a chance to explain,' I plead, my voice thick with emotion. 'What do you want me to do?'

Charlie shouts her answer at me, and I'm almost knocked backwards off the doorstep by its ferocity. I stand there stunned for a few moments, and then turn and trudge wearily towards the Impresser and drive back home.

I don't know what I'd been expecting her to say, but 'Get lost, Adam' certainly wasn't on my list of preferred responses. A wave of exhaustion washes over me, and when I reach my flat it's all I can do to make it to the couch, where I immediately drop off into a deep sleep.

That is, until my intercom buzzes.

Chapter 19

I sit up with a start and check my watch. It's ten o'clock, I've only been asleep for a couple of hours, and my heart leaps, hoping that it's Charlie. I hurry into the hallway, thinking that maybe I should have given her that spare set of keys after all, and nervously press the 'talk' button. But instead of Charlie's dulcet tones, what I actually hear makes me jump.

'Sorry about the punch!' says a metallic voice.

I buzz Nick in and fling open my front door in time to see him bounding up the stairs, holdall in hand. I'm so pleased to see him that not for the first time in the last thirty-six hours I have an insane urge to start crying.

'Nick! Thank God! Where the . . . what hap . . . are you okay?' I stammer.

'Calm down, mate, I've said sorry. No need to be so agitated. Where the fuck have you been, anyway?' he replies, as Mark comes puffing up the stairs behind him.

I usher them both in, and close the door behind them. 'But you . . . the Ferrari?'

'Tell me about it,' he says. 'Some bastard's nicked it

– and with my mobile. I didn't want to go anywhere near the flat while Sandra was there, and I've only just realized it's gone. I've had to rough it at bloody Mark's, seeing as you weren't around.'

Mark makes a face behind Nick's back. 'You're welcome,' he says, huffily.

I shake my head in disbelief. 'Why didn't you call?'

'We tried,' says Mark. 'But seeing as you weren't answering your phone . . .'

'. . . or doorbell,' adds Nick. 'And besides, we figured you could probably do with some space, what with Charlie and all.' He jabs a thumb in Mark's direction. 'Mark filled me in.'

Mark looks at me guiltily, and then a confused look crosses his face. 'Hold on. Adam, how do *you* know about the car being stolen?'

Nick frowns. 'Yeah. I've only just called the police; they're checking now to see whether it's been spotted. Organized gangs from Europe, they reckon. Come into town to nick a flash car, and it's across the Channel and out of the country before you even know it's gone.'

'Well for some reason they forgot to use a boat this time. You were insured, I take it?' I say, and explain the events of the previous evening.

Nick goes white when I describe in great detail the scene at Beachy Head, and then uses my phone to ring his mum, who we hear crying on the other end of the line. He calls the police, who tell him that the thieves were probably heading for the Newhaven ferry when something must have gone wrong – 'Probably broke down again, knowing your car,' suggests Mark – and they must have decided to dump it to cover their tracks. And then he does something he's never done before in the twenty-something years I've known him – comes over and gives me a hug. I don't know how to react to this and just stand there stupidly with my arms straight down by my sides until he's finished. He steps away, suddenly embarrassed, and punches me playfully on the shoulder.

'Bloody hell, pal – no wonder you look so bad. You must have been through it.'

'But what about Sandra, the kiss . . .' I say.

Nick grins awkwardly. 'Mate, I came in long before any of that started. I saw your car outside and decided I'd sneak in and see what you were up to. Thought you might be planning something for the stag night.'

'But you still hit me?'

'Yeah,' he says, giving me a sheepish look. 'Sorry about that. I overheard the whole conversation, about her only wanting my money, not loving me and so on. And then when she tried to kiss you, I thought no way can I marry someone with such bad taste . . .' He tries to make a joke of it, but his eyes are giving away the fact that he's obviously still pretty upset, although it occurs to me that it might be more about the Ferrari than Sandra. 'I was so angry I had to hit something, and I'd never hit a girl, so it was either you or the wall, and, quite frankly, punching the wall would have hurt.'

'Oh. Thanks,' I say. 'So the wedding?'

Nick shrugs. 'Off.'

'Sandra?'

'Gone off.'

'You?'

He grimaces. 'Pissed off, but okay, I suppose. Lucky I found out in time, really.'

Luck had nothing to do with it, I think, rubbing my bruised jaw.

I retrieve a bottle of Jack Daniel's from the kitchen and pour us all a drink. Downing his in one, Nick turns to me.

'Pretty dramatic turn of events, though,' he says. 'Why didn't you just tell me what you thought about her?'

I look at him incredulously, but he just smiles.

'Didn't you have any idea?' Mark asks.

Nick refills his glass and swills the golden liquid round, considering his answer.

'Sometimes you can be on the verge of getting what you think you want, and then you wake up one morning and realize it might not be as great as you thought it was going to be. And then what do you do? It's like standing on the deck of one of those supertankers and seeing that you're heading towards the rocks, but knowing that there's no way you're going to be able to turn round in time.' He takes a sip of whisky and continues. 'The only thing you can do is stay on board, brace yourself for the impact and try and convince yourself that it won't be so bad afterwards.'

'Or hope there's a rescue chopper on the way?' I suggest.

'Mate, it's always a "chopper" that gets us into these situations in the first place,' says Mark, ruefully, and I can't help thinking how right he is.

Nick stares into his glass. 'I'm not saying it was all Sandra's fault . . .'

I scratch my head. 'Well, was it your fault?'

Nick mulls this over for a moment. 'No. Actually, it *was* her fault. She was so transparent. I should have seen her coming.'

Mark coughs. 'Mate, technically, if she was transparent, you wouldn't have been able to see her coming.'

'Good point,' I say.

Nick laughs. 'Well, maybe she's just . . . a little misunderstood?'

'Yeah,' I tell him. 'Like Hitler was a little misunderstood.'

Nick sighs and shakes his head. 'I thought all this relationship stuff was supposed to get easier the older you were.'

'That's a popular misconception,' I say, somewhat bitterly.

'Speaking of, er, *misconception* . . .' says Mark, turning to face me.

'Yes. Well. And that's not the half of it,' I reply, and tell them both about my 'welcome' from Charlie this morning, and my unpleasant surprise at her flat the other evening: the mysterious Rick. I finish the story and slump hopelessly back into my chair, but despite my look of despair Nick seems to have an amused expression on his face.

'What's so funny?' I ask, a little hurt.

Mark opens his mouth to speak but Nick holds up a hand to silence him. 'Hold on a sec,' he says, rooting around in his holdall and producing a book from the inside pocket. 'Ta-da!'

I take it from him and glance at the cover: *French Lessons* by Richard Evans. 'Where did you get this?'

Nick shrugs. 'Charlie, of course. Well, Charlie's brother, to be specific. They came into Bar Rosa on Friday night,' he explains. 'I'd popped in to look for you, so we could have a chat about the wedding arrangements.'

'Not knowing that you were already on top of the situation round at his place!' laughs Mark.

Nick scowls across at him. 'Anyway,' he says to me, 'you might want to take a look inside.'

I shake my head and throw it on to the coffee table. 'No thanks, mate. My girlfriend—'

'*Pregnant* girlfriend,' interjects Mark. It's my turn to shoot him a look.

'. . . has just told me to, and I quote, "get lost", on top of which she might be having an affair, not to mention, thank you, Mark, that she's pregnant, and you think that reading a book written by her brother is going to help?'

Nick sighs patiently. 'Just take a look inside, where he's signed it. Tell me what it says.'

I pick it back up reluctantly and, turning to the first page, which is indeed signed, read out the inscription in, it has to be said, a somewhat childish voice. Despite the fact that the dedication may have been written for Nick, it certainly clears things up for me too.

'Hope this helps to explain! Rick.'

Even in my exhausted state it doesn't take me long to realize. Friday night. Richard Evans. Rick. Charlie's brother. *Her brother!*

Mark and Nick are both grinning like idiots. 'I see the penny has dropped,' says Mark.

'Unlike your testicles,' Nick says to him.

I stand up quickly and go to grab my keys from the mantelpiece, but Nick gets there before me.

'Hold on,' he cautions. 'What are you going to do?'

I take a deep breath. 'The right thing, hopefully.'

'Which is?' asks Mark.

I think about this for a couple of seconds, then sit back down again and look helpless. Nick moves to refill my glass, but I hold up a hand to stop him.

'Have you any idea what your strategy is going to be?' he asks. 'Because by the sound of things, you'll need one.'

'Wing it, probably,' I say, putting my head in my hands. 'I don't know. Even assuming she does actually want to see me again, you know what I'm like with children . . .'

Mark puts a reassuring hand on my arm. 'Listen,' he says. 'Don't put yourself down. You're great with India.'

I look up hopefully. 'Really?'

Mark shifts awkwardly in his seat. 'Well, not *great*, exactly, but at least you haven't dropped her on her head or anything. And remember, us making you her godfather wasn't just some ruse to get India more birthday presents. There's a serious side to it too. If Julia and I both die, for example, then she's your responsibility.

And I couldn't think of someone I'd trust more with my baby, the most precious thing in my life, than you.'

'Thanks, mate,' I tell him, getting a sudden lump in my throat as Nick mimes sticking two fingers down his, before turning to face me.

'What was the name of that girl you went out with a few years ago?'

Here we go again. 'Er, give me a clue . . .'

'The one with the kid?'

I swallow hard. 'Emma?'

He nods. 'Emma. That's right. You were pretty good with her little boy, I seem to recall.'

I give a short, bitter laugh. 'Obviously not good enough. She left me, remember?'

Nick sighs. 'She didn't leave you because you were no good with children. She left you because you were no good for her. She was slipping away from you long before you decided to propose.'

I look at him, miserably. 'Because she thought I'd be a crap dad.'

'No, but maybe because she thought you'd be a crap husband. She knew you weren't ready to get married, and she wasn't prepared for her son to get close to you and then lose another father figure.'

Mark turns to me. 'Nick's right. When women have kids, their priorities change. They have to do what's best for the child.'

I stare at Nick in amazement. 'How do you know all this? About Emma, I mean?'

He shifts uncomfortably in his seat. 'Because I asked her.'

'What? When?'

'After she dump— I mean, after the two of you split up.'

I shake my head in disbelief. 'Why the hell didn't you tell me?'

'I'm telling you now,' says Nick. 'Besides, what good would it have done to have told you then? Your ego was already bruised enough.'

'And, anyway,' observes Mark, in between cautious sips of his whisky, 'the experience didn't exactly turn you into a celibate monk.'

We sit in silence for a few seconds. Eventually, I just exhale loudly.

'So, how does any of this help me with Charlie? I'm still hardly a contender for Father of the Year, am I?'

'You might be surprised,' says Mark. 'It's different once you've got one of your own.'

I look at him disdainfully. 'Mark, that's easy for you to say. You're brilliant with kids. Charlie's seen what I'm like.'

Mark puts his glass down. 'But where children are concerned, women don't expect you to be brilliant. They just want to know that you're committed.'

Nick smiles at me. 'Adam, there was a time that I thought the chances of you ever settling down and starting a family were about as likely as, well, Mark running away to join the circus. But now you've met Charlie? Well, from where I'm sitting, it looks like the most natural thing in the world.'

I look across at Mark, but he just nods.

'There you go,' says Nick. 'And, anyway, whatever you decide, I know you'll make the right decision.'

'How can you be so sure?' I ask him.

He adopts a tone that can only be described as sincere.

'Because, unlike me, you always do.'

Nick checks his watch and decides he ought to go round and make sure that Sandra hasn't fire-bombed the flat on her way out. I show him and Mark to the door, and promise that I'll let them know how it goes with Charlie. As they leave, Nick stops halfway down the stairs and walks back up again.

'Mate, I just want to say thanks. For Sandra, and everything. I know it must have been tough for you, particularly with all this . . . stuff going on with you and Charlie. God knows how I'd let you know if I thought you were doing the same thing.'

I just shrug. 'Nick, that's what friends are for.'

'What, to try and shag their best mate's fiancée a week before their wedding?' calls Mark, from his position halfway down the stairs.

I grin, guiltily. 'Er . . . yeah.'

Nick grabs my hand to shake it, and holds on to it for a long time. 'I owe you.'

I'm moved by this display of affection, so I give him the only appropriate response.

'Let go, you big poof.'

I watch them leave, then go back into my flat, close the door and make straight for the phone. My hands are shaking, and it takes me two attempts to dial

Charlie's number, but when there's no reply I decide to head straight over to see her.

I'm just about to walk out of the door when I catch sight of myself in the hall mirror, and decide a shower, shave and change of clothes might be appropriate first, and so it's late morning by the time I find myself standing outside Charlie's flat. I wait a few moments for the street to clear, but when I nervously ring the doorbell there's no answer, so I call her home number again, and then her mobile, but still can't get hold of her. I sit down on her step in desperation for several minutes before I remember something. I've got a key to her flat.

With phrases like *now or never* running through my mind, I decide to go inside and wait for her. I let myself in, careful to knock loudly before I do so, but the place is empty. I walk round aimlessly for a while, and then collapse on to her bed, trying her mobile again, but it seems to be switched off. I call Mark for advice.

'Where are you?' he asks.

'Charlie's bed.'

'Blimey − that was quick work, even for you! What are you doing calling me?'

'No, you moron. She's not here. I let myself in. What do I do now?'

'Ah.' I can hear him thinking it over. 'So, you're on your own in her flat?'

'Yep.'

'No idea where she is?'

'Nope.'

'Well, aside from taking advantage of the situation to try on some of her underwear, all you can do is wait.'

I can't help but laugh. 'Mate, you're a pervert,' I tell him, adding, 'And a genius!' as a thought suddenly occurs to me. Charlie's underwear drawer. Or, more specifically, *her diary*!

I click the phone off on a confused Mark, root hurriedly through the drawer — a not too unpleasant task — and locate her diary at the bottom. I remember that she'd said she had to work today, so I flick hurriedly through and find out what she's up to. Sure enough today's entry confirms this: she's filming a commercial for mineral water in Notting Hill. I jot down the address and run back down to the car, careful to replace the contents of the drawer as I found them.

I find the place without any trouble, in a small mews just north of Hyde Park, but when I get to the door I freeze. What if I ring the bell and she refuses to see me? Nick's right — after my cool reception this morning I do need a strategy. According to Charlie's diary the shoot's only just started, so I reckon I've got a few hours to come up with a plan, or at least one that's better than spending the rest of the day waiting outside in ambush for her.

I leave the Impresser parked round the corner and decide to take a stroll through Hyde Park to clear my head, but given my current dilemma my point of entry to the park couldn't have been worse. As I cross the road and walk through the gates the screaming starts. It's the children's playground.

I force myself to walk past, and sit down on a nearby bench, from where I can watch the proceedings without looking like a pervert. As it's a Sunday, the place is packed, and everywhere I look children are either chasing round in a blur, or clambering along rope bridges, or whooping with delight as they spin faster and faster on the roundabout, their anxious mothers standing nearby in watchful attendance.

And as I sit here, resisting the impulse to stick my fingers in my ears, and feeling like the answer in a Spot the Odd One Out competition, a thought occurs to me. Where are all the dads? I check my watch, but I'm pretty sure the pubs aren't open yet. Sure, there are a couple, sitting on benches, obliviously reading the Sunday papers while their kids hang dangerously from the monkey bars, but the vast majority of parents here seem to be lone mothers. Try as I might, I can't help but read something into this.

But then I see him, over by the swings. He's probably my age, dressed pretty well, and I'm guessing he's got a good job, a nice car, maybe even a flat like mine. His son can't be more than four or five, and he's holding on for dear life as his dad pushes him higher and higher. I can't take my eyes off them, because, judging by the looks on their faces, they're both having the time of their lives.

My mobile rings, and it's Mark, phoning to see how I'm doing. I tell him I'm just on my way to see Charlie.

'Good,' he says. 'I'm glad I've caught you. Hold on, there's someone here who wants a word.'

Not now, I think, bracing myself for another of Julia's lectures. Instead, I hear a muffled fumbling sound, followed by Mark's voice saying, 'Other way up, darling.' There's a pause, and then India comes on the line.

'Uncle Adam?'

'Yes, sweetheart?'

'I love you, Uncle Adam,' is all she says, before accidentally pressing the 'end' button, but that's all I need to hear. I call Mark straight back, and when he answers with a guilty 'Yes?' I only have one word to say to him, and it's 'bastard', but I'm grinning as I say it and I know he can tell.

I put the phone back in my pocket, walk out of the park and head back towards where Charlie is filming. As I get near the building, the door opens and a couple of trendily dressed forty-something guys – advertising types, I guess, judging by the ponytails – come out and stand in the doorway, hurriedly putting cigarettes in their mouths and lighting them in the same movement.

Realizing that I probably can't just barge straight in with the two of them standing there, I keep walking, and go over to where the Impresser is parked. Waiting by the car, nervously biting my nails, I suddenly have an idea.

Once they've puffed their last and disappeared back inside, I remove what I need from the Impresser's boot, stride over to the door and ring the bell. The girl who answers looks enquiringly at me, particularly when she sees the huge toolbox I'm carrying.

'Hi,' I say, breezily. 'Emergency manicure service. I had a call from a Miss Evans?'

The girl hesitates for a second or two, then makes the 'shoosh' face, and ushers me inside. The set is a frenzy of camera crews, sound men, lighting technicians and make-up artistes – not the best place for a heart-to-heart, I suppose, but it will have to do. Charlie's sitting quietly in the middle of it all, perched on a stool in a mock-up of someone's kitchen (although why on earth they didn't just film it in someone's *actual* kitchen is a question that doesn't occur to me until much later). She doesn't see me, as she's concentrating intently on the bottle of what I recognize to be the latest trendy sparkling mineral water that she's holding. In one corner of the room a large group of people are gathered round the camera, so I stay where I am and stand inconspicuously by the door, watching the proceedings unfold in front of me while trying to calm my nerves.

After what seem like interminable checks of lights, make-up and camera angles, someone shouts 'Action', and the camera zooms in as Charlie pours water from the bottle into a glass. She's good, not spilling a drop – if there were an Oscar for Best Supporting Hands, she'd be bound to win it. There's a few seconds of pouring, then the same person shouts 'Cut', and someone else rushes in and gives Charlie a new bottle of water and an empty glass. After the fifth take, all of which seem identical to me, somebody shouts 'Still', lights and make-up are checked again, Charlie's bottle is replaced with one containing water of the non-fizzy variety, and the whole process is repeated.

Eventually, after I've seen so much water poured that I'm in danger of needing the bathroom, I decide that I can't wait any longer, and clear my throat nervously.

'Hi – is there a Miss Evans here?' I announce, holding up the toolbox as all heads swivel towards me. 'Someone called for a manicure?'

When she catches sight of me, Charlie's first reaction is, not surprisingly, one of surprise. 'I . . . I'm Miss Evans,' she whispers.

Marching confidently on to the set, I sit down in front of the shell-shocked Charlie, and take her by the hand, inspecting her nails. People are watching us, so I open the toolbox and remove the first thing that comes to hand. It's a . . . well, to be honest, I don't have a clue what it is. Some kind of pliers/wire stripper combination is my best guess.

'Charlie?' asks the chap who I guess is the director, but when she shrugs and looks at him blankly he just sighs. 'Take five, everyone,' he orders, and thankfully the set clears as everyone, except for Charlie and me, heads off towards the coffee machine.

Charlie just sits there wordlessly. 'What is that for?' is all she can eventually manage, indicating the pristine-looking . . . thing I'm holding.

I look at it quizzically. 'I don't know. It just came as part of a set.'

Charlie rolls her eyes. 'What on earth are you doing here?'

I can't think of a smart answer. 'Looking for you, actually,' I say, taking her other hand.

'Well, you've found me,' she says, shaking her head in disbelief, before adding, 'How did you find me?'

I think about trying to explain, but decide that as I'm probably skating on very thin ice already, and she's seen how bad my skating is, I'd better not mention the letting myself into her flat/rooting through her underwear drawer/reading her diary story. But before I can construct a less damaging answer a switch goes on in Charlie's brain, and she suddenly remembers that she's angry with me. Her face darkens, and she pulls her hand away and folds her arms.

'What do you want?'

Deep breath. 'You, of course.'

'Yes. Well. You're a little late.'

'A little late? Or too late?'

She glares. 'Do I really need to answer that?'

'Please, Charlie. Just hear me out,' I say, beginning to realize that this isn't going to be a walk in the park. But then I've just had one of those.

Charlie gives an exasperated sigh and stands up. 'Adam, I'm working. I don't have time for this now.'

'We've got five minutes, surely?' I plead, looking towards the director. My eyes feel red and watery from lack of sleep, and I guess this must give me an air of emotional fragility, because Charlie's expression suddenly softens.

'Okay,' she says, sitting back down reluctantly. 'Five minutes.'

I hold up the pliers. 'Whilst I'm here, did you want me to . . . ?'

'Not on your life!' says Charlie, sitting on her hands.

As we sit facing each other across a mock kitchen, I realize that, with time against me, it's time to play my trump card. I'm tired, but not too far gone to recognize that, even though it's a bit of a shameful tactic, the Nick incident is a fantastic excuse for my bad behaviour. So firstly I tell her about the Ferrari and Beachy Head, and how I thought I'd lost my oldest friend, which makes Charlie take hold of my hand in sympathy. Then I describe my 'encounter' with Sandra, reminding Charlie that it was her idea, which makes her let go of it again. And, lastly, I explain what happened when I came round to her flat and found Rick there.

After I've finished, Charlie stares at me for what seems like the longest time.

'Adam, that guy at my flat was—'

'Your brother. I know that. Now. Which is why I need to apologize for my behaviour. I've not been thinking straight. All this stuff with you and me, and Nick and Sandra, and then when I saw you with Rick, I just flipped. Particularly because . . .'

'Because he was so good looking?' teases Charlie.

'No. Because of what I felt . . . *feel* about you.'

Charlie looks puzzled. 'What?'

'I said, "Because of what I feel—"'

She rolls her eyes. 'No,' she says. 'Not "what" as in "pardon". "What" as in "What *do* you feel about me, Adam?"'

I take a deep breath and clear my throat. 'I love you, Charlie. And I haven't said that word to anyone before and meant it. Ever. Well, except for my mum. Oh, and my dad, of course. And Patch – he's my parents' dog. But I was a lot younger then. Anyway . . .'

Charlie stops my rambling by leaning across and placing a finger on my lips. 'And how do you feel about the . . .' She's having difficulty saying the word, as if she still can't believe it herself. '. . . Baby?'

It's my turn to correct her. 'Not *the* baby, Charlie. *Our* baby. And although you were right the other day, that, given the choice, I wouldn't choose to be in this—'

'Mess?' interrupts Charlie.

I shake my head quickly. 'No, not mess. *Situation*. Not right now, anyway. But we are. And I stress the word "we".'

People are starting to move back into position around the set, and I realize that my five minutes are almost up, particularly when one of the My Little Pony lookalike ad-men walks up behind Charlie, coughs loudly and points to his watch.

'Anyway,' I continue, ignoring him. 'The point is, I do love you, and, because of that, the more I think about our situation, the less it concerns me . . .'

Charlie swallows hard. 'It's the other way round for me.'

I soldier on, worried that I'll lose my nerve, which might lead to me losing something, or rather *someone* else.

'. . . and, quite frankly, I know you've seen how awkward I am with kids, and I'm actually more worried that you won't want me to be a part of our baby's life than the changes I'll have to make to mine.'

'Hmm. I hadn't thought of that,' she says, affecting concern.

'And all this stuff with Nick has made me realize some things too.'

Charlie grins. 'Not to leave the roof down on your Ferrari?'

'No, smart-arse. Not to take people for granted. And not to let opportunities pass you by. And how to recognize a good thing when you see it.'

Ponytail snorts derisively from where he's still standing behind Charlie, causing me to redden slightly.

'But aren't you scared?' whispers Charlie.

'Of course I am. But I've also realized that sometimes you can go along through life and spend all your time looking down just to make sure you don't tread in anything, when in reality all you're doing is missing what's going on around you. I know how much you want this baby. Our baby. And the fact that it makes you happy makes me happy too.'

'Oh per-lease,' sighs the ad-man, shaking his head and walking away.

I have a sudden brainwave. Picking up one of the bottles labelled 'still', I pour some water into a glass, placing it down on the table in front of Charlie.

'Look at this,' I tell her. 'Some people would say the glass is half full, and some would say that it's half empty, and there's a big difference between the two points of view.'

Charlie frowns. 'Thank you, Dr Freud.'

Placing another glass next to the first one, I find a

different bottle of water and remove the screw top
with a 'pssst'.

'Well, this is how I see my glass at the moment,' I
say, filling the second glass up until it spills over the
rim and on to the table. 'It's overflowing. And with
sparkling water.'

I sit smugly back in my seat, but Charlie just looks
at me as if I've gone crazy, and starts to mop up the
water with a tea towel. 'So what are you saying, exactly?'

'Didn't I make it clear?'

Charlie looks puzzled. 'No. Not unless I missed
something.'

Taking the towel from Charlie, I hold on to her
hands with both of mine. 'I'm saying that I want to
be with you, Charlie. And I want to be a part of a
family − *our* family − if that's the two of us, or three
of us, or however many. I'm sorry if you don't think
that I've been as enthusiastic as you'd ideally like, but
I will be. I promise.'

Her fingers tighten round mine. 'But I'd hate to
think that you were having to compromise,' she says,
quietly.

'Quite the opposite, in fact,' I say. 'You inspire me,
Charlie. You make me want to do the right thing all
the time. And while I realize that I might not be able
to make the rest of the world a better place, at least
I can make something of *our* world.'

Charlie doesn't say a word as I lean across and rest
my hand on her stomach. 'And I'm hoping that the
minute little Adam, or little Charlie—'

'Or Adam *and* Charlie,' she interrupts mischievously.

'. . . pops into this world I'll suddenly be imbued with dad skills, and turn into the best father I can be. And if not . . .'

'If not?' sniffs Charlie.

'If not, then I'll give it a damn good try.'

Not for the first time in our relationship, Charlie starts crying, but this time these tears are good.

I think.

Acknowledgements

Thanks be to Patrick Walsh and Kate Lyall Grant; so good at spotting talented new writers that they can afford to spend time on the likes of me. To Tony, Loz, John, Stew, Chris, Seema and everyone else who has played even a small part in this process, I will be eternally grateful. And lastly, but by no means leastly, to the lovely Tina. I couldn't, and wouldn't, have done it without you.